"I can't tell Daddy. He has enough to worry about."

Heather's face crumpled as she sagged back on the bed. "And Grandma and Grandpa are too old. Aunt Beth is the only one, but…"

"But what?" Amanda took Heather's frigid hand in hers and stared directly at the child.

"It's just that Aunt Beth is so much fun. Things are better when she's here and I don't want to spoil the time we have with her."

"Well, we'll just have to find someone else you can talk to, won't we?" Amanda squeezed the girl's hand.

"You?" Heather's voice was timid, yet hopeful. Then it dropped as she added, "But Daddy said no."

"I know that, Heather. But we'll take it as a good sign that he called me tonight. He doesn't seem to be against counseling. He just seems uncomfortable with me. I'm not exactly sure why."

Heather closed her eyes. They were clouded when she opened them.

"Because you remind him of…*my mother*."

ABOUT THE AUTHOR

Writing and teaching are two of Kathryn Shay's loves. She's been doing the first since she was thirteen, the second for the past twenty-four years, and has used elements of both in creating her first published novel.

"I've counseled many teenagers and gone through many harrowing experiences with them, as my heroine does. The two children in the book are the same age as mine were when I wrote it. My son supplied many of the corny puns in the novel. I've been married to their father, Jerry, for twenty-four years and feel he is responsible for most of what I know about romance."

Kathryn and Jerry—and their two children—live in a small suburb of Rochester, New York, "...very near the school where I teach and close to my friends and family."

Kathryn Shay would like to hear from readers. You can reach her at P.O. Box 24288, Rochester, NY 14624-0288.

Kathryn Shay

THE FATHER FACTOR

Harlequin Books

TORONTO • NEW YORK • LONDON
AMSTERDAM • PARIS • SYDNEY • HAMBURG
STOCKHOLM • ATHENS • TOKYO • MILAN
MADRID • WARSAW • BUDAPEST • AUCKLAND

ISBN 0-373-70659-6

THE FATHER FACTOR

To Jerry,
For all the love, laughter and romance
you've brought to my life.

CHAPTER ONE

"HI. You look dead."

"I am." Nick DiMarco closed the door to his small apartment and crossed the worn rug to plop down at the fake wood-grain table where his sister Beth was working at her laptop. "Tony sent me home early because he said I was too tired to work. And because I was grouchy."

Beth smiled at her brother's rueful expression. "Can I get you something?"

"No, it's bad enough you have to waste your nights here. You're not going to wait on me, too."

"I wouldn't call spending the evening with my two favorite people a waste of time."

Nick gazed fondly at his sister. At thirty-one, Beth was a very attractive woman. Three years her senior, he had been driven nuts as a teenage older brother trying to shelter her from the leering looks of eighteen-year-old boys. But he'd learned to enjoy how men made fools of themselves over her now. Mary Elizabeth DiMarco was more than capable of handling herself.

She added more information to her computer as she talked. "Besides, the kids have been in bed for an hour and I've been working on the figures for my bookstore. I think I'll be able to open by next fall."

"Well, I still don't like all the sacrifices you make for us." Nick scanned the cramped quarters—another thing in his life he didn't like. An exact square, the apartment in a downtown neighborhood of Syracuse, New York had an L-shaped living/dining area, a narrow galley kitchen off to the side and three bedrooms straight ahead. The mismatched furniture needed a good face-lift.

He rubbed his eyes, thinking of all he couldn't give his family, of all he *wanted* for them. Wearily he propped up his feet and laid his head back. Still wearing the black-tux-and-white-shirt uniform of all the waiters at Muscato's Italian Restaurant in Armory Square, he tried to summon the energy to go change into something more suitable for the night of studying that lay ahead.

"Tell me about the plans for the layout of the store," he said. "Will it be similar to the place you're at now?"

Discussing her imminent entry into the world of small business usually delighted Beth, so her frown concerned him. "What is it?" he asked.

"I'll tell you about the store later." His sister stopped typing and stared at him across the table. "Right now, you have to call Heather's English teacher. She phoned earlier."

"Her English teacher? Don't tell me my perfect child is in trouble. Not that I'd be too upset. It would do her good to act out a little bit."

"No, not trouble exactly," Beth responded thoughtfully. "Though she wouldn't tell me what it was about, the woman's concerned enough to insist you call her back regardless of what time you get in."

Nick's stomach knotted. As he got up and strode to the phone, he tried to quell his uneasiness. "Was Heather okay tonight?" He dialed the number Beth had scrawled on a message pad.

His sister closed down her laptop as she spoke. "Yeah. We did each other's hair and she played on the computer. She didn't eat enough at supper to keep a bird alive, though."

Her words unnerved him. His thirteen-year-old's eating habits had been erratic lately and she was already too thin. She'd also been unusually quiet and sad.

The English teacher answered on the fifth ring. "Yes, Ms. Sanders. This is Nick DiMarco. Heather's father. You wanted to speak to me tonight?"

"Thanks for returning my call. I've thought long and hard about contacting you, and once I decided it was the right thing to do, I wanted to talk to you immediately." The woman's voice was soft and soothing, and Nick could understand why Heather liked her.

"I'm concerned about the things Heather's been writing in English class these past few weeks. They were written in a journal format that we've all agreed would be confidential. But you need to know that they're very disturbing."

"What kinds of things?" His hand tightened on the receiver.

The teacher sighed and Nick could hear her hesitation across the lines. "I don't feel I can go into detail. But I've shown them to a guidance counselor at school and she'd like to meet with you as soon as possible."

"Can't you tell me any more than this?" Nick asked. He tried to stifle his irritation, knowing the woman was simply worried about his daughter.

"I'm afraid not. I don't want to be mysterious, but I try to respect the kids' privacy. I told Heather I wanted to speak to you and to her counselor, because I was concerned about her papers. She wasn't pleased, but I feel you need to be aware that she's been very sad these days and she requires some extra attention."

Nick closed his eyes. Heather had never been a happy child. "Of course I'll meet with her counselor. I want to do it as soon as possible."

"I was hoping you'd say that. I took the liberty of scheduling an appointment for you at three-thirty on Monday."

Right in the middle of my Securities Regulations class. The familiar frustration washed over him. Trying to balance a schedule, jam-packed with law school and two jobs, *and* be a good father was close to impossible. He ran his free hand over his face. "Fine, I'll be there. Thanks for your concern. Heather's lucky to have you."

After he hung up, he pinched the bridge of his nose and expelled a heavy breath before he recounted the teacher's comments.

His sister shook her head when he finished. "She's right, Nick. Heather's an unhappy little girl."

"Hell, Bethy, I know that. Why wouldn't she be?" Raking a hand through his hair, Nick sank onto a stool by the phone. "I know I'm not at home enough for her."

"It won't be for much longer," she said soothingly. "And it's not your fault, though it's too bad you can't quit one of your jobs while you wrap up your courses."

"I can't. I've got to make ends meet. Working at Muscato's and the construction site is the only way I can pay Jason's doctor bills and keep food on the table."

"I know." Her sympathetic eyes met his tired ones.

"I'll be home more when I finally finish school in May. Maybe that will help."

Beth went over and hugged him fiercely, then drew back and faced him. "You're doing what you can and you'll keep on doing that. Go to Heather's school on Monday and hear what her guidance counselor has to say. You'll make the right decision. You always do."

Edgy, Nick stood. "I'm going to get a beer. Want one?" When Beth shook her head, he walked through the swinging doors that led to the kitchen, grabbed a can out of the refrigerator, then came back and sprawled on a chair again.

"Did something else happen tonight?" Beth asked after a moment.

He started to deny it, but his sister leveled her knowing gaze on him. "Yeah. Some people at the restaurant were insufferable."

"Rude customers usually don't bother you."

"I know."

"Why tonight?"

He shrugged. "They ordered me around like I was a slave, for one thing."

"You deal with domineering clientele all the time as a law clerk."

Nick took a long swig of beer. "I guess it's because they reminded me of the Sullivans. The older guy had the same silver hair and tan Suzanne's father did, and the woman looked just as plastic as the condescending Mrs. S."

Abruptly, Beth's gaze turned frosty. It always did when they talked about Nick's ex-wife and her family. Suzanne's parents had objected strongly to the hurried, youthful marriage of their only child to a construction worker's son. They'd never considered Nick a suitable match. Thank God, Nick thought, the only contact his kids had with their grandparents was occasional mail from Europe, where they'd retired.

"Do you think about them often? About her?" Beth asked.

"Not much. But the younger woman in the restaurant tonight reminded me of her." Even now, Nick remembered the customer they'd addressed as Amanda. Wheat-colored hair. Wide azure eyes. High sculpted cheekbones. She was probably Suzanne's age, just shy of thirty, slender and average height.

"I'll bet she was the most condescending."

Begrudgingly, Nick remembered the slight blush that had colored the woman's cheeks and how apologetic her eyes had been. "Ah...no. Actually, she seemed embarrassed."

"Still got a weakness for that type?"

"Naw. My ardor for rich, spoiled blondes was cooled ten years ago when one of them stuck a crying infant in my arms, left a frightened three-year-old with my mother and walked out because she couldn't live without diamonds and gold." The words came out sounding more vehement, and bitter, than he'd intended.

"I'm sorry for bringing it up, Nick."

His grin was genuine. "Little sisters are entitled to snoop."

After Beth left, Nick sank into the chair once more and finished his beer, thinking back to his life so many years ago...

Things had been rough right from the beginning, but they took a turn for the worse when Suzanne got pregnant a second time, and the baby was born disabled. His son Jason was paralyzed from the waist down. It could have resulted from the birthing process when the umbilical cord had wrapped tightly around his stomach, cutting off the supply of blood and damaging nerves irreparably. Or it could have been caused by Suzanne's irresponsible behavior during the pregnancy. Most likely, it was a combination of things. A multifactorial birth defect, they called it.

Whatever the cause, Suzanne hadn't been able to handle it. Nick came home early one night when Jason was two weeks old because a strange foreboding had plagued him all afternoon. He'd been working on a building not far from their apartment and had entered the house tired, hungry and apprehensive.

When he opened the door, he heard Jason squalling. The boy was not just fussing. He was in a fit of crying. Nick strode to the nursery, picked up the child and cuddled him to his chest. "It's okay, little guy," he'd crooned to the baby as he made his way to the bedroom. The sight of Suzanne, sitting on the bed, her bags packed, a bottle of Scotch in her hand, would forever be etched in his mind. Her eyes were red-rimmed, and Nick wasn't sure if it was from crying or booze.

She'd stared at him helplessly. "I just can't do it anymore, Nicky. I'm not strong enough. I have to have more. These children," she said, holding up her hands as if discussing some alien species, "they demand too much. And he needs constant care, so many doctor's appointments, and he'll never be *right*. I'm ... not capable of doing this. I don't want my life to be like this."

Nick remembered the picture she'd created. Suzanne was a stunning woman with long silky blond hair and come-hither blue eyes that blazed with sensuality. She had a knockout body that she'd resented having spoiled by childbearing. But he'd never despised anyone more than at that moment when he realized what his wife was going to do. She was turning her back on him and two

innocent children. Without a word, he'd returned to the
nursery. Heather had been staying with his mother in an
attempt to give Suzanne some time to get used to the
new baby, so he was alone with his child.

"Shh," he told his imperfect son, rocking the infant
back and forth, long after Suzanne had gone. "I'll
make it up to you. I'll take care of you. I promise."

His hand clenched reflexively on the beer can, and the
crushing sound brought him back to the present. Ex-
haling, Nick set it down with a plunk. "Damn, where
have these memories come from?" he muttered, knowing exactly the source. *Table number four. And the
beautiful Amanda.*

He rose, threw back the chair and went into Jason's
room. The bedspread was uneven, the drawers half-
open and action figures spread in some kind of square-
off on the desk. Though the boy tried, he simply
couldn't keep his room straight. Small wonder, since he
was in a wheelchair. Nick walked over to the sleeping
child, brushed the light blond hair from his eyes and
kissed his forehead. Ironically, he looked perfect lying
there. His skin was porcelain clear, his nose turned up
in a mischievous pug. "Good night, buddy."

Reaching into his pocket, he pulled out the slip of
yellow paper Tony Muscato had sent home to Jason.
Small and stocky, with a heart as big as his bank account, the swarthy restaurant owner had no children of
his own, and had practically adopted Jason as a surro-
gate grandchild.

Nick unfolded the note and chuckled as he read: *Why
did the football team go to the bank? To get their quar-
ter back.* Jason would love it. Given the fact that the
child *had* never and *would* never walk, Jason's sunny

disposition and delight in corny puns like this one was a blessing and a miracle.

He placed the note on Jason's pillow and left his son to peaceful slumber.

When he entered his daughter's room, not a thing was out of place. An army sergeant would be proud of its orderliness. Nick winced. He, himself, was a stickler for neatness. But he tried not to be obsessive with the children. Apparently, on that score, he hadn't been too successful with Heather.

Squatting by the edge of her bed, he tucked the covers closer around her. She was as angelic looking in sleep as she was awake. Her almost waist-length blond hair fanned across the pillow. It was a shade darker than Jason's but she had the same translucent skin.

He spoke into the darkness. "Oh, sweetheart, what's going on with you?"

But there were no answers, and after a few moments he left the room, feeling a sudden streak of despair. He crossed to a rickety bookshelf in the living room, picked up his Securities text and dropped onto the worn sofa. The words blurred as he began reading, and he tried to sit up straighter to keep awake. Knocking himself out to take care of his family and become the best tax attorney in upstate New York carried a high price—one he was willing to pay. But ten minutes later, when his eyes began to close, he gave in to the fatigue and slumped down against the cushions. At least oblivion didn't hurt.

"HEY, Nick, how are you doing?"

Nick smiled at the short, gray-haired chemistry teacher he met in the hall as he walked through Eastside Junior/Senior High the following Monday and reached out to shake hands. "I'm fine, Mr. Damon. How about you?"

"Ready to retire," the teacher said, his brown eyes twinkling. It was the same line he'd used fifteen years ago when Nick had been a student at Eastside.

Although many people criticized and feared inner-city schools, Nick had had a positive experience here and hoped Heather would, too. Not that he had a choice, he thought ruefully. He couldn't afford to send the kids to a private institution. Not yet, anyway. Maybe when Jason got older, Nick would be able to afford a school that had special programs for the physically challenged. It was one of the things he was working so hard for.

"Your daughter's here, isn't she? I'll probably see you at open house," Damon said, interrupting Nick's thoughts.

"Wouldn't miss it." Nick liked going to school events. Many of his former instructors still taught here and hadn't forgotten him.

He'd been so different then, so cocky, so sure the world held only great things for him. Blessed with a high IQ, he'd worked fairly hard to maintain good grades and was captain of the football and baseball teams. Life had looked good then, he thought as he made his way to the guidance office.

Walking down the hall, he thought back to the conversation he'd had with his daughter at breakfast. He'd purposely waited until the weekend was over.

"Heather, your English teacher called Friday night."

"What did Ms. Sanders want, Dad?" She'd tensed instantly, dropping the slice of toast she'd been nibbling.

Touching her arm gently, he smiled. "She'd like me to see your counselor today. Do you know why?"

Nick had seen tough football players sick with apprehension before a big game. Heather's face mirrored that look now. His grip tightened. "What is it, honey? It can't be that bad."

Staring at his hand for a moment, she'd turned wary eyes to his face. "No, not exactly. Well...see, the counselor is..." Heather broke off, shaking her head, unable to continue. Then she'd bolted from the table, saying, "Look, Dad, I have to catch the bus. Just go see her, okay?"

When she'd left, Nick turned to Jason. The boy's eyebrows lifted innocently. "Maybe it's PMS," he quipped.

Nick's jaw dropped. "What do you know about PMS?"

"Aw, nothing." Grinning mischievously, Jason shredded his napkin. "I just heard it on TV and knew it was something embarrassing 'cause I asked Heather and she told me to ask you. Just like the time I wanted to know what a virgin was and she got all red in the face."

Nick chuckled and ruffled his son's hair.

"Hey, Dad," Jason had said then, obviously sensing his ability to ease Nick's mind. "How do you know an elephant has moved into the neighborhood?"

"You smell him?"

"Nope. You see his trunk."

Nick laughed, his somber mood suddenly dissipating.

What a kid, he thought later, as he headed down the corridor to the guidance office.

AMANDA CARSON WAITED for Heather DiMarco's father with some degree of apprehension. She fidgeted with the row of buttons on the front of her Liz Claiborne black-and-white dress and smoothed down the slightly flared skirt as she thought about the upcoming conference. She'd wanted to phone Mr. DiMarco herself, but the English teacher felt proper channels should be followed so Heather wouldn't feel anyone had acted inappropriately.

Consequently, Amanda didn't know what to expect. Would he be open to suggestions or would he be angry and defensive? She hated confrontations. Which was one of the reasons last Friday night had been such an ordeal for her.

She'd dreaded the dinner with her parents and Craig, but her father was so incensed at the changes she'd made in her life, she'd been reluctant to refuse the invitation. He'd been horrified that she'd divorced Porter last year and then doubly horrified when she'd taken this job. But Amanda didn't care. She knew what she needed and she'd pursued it.

Cringing, she thought of how badly her father had treated the waiter. Though the waiter himself hadn't seemed flustered. He'd appeared amused at times, annoyed once or twice, but all the while had stood tall and broad-shouldered, diffusing her father's treatment of him with the aplomb of a diplomat.

"Excuse me?" a deep male voice said behind her.

Amanda swiveled her chair toward the office door, and felt her face redden. She gripped the arms of the seat and struggled to breathe normally. "C-can I help you?" Shock made her sputter.

He pinned her with his gaze. "You look familiar."

Oh, God, how embarrassing. Though she knew her blush betrayed her, she stood up and faced him bravely.

"Yes, we've met. You were our waiter at Muscato's Friday night."

Leaning back against the doorjamb, he surveyed her with a discerning stare. "You look different today. No jewels. Casual hairstyle. Less makeup."

She tilted her chin, uneasy with the way he'd said that. "So do you."

Actually, he looked sexy. And big. At least six-two. His wide shoulders were encased in a gray T-shirt that hugged his muscular torso and trim waist. Over it, he'd donned a fine corduroy jacket. His eyes were steel gray, framed with long, dark lashes a woman would kill for. His hair was sable and just a shade too long. A lock fell over his high forehead. His cheekbones and jaw were stern, accenting the angularity of his features. There was a cleft in his chin. Overall, it was a rugged face, sculpted with hard years and bitter lessons. Yet there was kindness there, too.

Her response to him today, and Friday night—she'd noticed him right away—had been so unusual for her, she almost didn't recognize it. None of the men she'd known had had this effect on her.

"I'm sorry my father was so...demanding at the restaurant. He—"

But Nick cut her off with a chop of his hand in the air. "It's irrelevant. I'm only here to talk about Heather."

"You...you're Mr. DiMarco?"

Nodding, he scanned the room as if he was trying to get his bearings. Every inch of wall of the ten-by-twelve office was covered with a poster or a saying or a witticism. His eyes focused on one: *When you come to the end of your rope, tie a knot and hang on.* Then his gaze traveled to the bulletin board labeled Joke of the Day.

It read:

> Question: What does a baby ghost call his mother
> and father?
> Answer: Transparents

He smiled, then took in the window behind her and
the three chairs facing her desk. Not that you could find
the top of that particular piece of furniture. It was
buried beneath paper, folders, books and phone messages. He frowned at her mess. When he noted the
floor-to-ceiling bookcase, jammed full, she watched his
expression turn into a scowl. The titles included *Problems of the Young Adolescent; Sexual Abuse and the
Average Teenager; Teen Suicide, Did You Ever Want to
Kill Yourself?* and *Would My Father Do That To Me?:
Facts on Incest.*

Amanda realized a moment too late what he must be
thinking. He glared at her before she could explain that
she didn't suspect him of abuse. His mouth had thinned
and his nostrils flared, and he sucked in his breath.
"What is this all about?"

Amanda stood straight without flinching. This job
was too important to her to back down with her first
angry parent. And it was a chance to atone for Lisa.
"I'm concerned about Heather, Mr. DiMarco. Her
mental health, not her physical well-being."

It took a moment, but his whole stance relaxed. He
folded his arms and leaned back on the edge of the table that butted the wall. "Okay, what's going on with
her?"

Amanda relaxed too—but only fractionally. Matching his casual pose, she slid her hands into her pockets.
"Your daughter has been writing disturbing things in

English class for the past few weeks and Ms. Sanders sent them to me to read. I spoke with Heather about it today."

The grooves around his mouth deepened. Amanda had the unfamiliar urge to comfort him.

"The teacher mentioned Heather's writing. But she wouldn't tell me what it was about." His voice was low and raw.

Amanda automatically softened her tone. "How much *did* she tell you?"

"Not much. I expect to get some answers from you."

The dilemma was becoming familiar to Amanda. Confidentiality was vital to teenagers. Yet school personnel had a legal and moral responsibility to inform parents of their concern. Earlier that afternoon she'd received Heather's permission to talk to this man, but it hadn't been easy.

"Heather, the feelings of despair that you've written about need to be dealt with," Amanda had told her. "I'd like to talk to your father and get his permission to see you on a regular basis."

"No, please, Ms. Carson..."

Amanda had waited for her to continue. When the teenager seemed unable to do so, she'd prompted her. "He'll worry?"

Heather nodded. "He works hard and he's always tired. He's got so much on his mind already. I don't want to add to it."

"Why don't you let me talk to him. I think I can ask him in a way that will ease his concern." Amanda's heart had hurt for the child trying to be so adult.

In the end, Heather had agreed.

Now, Amanda decided to give the father *some* of the facts. She moved to the front of her desk. "Heather is a sad young lady, Mr. DiMarco. It comes out in her writing. She feels a lot of responsibility and guilt.''

Nick cocked his head. ''What does she have to feel guilty for?''

For being so healthy when her sibling is not, for one thing. Amanda glanced behind her at the picture of Lisa on her desk, then said, ''I can't get into specifics. We strongly believe in confidentiality, and the kids' trust is hard enough to earn without betraying them.''

''All right, I can accept that. You can't say much.'' Straightening, Nick took two steps and towered over her. ''Just give me the things she's written and I'll talk with her about it myself.''

His clean masculine scent, undiluted by cologne, gently assaulted Amanda. Surprised at its effect on her, she admonished herself. After all, this man was a student's father, for God's sake.

She crossed her arms and tried to ignore the churning in her stomach. ''I'm afraid I can't do that. They are Heather's to share or not to share at this point. It would be a breach of confidence for me to give them to you. You'll have to ask her for permission to read them.''

''So what do you want me to do?''

''I want you to allow me to help her.''

''I don't like to bring outsiders into family matters,'' he stated bluntly.

''Your daughter turned to outsiders, Mr. DiMarco. She's in trouble. And she needs the help of a professional. She needs *my* help.''

Nick's face paled as she spoke, and Amanda was disconcerted by his reaction. ''Would you like to sit down?''

Shaking his head, he stared over her shoulder. She reached out and touched the soft corduroy of his jacket.

Briefly, he looked down at her hand and then up into her eyes. For a moment, she saw a need there, and something else she didn't recognize, but in a second the look was gone and he backed away.

"I don't mean to insult you, Ms. Carson, but judging from what I witnessed Friday night, you aren't the one to help my family."

"Why is that?"

"Let's just say we've got some bad scars from women like you."

"And you've known a lot of women like me?"

"One too many."

Amanda stepped back and fought to control her temper. "Mr. DiMarco, I don't know why you dislike me, but I asked you here because Heather's in trouble. Despite your preconceived notions, I have a master's degree in counseling and a hundred and twenty hours of intensive study with some of the most prominent child and adolescent psychologists in New York City. I know I can help Heather. I told her this afternoon that I needed your permission to spend time with her after school. That's all I'm asking from you today."

Arms tensed at his sides, he stared at her intently for a long moment. He looked thoughtful, maybe even a little torn. But finally he shook his head. "I appreciate your having called this problem to my attention. I'll deal with it myself, though. Heather and I will deal with it. I really don't think we need to involve anyone else." Then, he walked around her and strode from the room.

Amanda crossed to her desk and sank into her chair openmouthed. She'd been so sure a plea to his fatherly instincts would get him to agree to counseling for Heather. But she'd been wrong and though he'd hinted at the source of his negative attitude, she had no idea how to break through it to help his troubled daughter.

Glancing again at the picture of her sister, she picked it up and spoke softly to it, a habit she'd taken to lately. "And we know just how high a price they'll pay if she isn't helped, don't we, Lisa?"

CHAPTER TWO

AMANDA WAS STILL thinking about Nick DiMarco four hours later as she sat in her parents' formal living room. Though it had been designed and decorated by the best, Amanda had always found it austere. She toyed with her slice of anniversary cake, not listening to the conversation around her. Her mind reeled back and forth to Nick DiMarco and how his gray eyes had warmed when he spoke about Heather. How torn he'd appeared at her advice about his daughter. How, in spite of himself, he'd eyed her with masculine appreciation.

"Amanda, darling, are you all right? You're flushed." Craig's voice penetrated the haze of her distraction. She was faintly surprised to see him there, so immersed had she been in her thoughts. She shifted uncomfortably in the wing chair.

"Yes, Craig, I'm fine. I was just thinking about...my job." *Well, almost.*

As she made her excuses to him, Amanda took in Craig Coleman's meticulous appearance. His fashionably cut short blond hair was perfect for his swank appearance. He wore a charcoal pin-striped suit, white starched shirt and a solid tie. Gold cuff links twinkled when he raised his arm to sip his sherry. He moved with the confidence instilled in him by years at prep school and Harvard Law and he spoke with the precision and polish of an affluent attorney. She winced inwardly at his similarity to her ex-husband, Porter. They exuded the same aura of self-importance and they even resembled each other physically. They were clones, both chosen by her father, both perfect catches in his opinion and theirs, both totally dedicated to their positions in society.

"How *is* your job, Amanda?" Joan Carson asked hesitantly, setting her plate on the Queen Anne table. Dressed to celebrate, she wore a black Chanel suit trimmed in white. Her latest bauble from her husband, Robert, a three-carat diamond necklace, hugged her throat. Because Amanda knew she was expected to dress for the occasion, she'd donned a peach silk blouse and a matching full skirt that swirled at her knees.

Turning to her mother, who sat adjacent to her on the brocade sofa, Amanda answered quietly, "Many of the kids at Eastside are really troubled. I'm needed there."

"I'm sure you are, dear."

"Well, get it out of your system now, darling," Craig put in as he patted his mouth with his napkin in a delicate way that irritated Amanda almost as much as his assumption that she would do whatever he wished.

Why shouldn't he? she thought ruefully. *I'm the model wife and daughter. At least I was.*

"When we're married, you won't have time for those kinds of activities."

Amanda felt the hairs on the back of her neck bristle. She picked up her chardonnay and took a sip to cool her temper. "Craig, I've told you, all of you, that I'm not ready to remarry. And I certainly don't intend to give up my job. I thought you understood that." There was iron in her tone beneath her velvet smile.

"Please, let's not argue," Amanda's father interjected. Robert Carson was a tall, stately man, still trim at sixty. Appropriately attired for the evening, he wore a navy blue suit, a light blue shirt and striped tie. He rose from his seat near the floor-to-ceiling Palladian windows and moved to the cherry wall unit that housed the bar. Pouring himself a second glass of wine, he added, "We've seen so little of you in the last couple of months." Amanda thought she heard a note of pain in his voice, but it was not there when he finished. "And we've had to practically beg for your time twice in one week. It's your mother's and my anniversary. I don't want to spoil it with squabbling."

Amanda bit her tongue so hard she could taste the coppery blood she'd drawn. She felt guilty for neglecting her mother in August and September. Amanda was—since Lisa's death—the only child Joan had. But Amanda had been unable to make the changes she needed in her life under her father's thumb, so she'd maintained her distance. Robert Carson's need for control was legendary in both his well-connected family and the well-established law firm where he was a senior partner. He directed everything—personal and professional—with the arrogance of the very rich and the securely powerful.

Lord knows, he'd been livid when she'd divorced Porter. Only her ex-husband's easy acquiescence, brought on by his own dissatisfaction with the relationship, had allowed her father to accept the split with even a modicum of grace.

She hoped Porter had already met someone who drove him wild in bed. The thought of the man she'd married, thin, tall and pale, writhing between the sheets with anyone was ludicrous. But then, she'd never imagined herself in such a situation, either. But maybe with Nick DiMarco... *Now where had that come from?*

"I talked to Porter today after our meeting with a new client." Her father announced this as he returned to his leather chair in the corner. "He said you're selling the condominium."

"What?" Joan Carson's fork clattered to her Lennox cake plate. "Amanda, do you have any idea how difficult it is to buy a co-op in that section of town?"

"Of course I know, Mother. But it was the best decision for me. I signed the papers at Porter's office yesterday. It's sold."

Robert's face revealed nothing, but Joan's jaw dropped in shock. Her mother was obviously hurt that her daughter had kept this from her. Amanda started to explain that these changes were part of her plan to take control of her life. But Craig intervened.

"Let me handle this, Amanda," he said condescendingly. Turning to her mother, he patted the older woman's hand. "Don't worry, Joan. She can move back here until we're married. Then you'll get to see her more often."

Amanda wanted to scream. Instead, she calmly ran a manicured finger around the rim of her wineglass before she dropped the bomb. "Actually, that won't be necessary. I've already bought a house."

Three well-bred, stoic faces turned white, then red. Craig recovered first. He set down his drink carefully and folded his hands. "Why wasn't I in on this? As your fiancé and as your lawyer?"

"You are *not* my fiancé, Craig." Amanda eased back into her chair and crossed her legs, discreetly taking a deep breath. "And don't speak to me like I'm a child."

"Then don't behave like one," he said crossly.

Silently counting to ten, Amanda fingered the simple gold chain around her neck. She forced her mind

elsewhere and it went to the DiMarcos, to the gratitude
on Heather's face when she'd told the girl she would
help her. The thought made her smile.

"Is something funny, Amanda?" Her father's mouth
was set in a thin, disapproving line. He'd crossed his
legs and encircled his knee with his hands. Glancing at
him, she noticed how his pose mirrored Craig's. Was it
a lawyer stance? She'd studied Heather's records yesterday and noted that Nick DiMarco was pursuing his
law degree. Somehow, she couldn't quite see *him* sitting like that.

For some reason, the comparison calmed her and she
was able to answer evenly. "No, it isn't funny, Father,
but neither is it some great tragedy. I told all of you that
I wanted to make some changes in my life. And I'm
going to do it. With or without your approval. If I can't
talk to you about it..."

Always astute, her father was the first to catch the
implied threat. He straightened in his chair, dug his
wing-tipped feet into the Aubusson carpet and crossed
his arms over his chest. His eyes held an undefinable
sadness when he spoke. "Don't do anything rash, Amanda. We all realize how affected you were by Lisa's...
death, and how strangely you've behaved in the last
year. We're just concerned about you."

Amanda's spirit was deflated by the memory of the
loss of her sister and the bleak days that followed. She
sank back into her seat, willing the moisture from her
eyes. Once more she pictured Lisa's ashen face, cold and
waxen in the casket. Once more she felt the grief that
had overcome her when the lid was closed and she knew
she'd never see her sister again.

But in her mind, she heard Lisa's calm, clear voice,
determined to cheer her up: *What did the people say*

when one hundred lawyers were killed in a plane crash . . . ? It's a good start."

Her sister had always loved the sacrilegious lawyer jokes that drove her father crazy. Amanda often repeated them to herself when things got tough with him.

Her mother coughed nervously and fidgeted with her bracelet. "Where is this house, dear?"

"About five blocks from my school," Amanda said, regaining some control. She ignored the two men who stared at her as if she were a newly discovered life-form. "And it has a lovely garden. I've always wanted to grow things."

Joan Carson's astonished look told Amanda she could not conceive of someone wanting to do her own digging when the world had gardeners. Craig Coleman scowled, as did her father. Amanda smiled serenely, and before anyone could comment, the maid knocked discreetly on the door.

Visibly trying to control his irritation, Robert asked, "What is it, Mary?"

"There's a phone call for Miss Amanda."

"Who is it?" Amanda asked.

"A Mr. DiMarco. He got this number from your service. He . . . he said it's an emergency or I wouldn't have interrupted."

Amanda shot out of the chair and flew from the room. She took the time to squeeze Mary's arm and murmur her thanks before she raced to the phone.

RINGING THE DOORBELL of apartment number four, Amanda shifted from one foot to the other. She was just about to push the button a second time, when the door opened. In front of her sat a ten-year-old towheaded boy, his blue eyes brimming with anxiety. In a wheel-chair.

Her heart clenched at the familiar sight. The chair was an older, cheaper model than Lisa's had been, but it summoned images, just the same. She saw herself pushing it as fast as she could, while Lisa screeched with glee. She remembered struggling with it through the grass so they could both feed the ducks in the pond they were forbidden to go near. She thought of the time she'd forged space in the bleacher aisles so Lisa could watch her cheer at a football game. And she recalled the pain of folding it up for the last time.

"Ms. Carson?" the young boy asked.

"Yes, you must be Jason."

"Yeah." He maneuvered the chair so she could enter. The agility with which he did it resurrected even more memories of Lisa, but Amanda forcibly shook them off. Nick DiMarco had been in a panic when he'd called her thirty minutes ago.

She scooted past the little boy and stepped farther into the small room to see an older woman sitting on a striped couch adjacent to the door. Obviously, this was Nick's mother, judging from the black hair liberally peppered with gray and the shape of her charcoal eyes. She clutched rosary beads and mumbled in Italian.

"Oh, praise the Lord," Rosa DiMarco said when she saw Amanda. "You from the school? Go down the hall. It's the first door. My boy and granddaughter are there."

The words tumbled out in a rush, and Amanda wished she had time to soothe the overwrought woman. But she went immediately to the room indicated.

Inside she found Nick slumped on a single bed against the wall. He held his thirteen-year-old on his lap and crooned nonsense words to her as he gently stroked her hair. He was still dressed in his waiter's tux and Heather wore a baby pink sweat suit. The contrast was incongruous.

Heather was weeping uncontrollably. When Nick looked up and saw Amanda, the relief on his face was so intense, it made her heart turn over. She longed to erase the lines of fatigue and anxiety that bracketed his mouth. But she couldn't, of course. His child came first.

Crouching in front of them, she touched Heather's arm to let her know she was there. The girl started and then eased her face out of her father's neck. Her china blue eyes were red-rimmed and puffy and her skin was blotchy. As Nick had told her on the phone, Heather had obviously been crying for a very long time.

Between sobs, the girl managed to gulp, "What are you doing here, Ms. Carson?"

"Your father called me, Heather. He thought I might be able to help you."

"No one can help..." A fresh bout of tears stopped Heather from going on.

"I can try. Why don't you tell me what happened."

Hugging his daughter tight to his chest, as if to protect her from the question, Nick said, "She dropped the sauce..."

Before he could continue, Amanda shook her head and held up her hand to stop him. "Heather, you tell me."

The girl quieted somewhat and turned in her father's lap to face Amanda. She still clasped his neck in a death grip.

"I...was...helping Grandma...and the bowl was so heavy. It slipped out...oh, God, all over the floor... the glass broke... we had nothing else for supper..." She began crying again and was unable to finish, but Amanda had the gist.

"Did your grandmother yell at you?" Amanda kept her voice purposely low and soothing.

Out of the corner of her eye, she saw Nick frown, but she ignored it.

"No, but she should have. It was my..." Heather released her father's neck and turned to face Amanda fully.

"Your what, Heather?" Amanda asked softly.

"My fault, of course." The girl said it without hesitation, scrubbing her eyes with her fists.

Hearing the silent *like everything else,* Amanda wondered if Nick had picked up on it. One glance at his face told her that pain hadn't blurred his perceptions.

"It was so messy. Daddy doesn't like mess," Heather said tonelessly.

Amanda tensed. Was something going on she hadn't anticipated? "Does Daddy get angry when something happens he doesn't like?" Leaning back on her heels, she risked a glimpse at Nick. His eyes were cold and seemed to look right through her. She met his stare unblinkingly.

"No," Heather said, without guile. "He'll just be disappointed."

"Ask him how he feels," Amanda said.

Heather pulled completely away from her father and looked at him questioningly.

Nick smoothed her silky hair with his large, strong hand, the muscles in his forearm bunching in an apparent effort to control his anxiety. "Oh, sweetheart, I don't care about the dinner. Grandma has quarts of that stuff stacked in the freezer."

"But . . . but you had to leave work to come home."

"Not because of what you did. I came home because you couldn't stop crying." Nick's voice was laced with regret, but he held her gaze unwaveringly.

Amanda waited a moment. When nothing more was said, she asked, "Why can't you stop crying, Heather?"

The tears were now a silent stream down her cheeks, but she'd stopped sobbing and her body no longer convulsed. As if just aware of her position, she eased off her father's lap onto the bed, but still held his hand. Amanda glanced at Nick and wondered briefly who needed the connection more. Nick had no color in his face and his eyes were haunted. She felt his pain deep in her heart.

"I don't know why I can't stop crying."

Amanda had heard that statement before. It was a common indicator of real depression. She rose from her crouched position and looked at Nick. "I'd like to see Heather alone for a few minutes."

Nick stared at her intently. Disapproval was etched in the taut lines of his forehead, and his mouth thinned with it.

Turning from him, Amanda removed her leather coat and threw it on the chair, as if the matter was settled. He had called her and she wasn't about to miss this opportunity.

Slowly, Nick stood and faced his daughter. He leaned over and stroked her flushed cheek. "This okay with you?"

Heather nodded. Nick backed away, then walked silently to the door. Even after he'd gone, Amanda felt his distrust like another presence in the room.

She pulled a chair up to the bed. Tears pooled in Heather's eyes now but didn't fall freely, and the child relaxed into the mattress. The strain of the evening was outlined in every muscle of her body.

"Sit back and prop yourself up against the pillows," Amanda told her. When the girl relaxed slightly, Amanda said, "Tell me what hurts so much."

Clutching the covers, Heather peered at her with vacant eyes. Amanda waited. Finally, the girl answered. "My heart."

Amanda felt her own contract at the simple yet poignant response. She reached out and touched the teenager's hand. Heather grabbed hers like a lifeline. After a moment, Amanda asked, "Why does it hurt so much?"

Huge fat tears coursed down Heather's innocent, pink cheeks. Leaning forward in her chair, Amanda searched for the right words to say.

"How about telling me just one little thing? Sometimes, when so much is wrong, it helps to start with something small."

The teenager looked at her with disbelieving eyes. Then, still grasping Amanda's hand, she shrugged her slender shoulders. "Well, Jason for one thing."

Amanda didn't have to ask why. A sudden image of Lisa's face watching her dress for a dance recital engulfed her. The longing etched there had been enough to drive Amanda away from the ballet bar for a full sixteen years. Only last year, eight months after Lisa's death, had she begun classes again.

Unaware of Amanda's associations, Heather plucked at the spread. "It's just so unfair, you know. He's so *nice*. He's never mean, he never resents that I can do things that he can't. It hurts so much to see him be happy for me. I'm . . . I'm miserable for him, Ms. Carson, and I can't stand it anymore."

Briefly, Amanda wondered if she was thick-skinned enough to handle the career she'd chosen. Heather's confession broke her heart in and of itself. But the fact that Amanda had felt exactly the same about Lisa made her wonder if she was capable of remaining objective.

She took Heather's frigid hands in hers and stared directly at her. "Heather, Jason's condition is *not* your fault. And you'll probably always feel some guilt for being whole when he isn't. I'm not sure there's anything you can do about that."

When the girl's eyes turned bleaker than a February afternoon, Amanda tightened her grip. "But what you *can* do is talk about it. Get it out. Yell and scream about how unfair it is. You *will* feel better about it, although the reality *will not* go away."

Heather's face crumpled and moisture welled up in her eyes once more. Her whole body slumped back into the bed. "I can't do that. Daddy has enough to worry about. And Grandma and Grandpa are too old. Aunt Beth is the only one I could ever be that way with, but she..." Her voice trailed off.

"She what?"

Heather shrugged. "It's stupid."

"So? Be stupid. It's just you and me."

Sinking deeper into the pillows, Heather hesitated before she added, "It's just that Aunt Beth is so much fun. Things are *better* when she's here. For Jason and for me. I don't want to spend the time we have with her whining."

Again, Amanda's heart constricted and she averted her eyes to a poster of a unicorn on the wall.

"Well, then we'll just have to find someone else you can yell about it with, won't we?" she finally said.

"You?" Heather's voice was timid yet hopeful, then dropped, defeated. "But Daddy said no."

"I know that, Heather. But we'll take it as a good sign that your dad called me tonight. And he doesn't seem to be against counseling. He just seems uncomfortable with *me*. I'm not exactly sure why."

Heather closed her eyes and they were cloudy when she opened them. "Because you remind him of... my mother."

And you've known a lot of women like me?

One too many.

It was beginning to make sense now.

When Heather didn't elaborate, Amanda asked, "How do you know he feels this way?"

The girl's face turned scarlet and she bit her lip. But she held Amanda's gaze, showing some of her father's grit. "Because I listen when he and Aunt Beth talk at night. It's the only way I find out what he's thinking. He doesn't say much about his feelings to me, so I... eavesdrop. It's how I found out about—"

Heather stopped abruptly. After a few moments of silence, it seemed confession time was over. Donning what Amanda had dubbed the DiMarco scowl, Heather finally said, "Please, I don't want to talk anymore."

Amanda knew the aftermath of hours of tears, from both personal and professional experience. Eyelids that felt like sandpaper. A queasy stomach. Every muscle screaming from tension the body could only hold for so long.

"Sure, honey. I think you should go to bed," Amanda said and drew the covers up.

Wearily, Heather lay down and allowed Amanda to adjust the quilt. She closed her eyes and reached out her hand. Amanda took it and gave the girl a moment to settle down before saying any more. Her eyes scanned the room.

The books on the shelves were arranged by size. The tops of the desk and dresser were spotless. Every surface reflected the same sense of neatness, the kind Amanda hated. When she was a child, she and her sister had given the maid prematurely gray hair. There was always a doll hiding behind a couch or one of Lisa's trucks peeking out from underneath. Her father's displeasure had not been enough to make the girls more tidy and Amanda often reflected that it was probably just another way they'd had of thwarting him. *And the reason you're so messy today.*

There was no rebellion in this room, though.

Smoothing Heather's fine, pale hair onto the pillow, she asked, "Feel better?"

"A little." Heather glanced at the door. "But you should send them all in to see I'm okay." Even amidst her pain, the child's concern for others surfaced.

"How about if I fill them in on how you are, instead? Would you trust me to do that?" Amanda squeezed Heather's hand.

Grateful blue eyes, exactly like her brother's, peered up at Amanda. The children must look like their mother, given Nick's dark coloring. "Okay."

But her father was clearly resistant to the idea when Amanda entered the living room a few minutes later. He'd shed his tie and jacket and rolled up the sleeves of his white shirt. Coarse black hair dusted his arms. He was sitting with his mother and Jason in a too-quiet living room. "I want to see her," he said implacably when Amanda told him his daughter was in bed.

"She's just about asleep. I think it's best to let her rest."

Nick's eyes flared with temper but he said nothing. Though his gaze caused her pulse to speed up, Amanda stood her ground. Turning from her, he glanced at the clock and then at Jason. "Come on, kid, you should go to sleep, too." When his eyes rested on his mother, he sighed and closed them.

Amanda read the fatigue and frustration in the slump of his shoulders. How could he take Rosa DiMarco home and get his son to bed and not leave his daughter alone?

She sighed inwardly. One minute, she was steeling herself against this man. The next, her whole being softened toward him and she wanted to massage away all the tension in that broad back. She took a few steps in his direction and spoke gently. "Why don't you take your mother home? She probably needs some comfort from you. I'll stay and get Jason to bed."

Nick looked at her with gratitude and something she couldn't define. Then, as if remembering to shield himself, he backed away from her and said, "Thank you. But I'll take care of Jason when I get back. It's tough getting him settled in."

"I know how to do it. I've had plenty of experience." Amanda smiled sadly and clasped her hands behind her.

Nick looked directly at her. "Really? Where?"

"I'll tell you about it sometime."

"HOW DO YOU KNOW how to do all this?" Jason echoed Nick's question when she locked the wheelchair at the bottom so he could brace himself on it and ease over the sink. She dodged the query, but he asked again later, when she tilted the chair slightly to let him roll into his mattress with some degree of autonomy.

Finding herself on the edge of a DiMarco bed for a second time that night, she pulled the covers up to his small chest. "Someone very close to me was in one of these. I know all the tricks."

"Yeah?" The devilish grin was there despite the gravity of the evening.

Amanda brushed back an unruly lock of his white-blond hair. "Yeah. And you know what? She loved jokes just like Heather told me you do."

"Tell me one."

Amanda pretended to think. "Okay, why was the little strawberry worried?"

Jason's grin broadened and his blue eyes twinkled. "I give, why?"

"His parents were in a jam."

Without missing a beat, the child responded in kind. "How do you know the ocean is friendly?"

Amanda lifted her chin and glanced at the ceiling, giving the matter consideration. Finally, she shook her head. "Don't know."

"It waves."

Both giggled.

Ten minutes later, Amanda was still smiling as she paced the living room waiting for Nick. There were framed photos of him, the children, his parents and a woman who had to be his sister. But there was no picture of the children's mother. It was as if she didn't exist.

And the order here reflected Heather's room. Though cramped with a tattered flowered sofa and two big chairs, a small television and a desk next to wobbly bookshelves, everything was neatly in its place. Even the books were tidy and each picture was straight. There was no lint on the throw pillows or aged rug. No magazines, newspapers or toys graced the coffee table.

So, Heather wasn't the only fastidious one in this house.

"God, can I do this, can I help them?" she asked aloud in the silent living room.

Sure you can, Mandy, she heard her sister say. *I know it!*

HALF AN HOUR LATER, Nick stood in the doorway. Now that the crisis had passed, and he'd had time to marshal his defenses, he didn't know exactly what to do with Ms. Amanda Carson, who looked so lovely standing before him. He hadn't had time to appreciate how the peach blouse accented the blush of her cheeks or how her short skirt flared sexily around her knees. Her honey-colored hair swayed about her shoulders when she turned from the bookshelf to face him.

"Hi. Is your mother all right?"

"Yeah." He raked a hand through his hair. He tried not to think of how well she'd handled the situation, how much he'd admired her expertise. He was grateful to her for her intervention, but it was difficult to show this. To let her see his vulnerability.

Amanda crossed her arms over her chest nervously.

"Thanks for everything," he finally said.

"You're welcome. I'd like to do more."

Again fear coiled in Nick. Letting this woman near Heather tonight had been hard enough. Could he do it long-term? Could he risk entrusting Heather's welfare to someone so different from them?

Amanda's eyes held his during his silence. Hers had darkened with frustration to a slate blue. Nick wondered if they would do the same in passion, if he slipped his hand inside that prim, buttoned-to-the-collar blouse and kneaded the full, ripe breast he could see outlined under the silk. Upset by his thoughts and the hardening of his body because of them, he said, "You just don't understand all of this."

Amanda expelled an exasperated breath. "I understand you more than you realize."

Nick braced himself for the attack.

"I understand how much you love your children and are trying your best to protect them and provide for them."

"If that's true, what was that all about in there, about 'Daddy getting angry'? I'd never lay a hand on her."

Moving closer to him, Amanda squared her shoulders to full height. Still, she only came to his chin. "You should be pleased I was protecting your child, Mr. DiMarco. There *are* families where fathers abuse their children. It's my responsibility to ferret that out. It wasn't the case here, but I asked because I needed to be certain I'd read the situation correctly, not to insult you."

He didn't respond, so she continued, "Listen, I didn't come here to argue with you. I came because you asked me to help Heather. I did that tonight, but she needs more. She's hurting and I know I can help her in the long term."

Impatiently pushing her hair back from her forehead, she forged ahead. "I've had a lot of training and experience with troubled teenagers. I think it's vital to Heather's well-being that you let me spend some time with her."

She paused, apparently having run out of breath, but just as Nick decided to rescue her by giving in, she looked away, then back into his eyes, and added softly, "Please."

He wasn't sure how he knew it, but he sensed that had cost her a lot. He'd bet Amanda Carson didn't beg anyone for anything. His voice was gruff but gentle when he answered, "All right, Counselor, you can see her."

Her smile was like the sun in October. It warmed him right down to his toes. He had the sudden urge to make her smile like that at another time, in another place. And she'd say, "Please . . ." for a far, far different reason.

He forced the fantasy to recede. He couldn't do this. Not again. Women like her were poison to men like him. But equally important was the fact that Heather needed her, so he'd make peace and treat her like a professional. Nothing personal could happen between them.

Straightening, he said, "I love my daughter and I'll do anything to help her. I didn't know things were so bad with her." Before Amanda could respond, he added, "And I don't mean to keep insulting you. The problem's with me, not you."

She stared at him for an uncomfortable minute, then smiled unsurely. "Good. I'll set up an appointment for tomorrow." Leaning over, she picked up the coat she'd tossed to the couch when she'd left Heather's room.

Nick took it from her. She looked so surprised, he almost laughed aloud. Turning her back to him, she slid her arms into the sleeves.

As she shrugged into her coat, he was barraged by the scent of her. Her thick, wheat-colored hair was inches from his face and the smell of flowery shampoo invaded his senses like the Garden of Eden in full bloom.

Unable to stop himself, he lifted his hand and freed the heavy locks from inside her collar. When he got a glimpse of her exposed neck, he had the sudden urge to press his lips into the fine down at her nape. She was a feast set before him, and he felt like a man starved for weeks... hell, for months, years. But, he'd partaken of this particular banquet before and paid dearly for it. The price was too high. He couldn't risk it again, no matter how enticing he found her.

So, he let her hair fall around her shoulders and lightly rested his hands there and squeezed gently. "Go home, princess, before you get more than you bargained for." His voice was raw and raspy with his wayward thoughts.

She turned to face him, her eyes huge and wary. There was a confusion in those sapphire depths, as if she had felt something unexpected. She bit her lip, a small gesture that sent shivers through him. Without speaking, she nodded and headed for the door. Which suited him just fine.

Or so he told himself.

CHAPTER THREE

NICK RAN like the devil was after him. It was true, in a way. His own personal demon had been on his tail since Suzanne had left him. Slowing to a jog and then a walk, he finally bent over, hands on his knees, sucking in air. He banished thoughts of his ex-wife, but then his mind turned to Amanda Carson, as it had done all too often since he'd touched her in his living room a week ago.

To outrun the memory, he took to the track again. Perspiration poured down his face from the too-warm temperature, and he inhaled the sweat-scented air as he ran. He was grateful for the fitness center at Syracuse University. The indoor arena with its basketball courts and the surrounding quarter-mile track had saved his sanity more than once when he'd needed a physical outlet.

"You're slowing down, buddy, showing your age."

Nick stopped his trek, smiled and turned to see Adam Sherwood gripping a basketball. He surveyed his friend from the top of his balding head to the toes of his wiry medium-height body. Outfitted in crisp white trunks and a loose polo shirt, Adam contrasted sharply to Nick in his cutoff sweatshirt and ragged shorts. "Yeah, well, I've still got years on you. Which I'm about to prove."

With that challenge, Sherwood tossed Nick the ball and the two began to warm up for their weekly one-on-

one match. Nick dribbled around his opponent and sank a long one from the three point line.

"You're hot today," Sherwood said.

"Yeah, at least I can do something right."

Adam stopped midshot. "What's going on?"

"Oh, just the usual. Family problems, not enough money, not enough time, overload just before finals." Nick stole the ball and went in for a lay-up, making the move smooth and sure. Lord, it felt good to enjoy the exercise and leave the mind games behind.

Sherwood took the ball from him and swished his own hoop. "Want to talk about it?"

"The last thing I want to do is talk, or think. Let's play."

For thirty minutes, there was little conversation, loud grunts and the cleansing sweat that accompanies a vigorous workout.

They finished their game, exhausted and exhilarated, and jogged companionably around the track to cool down. Nick glanced at the man beside him and remembered the first time he'd met Adam. He'd sought out the best divorce attorney he could find. Sherwood had been some kind of prodigy, only eight years older than Nick, but already a professor at Syracuse Law School and a member of a glitzy downtown practice.

"I've scraped together the money and I have evidence of my wife's unfitness as a mother," Nick had told Adam. "I want total custody of the children."

In the end, Suzanne hadn't contested anything, only too happy to legally sign away her right to all of them.

"Stay in contact," Sherwood had said when the papers were finalized. "I like you, DiMarco, and I believe in you."

So Nick had kept in touch, and Adam Sherwood had been instrumental in getting him into Syracuse University to finish college and apply for law school. Without his friend's help, Nick doubted he would have gotten the grants and scholarships that paid for his tuition, and he suspected the man had pulled other strings along the way. Like the clerkship Nick had started this semester. It was in a prestigious, coveted firm, and Nick knew that although he was third in his class, this was a plum position not easily attained. He couldn't have done it without Sherwood's recommendation.

"Let's grab something cold in the Union," Adam suggested, tearing Nick away from his reverie.

Nick glanced at his watch. "I need to pick up Heather in an hour."

"I, ah, want to talk to you," Sherwood said.

Alerted by his serious tone, Nick followed his friend into the break room next to the gym. When they were seated with their drinks, Adam turned to face him. "I've quit my job."

Nick's jaw dropped. "What?"

"I've resigned from Lowell and Bean, effective today."

"Why?"

"Because I've been in a rat race. Because I want to spend time with my family." Adam wiped his face with a towel from his gym bag and took a swig of his drink.

Shaking his head to clear it, Nick took a sip of his water. "But you're giving up exactly what I'd sell my soul for."

"*Soul* being the operative word here," Adam said sadly, and Nick felt ominously chilled. "You may have to do that, buddy, especially if you go with Joris, Beech and Stowe. Once they've decided they want you, which will probably be at the end of December, they'll really test your mettle. Be careful what you wish for.''

Nick drew circles on the tabletop. God, he couldn't fathom giving up what Sherwood had. This was the goal Nick had nearly killed himself to attain, had worked day and night for years to achieve and for which he had sacrificed everything. He was finally close to giving the kids all they'd missed out on, and never having to worry about Jason's doctor bills. *And prove yourself to the world, DiMarco. Be honest about that.*

"What will you do?" Nick asked, trying to ignore the prick of his conscience.

"I start with the public defender next month. I'm taking a few weeks off to be with Joanna and the new baby. I don't want to miss his infancy like I did the others."

"So you're going to spend your time, expertise and considerable intelligence freeing criminals?" Nick propped his elbows on the table, his smile sardonic.

Adam shook his head. "There are criminals everywhere, Nick. At Lowell and Bean, I did a lot of things, got a lot of people out of things, that I'm not proud of. As a public defender, I'll be honest about what I'm doing and I'll be able to retain my integrity when I do it.''

"At least you got paid well for it at Lowell." Nick heard the bitterness in his tone and fought it.

"But the personal price was too high," Adam said sincerely. "For me, at least."

Nick was at a loss for what to say, so he kept silent. He used to feel like Adam did about law and about life. Sometimes he missed that idealism.

As if he'd read Nick's mind, Adam said, "You'd be a natural for a job like this, buddy."

"What makes you think so?"

"Your desire to take care of people. Your basic integrity."

"Naw, it's not for me anymore. I'm not idealistic about anything anymore." To change the subject, he asked, "How's the baby?"

Adam gave him a shrewd look, then took out his wallet.

As Nick studied the picture of the smiling boy, he said, "I still can't believe you're this happy about a completely unexpected baby. Your other children are practically grown up."

Adam's grin was wide as he peered at the child. "Yeah, well, after all Joanna put up with those first few years, I never thought we'd make it together. This is like a whole new chance with her and the baby. Even if he does keep me up half the night." The lawyer glanced at his watch. "Speaking of which, I've got to get home. I like to give him the dinner feeding."

Nick watched his friend retreat and experienced such poignant regret, his chest ached with it. He'd never had a chance to enjoy his children's infancies. Those years had been too fraught with tension and despair to ever fully appreciate the wonder of their babyhood. Ah, hell, maybe once he finished law school and got that prize job, he'd have more time with his kids and could begin to enjoy them. He vowed he'd make up to them, and to himself, all that they'd missed. Unbidden, a picture of Amanda Carson came into his mind, his child at her breast, undiluted joy burning with blue intensity in her eyes. Though he banished it quickly, the image stunned him.

Adam was right, he thought, gathering up his gym bag and heading for the door. "Be careful what you wish for..." It would be a curse to get involved with her.

He vowed ten years ago he'd never risk that kind of pain
again. No woman was worth it. Better to concentrate on
his goal to become a hotshot lawyer and give up the
wishes and dreams that Nick had learned were meant
for other men.

HEATHER TRIED to hold back the tears, but it just hurt
too much. She couldn't keep it inside any longer. Wiping the moisture from her face and squaring her shoulders, she adjusted the collar of her pink oxford shirt,
smoothed down her clean, pressed jeans and knocked
on the guidance counselor's door.

"Come in."

The small office had a big window and the precious
sunlight warmed Heather when she entered. Ms. Carson swiveled her desk chair around, and it took all the
courage Heather had not to turn tail and run. It was her
third time here, and it didn't get any easier. But her dad
was big on guts and Heather DiMarco decided it was
time she showed some. She hated the tears that escaped, but she hated even more the horrible pit she felt
in her stomach every single day now.

Ms. Carson rose and and came to stand beside her.
"Heather, it's okay. I know you're hurting. I can help
you, that's why we set up another meeting today."

Nodding in shaky agreement, Heather let the counselor lead her to one of the four chairs that formed a
semicircle across from the desk.

"Can I get you something?" Ms. Carson asked.

Heather shook her head and clasped her books
tighter to her chest. Ms. Carson eased into a chair,
folded her hands and watched her.

Tears continued to slip down Heather's cheeks and
she brushed them away with the sleeve of her blouse. "I

knew I shouldn't have written those things for English class, but they just wouldn't stop coming." It felt like a million tiny paper cuts to say this out loud, but she couldn't stop herself.

Handing her some tissues, Ms. Carson coaxed, "Let's start with those things you wrote for English."

Once the floodgates were open, the pain kept coming. An hour and a half later, Heather had about reached her limit. She buried her face in her hands and spoke through her fingers. "He does his best. He just can't do all the things most fathers can, so I have to do lots of them."

"But that doesn't mean you have to accept it as fair, does it?"

Heather took a tissue from her lap and blew her nose, then scowled up at the counselor. "What do you mean?"

"I mean that there are a lot of things in life we have to do, but we don't have to pretend they're fair."

She just doesn't understand. No one does.

Scooting her chair closer, Ms. Carson leaned over to take Heather's hands. "In the last ninety minutes, you told me that you feel bad about not having the kinds of clothes other kids have. You said you don't like all the chores you have to do after school. And you indicated that you wish you could have a messy room and play the radio like most teenagers, right?"

"Uh-huh."

"How do you feel now?" Ms. Carson asked. "Take an internal inventory. Do you feel any better than you did at three o'clock?"

Heather dug deep inside herself. Something felt different, a little lighter, not so dark and scary. "I do feel better. But I don't understand why. Nothing's changed in the time I've been here."

"Sometimes, just getting all that stuff out, looking at it, seeing what it really is, and isn't, makes a difference in how heavy it feels inside." Smiling, Ms. Carson squeezed her hands.

Heather looked at her for a moment and felt the tears welling in her eyes again. Tugging her fingers free, she swiped at the wetness on her cheek. This just wasn't it, Ms. Carson just didn't know. She closed her eyes to keep from saying it aloud.

"What makes you so sad now?"

Heather shook her head. Too nervous to sit still, she got up from the chair and went to stare out the office window. The warmth of the sun bathed her face. It felt good.

After a long time, Ms. Carson said, "You're thinking that you've only told me surface stuff, aren't you? That maybe talking about *these* issues helps, but nothing could possibly affect the important secrets you're keeping inside."

Heather whirled on her. "How do you know that?"

The counselor smiled, as if Heather had just admitted something. "We all have our secret fears." Then, she stood slowly, made her way to the window and ruffled Heather's hair.

"I think that's enough for today," Ms. Carson said. "But I'd like to ask one more thing before you leave." When Heather nodded, Ms. Carson leaned against the wall and sighed. "I'd like to see you more than once a week. I'd like you to be part of a group of kids I meet with regularly."

Heather wrapped her arms around herself and stepped back. She struggled to catch her breath.

"What bothers you about that?"

"Everything!"

"Try telling me one."

Heather sucked in some air and spoke. "I . . . I can't talk about this in front of anybody else."

"Okay, then listen to what they say. Maybe you'll find you're not the only one with bad feelings inside."

"Why do you want me to do this?"

"Because sometimes hearing how others feel helps you understand how *you* feel. You find out that a lot of people have some nasty things plaguing them. And you can learn to cope better from those same people."

"Daddy won't like it. He didn't even want this at first," she said, waving her hand to indicate the office.

Ms. Carson didn't look intimidated. "Okay, then, I'll talk to him personally. Will he be home tonight?"

"Yes, Grandma's staying with Jason now, but Dad's supposed to be done at five-thirty."

Nodding her head, the counselor walked over to the closet and took out a beautiful gray raincoat with a wide belt and silver buttons. "Good. Come on."

"Where are we going?"

Ms. Carson smiled and Heather realized how pretty she was. The sunlight made her hair different shades of gold, and the color of the coat made her eyes more blue. Eyes that were now filled with humor. "We're going to beard the lion in his den."

"What does that mean?"

"To meet him on his own turf and convince him," Ms. Carson said.

Despite herself, Heather grinned. "He can't be bearded."

"Okay, then we'll shave him," Ms. Carson joked, shrugging her shoulders and crossing her arms over her chest, "or we'll tie him up, or we'll feed him to the gladiators."

Heather laughed outright.

Ms. Carson joined her. After a moment, the counselor sobered and reached out to touch Heather's arm. "You're important enough to fight for."

When the tears welled in Heather's eyes again, Ms. Carson grabbed her hand and led her out the door, saying, "Did you hear the joke about the nurse who interrupted the doctor's phone call to tell him, 'There's a man in the waiting room who thinks he's invisible.'"

Heather's smile returned. She rolled her eyes but shook her head, indicating she would play along.

Ms. Carson finished, "The busy doctor responded, 'Tell him I can't see him.'"

On that silly but mood-lightening note, Heather left with her counselor, hoping the woman knew what she was doing, because she herself was more confused than ever.

"GRANDMA, I'm home," Heather called as she and Amanda entered the apartment at five o'clock. The late-October afternoon sun made a crisscross pattern on the living room furniture. Though it accented the worn patches on the sofa and the stains on the rug, the place looked more cheerful than on the gloomy night Amanda had last been here, fifteen days ago.

Amanda's thoughts were interrupted when Rosa DiMarco walked in from the kitchen. "Hello, Heather. Ms. Carson!" The older woman's shoulders tensed. "Is everything all right?"

Amanda smiled reassuringly. "Yes, we're just fine, Mrs. DiMarco. I was hoping to catch your son, so I offered Heather a ride home."

"He isn't here." Mrs. DiMarco glanced at her granddaughter. "Sweetheart, I have to go to the church supper tonight. I'm in charge," she added proudly. Then, her forehead furrowed. "But you'll have to come with me. Your papa called a few minutes ago to say he'd be late, and I don't like to leave you here alone." Mrs. DiMarco's frown deepened. "It's just that my arthritis is acting up today and I'm not sure about Jason's wheelchair on the church steps."

"It's okay, Nana. We'll be fine here."

"I don't know. This neighborhood isn't like it used to be." The older woman's eyes darted to the clock on the wall. "Maybe I could go across the hall and see if Mrs. Castellana can come over for a while."

Amanda stepped forward. "I'd be glad to stay with them, Mrs. DiMarco. As I said, I want to talk to your son, anyway."

Peering closely at Amanda, Rosa said, "I guess it would be all right. If it wasn't my first time in charge... Maria Martino would just love to see this go bad and then tell everyone I couldn't do a good job like she did last year."

Heather, who had stood by with her hands clenched and her shoulders stiff, obviously waiting for the adults to agree, visibly relaxed and smiled at her grandmother's comments. "Go ahead, Nana. Dad will be glad we're not alone."

After Nick's mother left, Jason, outfitted in denims, a superhero sweatshirt and hightops, whizzed in from the bedroom. "Hi, sis," he said cheerfully. "Hi, Ms. Carson." His blue eyes shone with mischief. "I waited in the other room for you to convince Nana to go."

When Heather seemed to comprehend his obtuse comment, Amanda asked, "What do you mean?"

The two children exchanged a look of mutual understanding, so deep, so poignant, that Amanda's heart
sank. How well she remembered having the same connection with her sister.

Jason moved the wheelchair back a few inches then
forward a few. He repeated the process as he talked.
"Grandma worries about me the most," Jason said
matter-of-factly. "If I'd come into the room and reminded her again that I'm in this thing, she would have
changed her mind about leaving. Heather and me, we
know how to get around older people." Again his eyes
glittered and his smile was impish.

"I'll remember that," Amanda drawled.

Heather's face suddenly sobered and she headed for
the kitchen. "Okay. Now we have to finish our homework, set the table, fold the towels and get the lunches
ready for tomorrow."

Digging her heels into the rug, Amanda held her
tongue.

"Aw, sis, can't we play one game before we do that?
We've been cooped up in school all day."

Heather stopped her trek to the waiting chores and
turned to them, her face a study in conflict. Amanda
knew she was getting a glimpse at the kind of pressure
Heather felt every day. Torn between her own teenage
response to crash for a while and her father's rules, the
girl stood rigidly in the middle of the floor. Well,
Amanda knew she could help with this.

Shucking off her coat, she suggested an alternative.
"How about if you set the table, Jason makes the
lunches and I fold the towels. Then we'll all play a game
of..."

"Monopoly," Jason interjected cheerfully.

"Monopoly," Amanda confirmed, "and then start homework." She looked at Heather. "Would your dad really mind so much?"

In the end, Heather succumbed to her instincts and agreed. Soon the three were ready to play. Jason had to be assisted out of the wheelchair, and Heather showed surprise when Amanda secured the break, held on to the sides and allowed Jason to ease onto his knees and then his seat.

As they set up the board, the radio blaring behind them, Jason asked, "Did you hear about the duck who went to the drugstore?"

Taking out the game pieces, Heather groaned but refrained from supplying the punch line. Amanda shook her head as she kicked off her pumps and sank to the floor, placing a bowl of popcorn beside her.

"He bought some lip balm and told the clerk, 'Put it on my bill.'"

Chuckling, Amanda settled into the rug. "Okay, smarty. Why did the tomato cross the garden?" When Jason shook his head, she said, "To get a head of the lettuce."

The ten-year-old guffawed. Amanda quelled the tears that threatened. He was so like Lisa.

That was how Nick DiMarco found them sixty minutes later. Amanda had just demanded rent for two ho tels on Park Place, when she looked up to find Heather staring past her in panic. "Heather," she teased. "It's only five hundred dollars. Listen, I'll lend you—"

Then she realized more was wrong than an unlucky roll of the dice. She tracked the girl's gaze to the door where Nick stood like an avenging angel. Or devil. Amanda bit her lip as she took in his taut stance and narrowed eyes. She also noticed the way his white

T-shirt stretched across his broad chest, outlining every line of his torso. His blue jeans were grubby but didn't detract from what was inside. His chestnut hair was in disarray and his chiseled features stood out more clearly due to fatigue. He looked tired but so sexy that Amanda once again experienced an unfamiliar, but thoroughly intense, feminine rush of response.

"What's going on here?" he asked, his voice low and somewhat impatient. Amanda guessed that Nick Di-Marco didn't like surprises, couldn't afford to like them.

Heather sat up straight and pulled her knees to her chest, hugging them with her arms. "I'm sorry, Daddy, we lost track of the time. We only planned to play—" Her voice broke off and tears welled in her eyes. She lowered her forehead to hide them.

Jason jumped in. "No, Dad, it's my fault. I begged everyone to play. I—"

"Hey, you guys, when did I become such a monster that you have to stick up for each other?"

When neither answered, just stared at him, he glanced around the room as if looking for some way to break the tension. Spying the popcorn, he automatically bent down, picked up the bowl and some of the kernels scattered over the rug. "I'll be right back," he said and headed for the kitchen.

In the small room, Nick tromped to the sink and ducked his head under the faucet, trying to get rid of the dirt *and* his irritation. Exhausted from four hours of construction work, after a morning spent studying for final exams, Nick could taste the grit in his mouth and smell the sweat that had covered him all afternoon.

But it didn't mask the expensive and provocative perfume wafting from the woman who sat on the floor with his children. He pictured them as he wiped his dripping face with a dish towel.

They'd made quite a sight and Nick's heart sank when he realized how natural—and how rare—such a comfortable scene was in his home: his son, propped on pillows, leaning forward like a normal kid, intent on the game; his daughter—until she'd seen him—sprawled lazily on the rug like a typical teenager. He felt guilty for ending this blessed normalcy.

Amanda had been sitting with her legs crossed and her flowered skirt bunched around her knees into her lap. As she'd bent her head to study the board, her scoop-neck sweater had molded to every curve. Her hair was down again, and his hands itched to feel the texture, bury his face in it and inhale the scent of the shampoo she used.

It wasn't just that, he concluded as he dried his hair and combed it back with his hands. He was annoyed because he'd thought too much about Amanda Carson today as he'd hoisted girders, and here she was in his house, as if he'd conjured her. Although the kids had specific tasks to do after school, he wasn't upset with them for taking a needed break. *She* was what got to him. Hearing a flurry of activity in the living room, he grabbed a can of soda from the refrigerator, popped it and took a slug before he returned to the scene of the "crime."

His heart fell to his stomach when he saw the trio lined up before him as if facing a firing squad.

The counselor and his daughter flanked Jason, who bravely said, "Hey, Dad, why did the tomato cross the garden?"

Nick saw Amanda bite her lip to keep from laughing. When he caught sight of the misery on Heather's face, and the hope on Jason's, he let the corners of his mouth turn up fractionally. "I don't know, Jase, why?"

With his compliance, all three visibly relaxed, and Nick's heart plummeted further, realizing again how intimidated his own children felt. Lord, when had this started?

After the punch line, Heather scrambled to pick up the game, while Jason tried to collect the stray popcorn and Amanda unsuccessfully sought her shoes. Nick intervened in the frantic motions.

"I see the chores are done, but my guess is that the homework was saved until last." When both children nodded, he said gently, "All right, now that you've relaxed, go finish it before supper."

As they hurried past him, Nick grasped his daughter's arm. "Heather, it's okay. You're entitled to some fun. I never meant for your afternoons to be so grim."

"I know, Dad. I just don't want to disappoint you."

"Honey, you never disappoint me." He gave her arm a tender squeeze.

When they were settled in their bedrooms, Nick closed their doors for privacy. Looking at Amanda standing warily before him, he was torn between confiding in her and ushering her out the door before he did something stupid. In a weak moment, he said, "I seem to keep making mistakes with Heather, don't I?"

"I don't know if that's true, but I do have some suggestions." Barefoot and beautiful before him, she looked like a spring garden of greens, yellows and purples.

In a gesture of frustration, Nick ran a hand through his hair. "Is that why you're here?"

Amanda took a step back but held his gaze. She might look soft, he thought fleetingly, but there was steel underneath. "Yes, it is. Heather needs psychological help."

"She's seeing you, isn't she?"

As if she was buying time—or was she mustering up her courage?—Amanda turned and searched for her shoes. When she found them, she faced him again, her jaw set. "Heather needs more, Mr. DiMarco. After our session today, I drove her home so I could speak with you about it."

The formal title sounded strange on the lips of the woman who had done wicked things to him in more than one fantasy.

"How much more?" Nick jammed his hands into his jeans.

"Heather is a sad young girl. I want her to join a group of students I counsel. I think it will loosen her up a little, give her kids to identify with." She bit her lip and shifted uncomfortably. "It's a suicide prevention group, Nick."

"*What?*" Too late, he realized he'd raised his voice, and he hoped it wouldn't draw Heather from her room. He grasped Amanda by the arm and pulled her into the kitchen for more privacy. When they reached it, he faced her squarely. "Are you telling me that my daughter wants to *die?*"

The plain words seemed to restore Amanda's courage. She stood up straight, though she didn't nearly match his imposing height. "I'm telling you that from three ninety-minute sessions with your child, I'm concerned that she has so little self-esteem, such a bleak outlook on her future and such dissatisfaction with her present that she is dangerously depressed. Yes, I think she has suicidal tendencies. And ignoring this carries a price you don't want to pay."

Gulping for air, Nick said, "I can't believe this. Not Heather, not my child."

"I know the feeling." Amanda reached out and touched his arm.

Something in her tone made him scrutinize her. "Do you?"

"Yes. More than I want to." The color drained out of her face as she withdrew her hand and gripped the edge of the table.

Every single protective instinct Nick had kicked into overdrive, and he involuntarily grasped her shoulders. "Amanda—"

"I can help your daughter, Nick. Please, give me a chance... Trust me."

It's too much, Nick thought desperately, his fingers sliding down to her upper arms. The worry. The guilt. The fear of the future. And now this. Could his little girl possibly be *that* unhappy? Could he trust this woman, who'd obviously buried deep inside her a kindred pain?

As if to override his doubts, or to underscore them, she raised huge, vulnerable eyes to him. An arrow of desire pierced him. Suddenly, all his fantasies about Amanda Carson swirled before him. And, wanting to escape the grim reality that had become his life, he pulled her close.

He expected her to feel frail, as she looked, but she felt supple, solid, strong. The soft cotton of her clingy sweater teased his palms when he slowly slid one up to her neck. He watched her watch him; she didn't flinch and he liked that. He liked it too much, just as he liked the way she helped Heather, the way she stood up to him despite his doubts, and the way she insisted on

changing her own life. He liked all of her a little too
much.

Don't do it, DiMarco, he warned himself. *Don't do
it,* he thought as his arms banded around her. The brush
of her breasts against his chest was electric, but he welcomed the shock of her. As he bent his head, he wondered fleetingly if he'd regret this later. But he did it,
anyway.

His lips met hers in soft need. They were firm against
hers, but gentle. He pressed hard, but coaxed, too, until she was pressing back, and her hands slid up his to
tangle in his hair. Trembling slightly, she threaded her
fingers through the locks at his nape and he angled the
kiss to get more of her. *Lord, she tastes sweet.* She
opened her mouth willingly to his probing tongue, and
he slid his arm around her slender waist, pulling her into
intimate contact with him.

The phone rang, dragging them both back to reality.
Nick was horrified at what he'd done and stepped away
from her. Shaking her head in denial, Amanda raised
her hand to her lips and rubbed them, as if the gesture
might erase what they'd shared. That she would be so
upset by it was understandable, though. He was a student's father, for God's sake. What had he been thinking?

He turned to answer the phone. "Yeah?" he said into
the receiver. Then, after a pause, his voice softened.
"No, Beth, we're okay. You just caught me at a bad
time. Can I call you back?"

After he hung up, he faced Amanda. Her hair was a
mess from his hands, and her lips were puffy from his
mouth on hers. Even her skirt was askew. He leaned
against the wall, dug his fists into his pockets and
crossed his ankles, trying very hard to look casual and

calm. Inside, his gut was churning. She'd really gotten to him. The kiss had meant . . . too much. "You'd better go, Amanda." His voice was a hoarse whisper.

She put her hand to her mouth again and touched her lips where his had just been. This time, the gesture was both tender and sensual. His stomach dropped to his knees. "Nick, I . . . I . . . you don't . . ."

Caught off guard by her vulnerability, he raised his palm to halt her explanations. "Don't say anything." *Please, God, don't make this worse than it already is.*

Turning from her, he exited the kitchen. He thought he felt her hand on his arm, but he kept going. He had to get away from her before he did anything else foolish.

"Nick, you don't understand. We need to talk about Heather. And we need to talk about *this,*" she called, following him.

"No." The word ripped from him as he faced her at the door. "We can't talk about this. We don't even speak the same language."

Amanda recoiled, then sucked in her breath as if to calm herself. "All right, we won't discuss us. But can we talk about Heather?"

"No, not tonight."

"Can she keep the private sessions, even if you won't let her attend the group?"

Hands fisted at his sides, he said raggedly, "I don't know about either right now. I can't think straight."

"Nick . . ."

"Please . . . just . . . leave." He enunciated each word, but his voice was raw and raspy with emotion.

He could tell she was startled by his reaction. Her cobalt eyes widened and her lips parted. Then, scanning the room, seeming disoriented, she grabbed her coat and fled without another word.

After she'd gone, Nick sank onto a kitchen stool and, in the loneliness of his apartment, admitted to himself that he'd lied. They'd spoken a language as old as time itself, communicated in a way men and women had for centuries, and all the denial in the world couldn't change that fact.

CHAPTER FOUR

SHE WAS KISSING *him again, only they weren't in his kitchen this time, as they'd been four days ago. They were completely, dangerously alone, with no chance for interruption. Thank God, since he was so hard, Nick thought he'd burst. Easing the buttons open on his denim shirt, Amanda ran slender, supple fingers along his bare chest. He pulled her closer and tangled his hands in the thick hair he'd slowly unwrapped from its chic coil. Just as he'd unwrapped her—like a gift from the gods—from the Victorian dress she'd worn earlier. Stepping back slightly so she was standing before him, he could see her lush curves outlined in a sheer, pale blue combination of bra and slip. The smell of expensive perfume filled his nostrils. It drove him wild and he reached for her . . .*

"Hey, Grandpa. What do you call the dumbest fish in a school?"

Jason? What is he doing here? God, was I so hot to get at Amanda that I took her to my house?

Nick heard his father's groan, a put-on since the older man loved Jason's corny puns. "I don't know, Jay. What's it called?"

"Dinner." The boy erupted into a giggle, enjoying his own jokes, as usual, more than anyone else.

Several voices joined in, mocking his son and bringing Nick awake with a start. He found he was sprawled on a green corduroy recliner in a corner of his parents' living room. The familiar smell of spaghetti sauce radiated from the kitchen.

"Oh, Dad, we're sorry we woke you." Heather's voice came from across the room where she was perched next to Beth on the flowered worn sofa, leafing through a magazine his sister had brought her.

Nick wanted to moan in response. Instead, he took a quick inventory, grateful that the paper he'd been reading before he dozed off was camouflaging the effects of his dream.

"No, honey, it's okay. I've got no business falling asleep in the middle of a Sunday afternoon. And don't tell Grandma, any of you." He scanned the room, taking in his son and his father playing checkers at a low corner table. Adjacent to them, his daughter and sister were poring over the latest hairstyles. "She'll badger me about working too much."

"Hmmph!" His father put in his two cents but didn't remove his eyes from the board.

"Well, if the shoe fits, bro," Beth teased.

"Careful, sis," Nick warned with mock severity as he righted the almost-prone chair and ran a hand through his disheveled hair. "If you start on my life-style, I'll feel free to casually mention to Ma that I'm worried about your biological clock ticking away. A whole thirty-one and not married, not even any prospects. I'm sure there's some 'nice Italian boy' she has waiting in the wings that's she's just dying to spring on you."

Everyone laughed at the brother-sister routine, played out with warm affection. Nick himself gave Beth one of his rare, genuine smiles, thinking how much this woman meant to him. The man who eventually cornered her, he mused, would be a fortunate one.

His black jeans were still uncomfortable, but the repartee had cooled his ardor somewhat, and Nick rose from the recliner to turn on the Jets game. He'd been the quarterback for his high school football team and usually loved watching the pros play. But today he kept seeing Amanda Carson superimposed on the screen. She had stood before him last Thursday, wonderfully mussed from his hands and mouth, and her face had showed...surprise. Each time he'd conjured that evening, he'd seen the shock.

Had it been more than her fear of behaving unprofessionally? He couldn't believe her reaction to him was foreign to her, as if she'd never responded to a kiss that way before. Surely some country-club boyfriend had kissed her senseless. He banished the thought quickly, the image of her with another man causing a dull ache in his heart.

Dinner was announced and Nick joined his family in the dining room, as he did every Sunday he could get free. Even when Suzanne had refused to go with him, he had taken Heather to his parents' for spaghetti and socializing.

As he sat down at the large oak table and pushed up the sleeves of his polo shirt, Beth asked, "Nicky, how's the clerking going?"

"Great. Joris is really wooing me, and two other firms called last week." At the thought, Nick felt anticipation swell in him like an athlete before a play-off.

Beth whistled and gave him a thumbs-up sign. "Wow, big time."

"Very big. And exactly what I want." He reached for the plate of meatballs and braciola.

His father's brows knit over his black eyes and his normally swarthy complexion flushed. Nick knew Ange

DiMarco was proud of him, but also that the Italian laborer had strong objections to his son's ambitions. They had argued vehemently over what Ange saw as Nick's sacrifice of time and health just to climb the corporate ladder. They had come to a tenuous truce, but Ange's concern hadn't changed.

Sipping her beer and twirling her spaghetti, Beth casually changed the subject. "So, Heather, how's school?"

"Okay." Heather shifted uneasily. She tugged at the collar of her green and blue rugby shirt and looked apprehensively at her aunt. Nick realized she was afraid Beth would mention the counseling in front of Heather's grandparents.

Beth winked, acknowledging the silent message. "Any good-lookin' guys in your class this year?"

Heather blushed and Nick groaned inwardly. His daughter was thirteen. She was noticing boys. What would he do when she wanted to date? The thought was too frightening to entertain.

"Speaking of dates," Rosa DiMarco interjected, clasping her hands across her hefty bosom, "Mrs. Pacetti's niece is staying with her for a while, Nicky."

"Whoa, Ma, right there. I'm not in the market. I'm too busy to date." Nick took a long swig of beer.

His mother frowned that 'you won't get off that easily' look she had perfected over the years. "It's not normal, you never going out with a woman. You got to get over..." Stumbling on her last words, Rosa's face turned as red as her sauce.

Everyone in the DiMarco family avoided speaking Suzanne Sullivan's name. At Nick's request. He felt it would be too hard on the kids to hear her mentioned. They hadn't seen or heard from her since she'd left.

Every Christmas and on their birthdays, they got cards from Suzanne's parents and that reminder hurt them enough.

Beth coughed to cover the silence, and the scrape of Heather's chair filled in the rest of the void.

Smiling weakly at everyone, Heather stood and picked up her half-filled plate. "I'll start cleaning up, Nana. You did all the cooking and it's the rule that if you make dinner, you don't have to take care of the mess. Jason will help when he's done."

Nick squeezed his fork tightly. Anger that Suzanne had intruded on this meal swept through him. He knew the kids were shaken when his son merely nodded instead of giving his sister an argument about helping with the chores. Nick wished they never had to be reminded of Suzanne. It was best for Heather and Jason to excise her from their lives completely. Wasn't it?

The tension at dinner did not dissipate and he mourned the fact that his one day to be with the people he loved most had been spoiled. Heather said almost nothing after Rosa's slip, picked at the apple pie her grandmother had made especially for her and retreated to another part of the house as soon as she could.

He was still thinking about Suzanne an hour later when he walked into his old upstairs bedroom and found his daughter huddled on the side of the bunks, with an open photo album on her lap and tears streaming down her face. She didn't hear him enter. Realization slammed into Nick like a sucker punch as he stood before her bent little form. Unbidden, Amanda Carson's words came back in full force. *Heather is a sad young girl.* and his own reaction, *Are you telling me that my daughter wants to die?*

Was she right? Was his little girl so hurt she might try to harm herself? Bile rose in his throat and he clamped his hand over his mouth. This was his greatest fear in life. He'd always known that the only thing on earth he could never handle was losing one of his children. The idea that it could happen to Heather—and happen by her own hand—was abhorrent.

Was it an indication of her tenuous state of mind that Heather didn't know he was in the room until he crouched before her and lifted her chin? She peered up at him, dazed, and the agony he saw etched in her youthful face undid him. He sank to his knees and whispered, "Honey, what is it? Tell me. I can help."

Heather shook her head and curled her body into a ball. Nick looked down at what she was holding and recoiled physically as if he'd been struck.

The photo album was open to pictures of Suzanne. Nick had destroyed most of them the day Suzanne walked out, but his mother had kept some because they were the only baby pictures of Heather she had. He'd insisted she store them out of sight but apparently Rosa hadn't buried them deep enough. How many times had his daughter snuck up here to torment herself? How many times had she sat isolated in this room and looked at pictures of her mother, holding her, pushing her stroller, giving her a bath?

"Talk to me, honey."

For a moment, he thought she wouldn't answer. Sitting down next to her, he reached over and stroked her hair, feeling the silky strands that were exactly the same texture and color as her mother's. God, would it help to tell her this? Originally he had thought not. But he was beginning to question his decisions about his ex-wife and his children.

"I can't talk to you, Daddy." Heather's voice was so soft, he had to strain to hear her. She hunched over, still and lifeless.

"Why not?"

She began to cry harder and Nick pulled her to him, tucking her head under his chin. Her hair smelled like baby shampoo. Sobs racked her young body. Tears misted his own eyes but he willed them back, knowing she needed his strength. When she quieted somewhat, he said, "I just want to help."

Heather looked up at him and smiled weakly. He saw a wisdom there far beyond her years and was shaken by the fact that his daughter had obviously experienced enough of life's disappointments to have earned her that look.

"I know you do, Dad. It's just that I'm afraid of—" She broke off, unable to finish the thought. Nick closed his eyes at the sight of her burrowing into him for the only kind of comfort she thought she could get from him.

"You're afraid of what, sweetie?"

"Of... of letting you down," she mumbled into his shirt, grasping a fistful of the cotton in her slender hand.

It was as though someone had doused him with cold water. Nick clasped her tighter to him. "Heather, how could you possibly let me down?"

"I can't tell you. I just can't."

Nick didn't know what to do. Should he push her to tell him? Should he insist? He just couldn't fathom the appropriate response.

But someone else could, you jerk.

I've got a hundred and twenty hours with some of the most prominent child and adolescent psychologists in the city.

Suddenly, the folly of resisting Amanda Carson's aid came crashing down on him like a falling girder. How could he have been so stupid? There was help for his kid right at his doorstep and he had refused it like a stubborn jackass because of his fears for Heather and himself.

His arms loosened around his child and he lifted her chin to look into her sad eyes. "Honey, listen to me," he said hoarsely, fearful his concession might be too late, praying that it wasn't. "I know Ms. Carson has been helping you. Do you think you could share this with her?"

He felt Heather stiffen in his arms.

"What is it?" he asked.

She simply stared at him. Seeing the cold resignation in her eyes, he felt a deep, searing shame. He knew, God help him, what she was going to say even before she got it out.

"You haven't said if I could see her again. I know you didn't like the group thing." Heather gulped as if she was unable to express the untenable thought, and Nick felt like one of the ogres in the fairy tales he used to read to her. "I thought you might say no to it all now."

He'd save the pain and the rage at himself for later. His daughter needed strength now, not his self-flagellation. Running his hand down her arm, he said, "No, honey I'm not saying no to it all. As a matter of fact, I've decided it might be good for you to go to the group, too."

Heather's gasp of surprise only twisted the knife that had lodged in his gut. But he went on. "She makes you feel better, doesn't she?"

When Heather nodded warily, he guessed she was afraid that he would retract his statement.

"Why is she so helpful?"

"I don't know." Heather paused, then relaxed her shoulders and leaned against him so his chest pillowed her cheek. "She seems to like me, Dad, though I don't know why she'd bother with a nobody like me."

Warning bells went off in his head. *I'm concerned that she has so little self-esteem,* Amanda had said.

Nick took a deep breath and raised his hand to brush back his daughter's hair. "Why wouldn't she like you, honey?"

"Why should she, Dad?"

Nick's throat clogged and he was unable to speak for a few seconds. Finally, he eased away from her and tilted her chin. He looked directly at her and asked one of the most difficult questions he'd ever posed in his entire life. "Heather, do you know what kind of group this is?"

The silence of ancient tombs surrounded them for so long that Nick began to worry. Then, in a shadow-filled room on Second Street in Syracuse, New York, Heather DiMarco made the biggest and bravest confession of her young life with a few softly whispered words. "Yes, Daddy. I know what kind of group it is."

Unable to hold them back, Nick's tears escaped. They fell down his cheeks and he turned his head to shield his daughter from his show of emotion. He saw a tear fall onto the open photo album, onto a picture of Suzanne holding Heather as if she had really cared about her.

Nick wiped his eyes. "When does this group meet?"

Reaching up, Heather slid her small palm over his cheek. She pulled her hand away and fingered the wetness that had collected there. Her gaze flew to her father's eyes then back to the tears. "Daddy..."

But Nick grabbed her hand before she could turn the talk to him. "Shh... When, honey?"

"Mondays and Fridays. Right after school." Her voice was husky when she answered.

He closed his eyes and kissed the top of her head. "Stay then, tomorrow. I'll meet you there."

Heather leaned into him the way she used to when she was little and when she was sick. Nick felt nausea churn in his stomach with the realization that she was no longer a little girl and that she was—he could hardly bring himself to say the word. His daughter had just admitted that she was suicidal.

"HOW DID the raccoon get to the bottom of the hill?"

Several groans responded in unison. Amanda sat back in her office chair looking at the tall, thin black boy who sprawled before her. Shunning the popular African-American cornrows, he wore his hair clipped short all over, the style usually accenting the bleakness in his black eyes. Today, though, they were alight with humor. "I give, Ron. How?"

"On the end of a fender."

"Sick, Marshall. Really sick." The gibe came from Sandi Berrios, and was made affectionately as she finger-combed her dark curly mane out of her almond eyes. She sat across from Amanda, next to Ron, swinging her foot rhythmically back and forth. Once again, Amanda was impressed with how nice the three kids before her could be to one another, though Ron remained the most distant.

"Any more jokes to start the session?" Amanda asked.

Matt Barone hooked a straight chair with his foot, turned it around and straddled it to become part of the semicircle. At only seventeen he was almost six feet tall. His unruly sable hair skimmed his collar and fell rakishly over his jade green eyes. He wore his usual deep brown leather jacket. "No, please, Teach, yours was almost as bad as Lee-ronne's." Matt often taunted Ron by using the full name the other boy detested. His smile took the sting away. It was said around school that that dimpled grin had gotten him in more trouble with teachers, and into more girls' pants, than anyone could count. Although the kids' crudity still shocked Amanda at times, the description was apt.

"How's everyone doing today?" Amanda casually guided the talk around to why they were all there.

Shoveling a chocolate chip cookie into his mouth, Matt reached for another of Carson's Cache, as they had dubbed her treats. "Aw, just the usual depression, a little schizophrenia, one or two suicide warning signs poppin' up here and there." Again, his grin softened his sarcasm and Amanda made a mental note to thank him later for breaking the ice. He'd done it often in the six weeks they'd been meeting.

These three students were high-risk, potential suicide candidates who'd been referred last year before Amanda came to Eastside High. The number of suicidal teenagers at the school had spurred hiring someone specifically trained in this area.

Sandi was about to make a comment, when there was a knock on the door. Amanda frowned, knowing the secretaries had strict instructions not to interrupt these sessions. She rose from the chair, opened the door and came face-to-face with Heather DiMarco.

The young girl stood tall before her and only the trembling of her lower lip indicated how scared she really was. Amanda's heart sank at seeing her. Much as Heather needed the help this group could give her, she could not be included over the resistance of her father. Damn his stubborn hide.

Excusing herself, Amanda stepped into the hall to explain this to Heather, only to come face-to-face with the hide she'd just cursed. She was so surprised that she was momentarily speechless.

"Hi," Nick said, his tone oddly humble. "I hope it's not too late for Heather. To make this session, I mean."

The statement was fraught with other meaning. Standing before her was a proud man who had overcome his own fears to admit his daughter needed help that he couldn't give her. Amanda was sure it was one of the most difficult things he'd ever done.

"Of course it's not too late. We just got started." She smiled warmly, then addressed Heather, "You ready for this?"

"I don't know."

"Well, I think you are." Amanda turned to open the door, but saw, from the corner of her eye, Nick reach for Heather and give her an encouraging hug. He whispered something in her ear, then backed away.

Inside, Amanda seated Heather next to her and began the introductions. "This is Heather DiMarco. I mentioned last time that we might possibly have a new member soon and here she is. How about some introductions?"

Silence reigned. Heather's wary eyes were glued to the schoolbooks she held on to tightly. At last, someone spoke up.

"Hi, Heather. I'm Matt Barone. Don't believe all you hear about me from the other kids, except what a cool dude I am." Then he winked at her, his green eyes sparkling.

Amanda smiled, noting Heather's blush. She could have hugged Matt for his teasing.

"Sandi Berrios," a sultry voice put in. "Glad we got another chick to even out the odds here, no offense, Ms. C."

"None taken." Amanda turned to the last member of the group and arched an eyebrow.

"Ron Marshall" was all he said, but his cold clipped tone spoke volumes. Amanda saw Heather's whole body tense in reaction.

"Don't mind Lee-ronne," Matt told her. He's just p—sorry, ticked off that we don't like his joke for the day."

A good place to start. Amanda folded her hands in front of her to present a relaxed pose. "We usually begin with a joke every time, Heather, and Ron's was particularly, ah, sick, today."

The teenagers chuckled and Amanda continued. "Then we go around the table and tell how we've been doing since the last meeting. Usually, we find something to zero in on for the remainder of the hour and a half."

Heather lifted her eyes from her books. "Okay."

"If anyone wants to pass, he or she can," Amanda added, and smiled encouragingly at the girl. "You can just listen today to get the lay of the land, if it's okay with the rest of you."

Amanda scanned the group, holding her breath they'd agree. She knew how important it was for them to make decisions and feel ownership of their time together, but she was hoping they'd take pity on the youngest and newest member.

Matt jerked his chin upward. "I'm cool."

"Yo," Sandi agreed, staring at Heather with assessing eyes. Amanda knew she was taking stock of the blond-haired, blue-eyed aristocratic looks Heather had inherited from her mother, so different from Sandi's Hispanic coloring.

She turned to Ron. He'd averted his eyes and was studying a poster. Quicker than a finger snap, he could create a shell around himself harder than any turtle's and almost as impenetrable. "Ron?"

He nodded somberly.

After a pause, Amanda asked, "Sandi, you were about to say something before."

The girl's usually sad eyes lit up like sparklers on the Fourth of July. She made a fist and punched the air. "My ma's back."

Amanda was glad for Sandi, but wished this had not been the first thing shared today. The counselor in her sensed that Heather's abandonment by her mother was at the heart of her difficulties, and the way the girl stiffened at Sandi's comments seemed to confirm this.

"She clean?" Matt asked.

"Think so." Slouching back into the chair, Sandi crossed her legs and fidgeted with the buttons of her shiny blouse. Some of her enthusiasm waned visibly. "She says she is, anyway. Geez, how can you tell?"

When no one responded, Amanda said, "I guess you can't ever be sure. Rehab centers are often bad-mouthed for the fifty percent relapse rate, but don't forget, that means fifty percent stay straight.''

When the teenager said nothing, Amanda turned to the others. "Guys? How's it going?"

"Got my bike fixed after that bust-up." Matt drummed his fist into his denim-clad knee, indicating he was upset. When there was no response, he scowled. "Had to borrow the money from my brother, though."

Matt Barone, the bad boy of Eastside High, had had many crack-ups with his motorcycle. Amanda worried about him constantly. The facts were chilling. Accidents made up a large proportion of teenage deaths, and who knew how many were real *accidents* and how many were intentional?

Matt's home life was also in an upheaval. He lived with his brother and sister-in-law, but Amanda wasn't sure how healthy the arrangements were. All he would say was that it was better than staying with "that bitch," a term he always used for his mother. So far, he'd never said why he hated her so much.

Slumped in his chair, an ankle crossed over his knee, Ron toyed with the laces of his combat boots. "'Least somebody helped you, bro."

Ah, the power of group therapy. Amanda knew that on her own, she would never have gotten Ron to open up; he would have remained a clam for the entire session as he had in all the private meetings she'd had with him. Maybe the same would happen with Heather, with those things the girl couldn't articulate.

And so it went. Bits and pieces of their misery were revealed, falling together like some macabre tapestry, one tiny comment at a time, usually said in casual, understated tones. Amanda was sure it hurt more than picking glass slivers out of your arm. By the time the group ended, she was exhausted.

But she asked Heather to stay for a minute when everyone had gone, and took the seat next to her. "What did you think?"

"They hurt a lot." The teenager sighed heavily, twirling a long strand of hair in her fingers. A look of commiseration shadowed her face. "Like me."

"You want to come back?"

Heather nodded.

"Is it okay with your dad?"

Heather bolted upright. "Oh, my God, I forgot. He's waiting for me. He's been out there an hour and a half."

Scooping up her books, she rushed through the open door. Nick raised his eyes from the text he'd been studying and smiled at her. There was no impatience in his demeanor and Amanda wondered where Heather got the idea she was impinging on his time.

"All set?" he asked calmly.

"Yeah. Sorry you had to wait so long." Heather struggled with her khaki jacket.

Nick's grin was meant to ease her anxiety. *He's had a lot of practice.*

"Don't be," he said easily, shrugging into his coat and bending over to gather up his books. "Got three chapters read for my course tonight."

Amanda saw the air seep out of Heather like a deflated balloon. Clearly, she'd counted on her dad's presence this evening. Nick's time at home, or lack of it, was going to be a problem, Amanda could feel it at a gut level.

Instead of picking up on Heather's cue, Nick reached out to grasp her arm. "Honey, I want to talk to Ms. Carson for a minute, okay?"

"Sure. I'll wait in the hall."

"No, Heather, wait right here. The school officially closes at five o'clock and there are guards posted to keep visitors out. Your dad and I will go into my office."

She smiled at Heather, then led Nick into her office. He filled up the small space. Looking at his rock-solid body in an ancient bomber jacket and faded denim jeans, she was reminded of the night in his tiny kitchen. Amanda tried to banish the memory, for several reasons, not the least of which was the professional conflict.

"I'm sorry about overreacting to this," he said, wrapping one hand around his neck and massaging the tightened muscles there. Though his tone was casual, the creases around his mouth were deeper today. Amanda knew what it was like to admit someone you loved was unable to cope with her own life. Maybe he'd be able to in time, she thought.

She hadn't been.

Rubbing the sleeves of her coral jersey dress, Amanda tried to ward off the chill that spiraled through her. "I understand, Mr. DiMarco. You did what you thought best."

A flicker of annoyance crossed his face. "Don't you think we're a little past that formality, Amanda?"

It was the way he said her name that terrified her. He breathed it. He caressed it. It was too intimate. She cleared her throat and dug her nails into her palms to quell her reaction. "Maybe we shouldn't be."

Apparently frustrated, he ran his hands through his hair, then slid them into his pockets. But he kept his eyes on her. "Maybe you're right. Listen, a lot of things have happened to me in the past. I guess I have a chip on my shoulder. You seem to trigger some of them . . ."

Amanda's heart went out to him. She relaxed her stance and perched on the edge of the desk. "It's okay, Nick. I have some things in my own past that make me touchy around you."

Nick seemed primed to talk. He straightened and stood tall, as if it would make what he was about to say easier. "Look, you know Heather's mother doesn't live with us."

"Yes, it's in the records."

"I suppose I seem like a failure to you, but there were circumstances at the time . . . that I don't want to get into." The muscles in his jaw tightened.

"No, you don't seem like a failure to me. I have a divorce behind me also. I know how difficult it is when a marriage is falling apart."

"Thanks."

"You're in law school, aren't you?" she asked, trying to keep the conversation going.

"Yeah. I've wanted to be a lawyer for a long time. I've worked for years to get within reach of it. But with my classes and with Jason's financial and physical demands, time is tight and Heather doesn't get enough from me. But I'm almost done now. As soon as I am, things will be better."

Amanda came off the desk and stood before him, seeing an opening to plead her case. "In the meantime, I can help your daughter, I know I can." When he just stared at her, she asked, "You're going to let me try, with the group, too, aren't you?"

He nodded. "Yes, I am. And I'm making you a promise. She can see you as much as she wants and I won't sabotage anything you do with her. No matter what happens." Nick's voice was hoarse with emotion and Amanda felt her own throat clog. "As her father, I'll do anything I can to help."

To cover her response, Amanda stepped away and clasped her hands behind her back. "I really admire you, Nick."

His eyebrows arched and he angled his head, his surprise evident. "I'm just doing what I should have done when you first brought this up."

Then he straightened and seemed to search for some way to break the tension. Scanning her messy office as he'd done before, his eyes landed on the joke of the day.

He smiled, and all thoughts of *admiration* fled from Amanda's mind at his sexy grin.

"Do you know how many guidance counselors it takes to change a light bulb?" he asked glibly.

Surprised at his levity, Amanda shook her head.

"One. But it's *really* got to want to change."

His chuckle added unnecessary wattage to his grin and he left her with the image of him whistling as he exited her office. Nick DiMarco could be lethal, Amanda thought. As she plopped into her chair and plunked her feet up on her desk, she wondered what it would be like to be held in his arms, free of professional conflict and its effect on all of them.

CHAPTER FIVE

THE SINGER BELTED OUT her undying love for the only man who could make her happy and Amanda wondered if she would ever feel that kind of passion and commitment. She looked over at Craig who sat in the civic center peering through the opera glasses he didn't need because their box seats were, as usual, the best.

I'll never feel it for him, Amanda thought sadly. Truth be told, she wasn't certain she even *liked* him anymore, given the way he'd been treating her since she'd "moved into that unacceptable neighborhood" and "gotten involved in that ghetto school." His terminology had incensed her but she'd been unable to express her anger. As usual. What was she doing here with him, anyway? And why couldn't she stand up more to the men in her life?

Without warning, an image of Nick DiMarco appeared before her. She'd stood up to *him.* Why? There was something about him that encouraged her spunk. Perhaps it was because he thought enough of her to challenge her. It was a crazy notion, but no more lunatic than the other thoughts she'd had of him. The sexual thoughts. The *graphic, detailed* sexual thoughts. Pretty intense for a woman who had never really found any of the men she'd known attractive enough to respond to them as a woman should.

She'd seen Nick only once since the afternoon Heather joined the group two weeks ago. Heather's aunt Beth had picked her up the other times, but the day Nick came for the teenager, he had asked for a few minutes alone with Amanda again.

He'd looked sexy in beige painter's jeans and a navy pullover that deepened the gray of his eyes. But it was the look on his face that had prompted her to readily agree.

Sinking into a chair, head down, knees spread, he'd clasped his hands between them. He was silent for a moment, staring at the floor.

"I want to talk about my daughter. I've been doing some reading about—" When he stopped suddenly, Amanda realized he was unable to articulate the thought. She wanted desperately to supply the words for him, but bit her tongue to keep from doing so. It was best if he said them himself.

Cautiously he looked up at her, his shoulders tense, his knuckles white, and that piercing silver gaze made her weaken. It was at that instant—longing to comfort the man before her—that she admitted her feelings for Nick DiMarco went beyond physical attraction. Maybe it was his willingness to put Heather's welfare above his fears. Maybe it was his struggle to do the right thing, no matter how difficult. But she was beginning to see the man inside, and liked him every bit as much as the very appealing outer one. That she felt this way about a student's father was something she'd have to deal with later, but it felt so right that she allowed herself to bask in it temporarily.

"I've been reading about adolescent suicide," he finally finished, the words like fingernails scraping a blackboard. He winced. "It's so prevalent."

"Almost six thousand teens a year die by their own hand."

Nick sat back and thrust his hands into his pockets. His eyes were grim. "I think Heather has some of the warning signs."

"I do, too, Nick."

"I, ah, talked to her about it. The books said to be careful not to create a conspiracy of silence, I think they called it."

Realizing he needed some reaction from her, Amanda said, "I agree with that theory. What was Heather's response?"

"She was pretty noncommittal. She seems to have a hard time telling me things, almost like she's afraid." Nick rocked his chair back on its back legs and tilted his head toward the wall.

This was the second time fear had come up. Amanda would stake her life on the fact that Nick would never hurt his kids, but a counselor had to be objective and protect the child. It was hard to ask, but she did it, anyway. "Why would she be afraid of you?"

His chair plunked down with a thud and awareness glinted in his pewter eyes, making them steely with accusation. "I thought we were beyond that, Ms. Carson."

Amanda's spine stiffened. She would not apologize for doing her job. "We are. But look at it from my perspective, or better yet, look at it as her father. Wouldn't you rather that I cover all the bases and not let anything slip by?"

"Yes, I would." Some emotion she couldn't identify warmed his flinty stare. Admiration, maybe? He shook his head and looked up at the ceiling. "I don't know why I'm so prickly with you. Or maybe I do . . . but I'll try to keep it in perspective.''

When Amanda smiled her encouragement, Nick rose and began to pace in the small room. ''What I really think is that she's afraid of hurting me. Afraid of worrying me.''

''Afraid of taking up too much of your time.''

Stopping midstride, Nick circled and peered down at her. ''My schedule is tight, but I try to make time for my daughter. This degree is important to me. I've sacrificed too much to stop now.''

Torn between what she knew Heather needed, and a very real understanding of Nick's need to succeed, so much like her own, Amanda answered slowly. ''All right, let's not debate this. I think it would be a good idea if you kept trying to get Heather to talk about it. And about what's causing her depression.''

''Should I do anything about her eating?'' Nick rubbed his neck with his hand as he spoke. At Amanda's quizzical look, he explained how Heather had been picking at her food. Suddenly, Amanda remembered seeing her at lunch a couple of times without anything in front of her. And she never sampled the cookies that were a staple on Amanda's desk.

''Was she a good eater before?''

Nick's shrugged. ''We don't eat together a lot . . . but I don't think it's ever been this bad.''

Amanda smiled reassuringly. ''Nick, we'll help her, I promise.''

''I know that. I know you're good for her and that you can help. But what I don't understand is why someone like you takes a job like this. You obviously don't need the money.''

She'd been tempted to brush him off with some cliché, but the intensity of his gaze, and his earlier confession, prompted her to share her reasons. At least some of them. Sighing heavily, she jammed her hands into the pockets of her pink woolen skirt. "You're not the only one who needs to succeed, Nick. I've done absolutely nothing useful with my adult life and this job is the first chance I've taken to do something worthwhile. Along the way, I get to prove to myself that I can do it." She looked at him intently for a moment, then went on. "Don't get me wrong. I care deeply about Heather's welfare and that of the rest of the kids. It's just that it's vital to me as a person to do this job well." She grinned sheepishly at him, then shrugged. "I just thought since you'd shared... I would, too."

Nick had moved from the middle of the room to stand before her. Empathy had darkened his stormy eyes. "Thanks. For helping Heather," he'd said huskily. "And for telling me this..."

"Amanda!" Craig snapped his fingers to get her attention. "Where are you? The first act is over, and you didn't even clap."

Coming back to the present, she looked vaguely at her date and muttered some excuse, enough to pacify him so they could go to the lobby for a drink... where they unfortunately ran into her parents.

"How nice to see you, dear," her mother said, giving her a peck on the cheek.

"Yes, it is." Her father kissed her briefly. "It's been days since we've heard from you."

"I didn't know you two would be here tonight."

As her father sipped his martini, a flicker of sadness shadowed his face. She'd noticed it once or twice lately and wondered at it. Finally, he said, "How would you know our plans? We talk so little. Really, Amanda, it hurts your mother when you ignore her like this. Is this job more important than your family?''

Amanda looked, really looked, at her father. Classically handsome, he had a full head of silver hair and eyes that were the same color as her own blue ones. But his housed a smugness she knew hers didn't possess.

''Amanda, your father asked you a question,'' Craig said, stroking the shoulder of her crepe sheath.

His touch made her shudder. She stared at him blankly for a moment and then shook her head. ''Yes, Craig. I heard him.'' She turned to Robert. ''And yes, Father, this job is important.'' She recalled Nick's words. *I know you're good for her. I know you can help her.* His statement wrapped around Amanda like a blanket, shielding her from the chill of her father's displeasure. ''Now, if you'll excuse me, I've got to use the ladies' room.'' Taking her mother by the arm, she suggested, ''Why don't you come with me? We can chat for a few minutes. I really like the way that mauve jacket highlights your complexion.''

As they repaired their makeup in the huge powder room, Amanda saw her mother peer at her in the mirror. Joan's hair was twisted into an elegant knot that accented her clear sea blue eyes and high cheekbones. At fifty-five, her mother was still a lovely woman.

''That teal color is exquisite on you, dear, but you look tired,'' Joan observed.

Amanda glossed her lips, then stared back at her. ''Mother, doesn't his arrogance bother you?''

Joan grasped her Gucci purse tightly but held her daughter's gaze in the mirror. ''Yes, it does. Especially when it's directed at you.''

"Really? I never knew that." Amanda had expected denial. Joan's confession shocked her.

"I'm not surprised." Taking a deep breath, her mother pushed away from the wall and stepped closer. "Amanda, let's do something together. What if I helped you with your house? Decorating, perhaps?"

She thought of the fifty-year-old house she'd bought and the major renovations it required. Slowly, Amanda turned and leaned back against the vanity. "I'd love your help, but the house is still in the remodeling stage. Right now, I need someone who's handy with a paint-brush, not a fabric swatch."

Joan raised her eyebrows and angled her chin in a gesture that made her look years younger. "I'll have you know I painted my dorm room at Vassar, *and* my first apartment."

"Honestly? I can't picture it."

"I'm afraid there are many things about me that you don't know."

"Why is that, Mother?"

"Sometimes, things don't happen the way you plan. My life took turns I hadn't expected." She stared over Amanda's shoulder.

"You mean Lisa?"

"Partially." Her mother's eyes held a wealth of pain. "But I also mean you."

Impulsively, Amanda reached out and hugged her mother, a real hug, not a polite, formal hello.

Joan hugged her in return. Then, stepping back, she hooked her sequined arm in her daughter's to lead her out of the powder room, and said, "Now, about that painting..."

As they returned to the foyer, Amanda was struck with a double awareness. Reaching a new plane of communication with her mother gave Amanda a real sense of pleasure and satisfaction. And if that was true for her, the need Heather DiMarco must feel to know and understand something about her own mother must be great.

Later, Craig was still grumbling as he walked her to her door. "It's all so unlike you, darling, arguing in public with your father, buying this ramshackle place and insisting on living here." He reached up and touched her cheek. "Are you sure you're feeling all right?"

Annoyed by his petulance, Amanda shrugged off his caress. "Actually, Craig," she said, "I'm feeling rather tired right now. I'd like to go to bed, if you don't mind."

She hadn't realized her unfortunate choice of words until she saw the masculine glint in his eyes. He grabbed her waist and pulled her to him. He felt thin compared to the sinewy strength of Nick's body. *Oh, God, now I'm thinking about him when...*

Briefly, she closed her eyes and Craig apparently misinterpreted the gesture. His lips swooped down and took hers like a crane after an ocean fish. Amanda felt the studs of his tux dig into her, and put her hands on his chest and pushed. He ignored the sign of rejection.

"Let me come to bed with you," he whispered silkily.

Straining to step back, she didn't try to hide her irritation. "No, Craig. I told you, we're not—"

Amanda could feel his grip tighten on her shoulders as he interrupted her. "I'm getting tired of this, Amanda."

In answer, she jerked away from him, crossed her arms defensively and glared at him. She was about to tell him what to do with his exasperation, when he added, "I know you haven't been yourself in the last year and a half. And I've been patient. But I won't tolerate this much longer. And I'll certainly expect you to warm up to me after we're married. Lisa's dead. Not you."

Amanda had once slammed into the concrete side of a house while sledding with her friends when she was thirteen. Craig's gibe hit her with similar force. It took her a moment to realize the full impact. He was halfway down the sidewalk, strutting with righteous male indignation in his six-hundred-dollar tux, before she recovered enough to respond. She said into the darkness, "You bastard."

Next time, she vowed she'd say it to his face.

DURING HER third private counseling session since she'd joined the group, Heather was struck by a scary thought. She was coming to care too much for her guidance counselor. Ms. Carson's genuine smile always warmed her. Today, the shiny purple outfit the counselor wore called attention to her blue eyes that, as usual, sparkled with sympathy and humor. Each time Heather saw her, she liked being with her more than the last.

Heather frowned, knowing it didn't pay to get too close to anyone. That's why she had so few friends. But she needed help. Ms. Carson *did* make her feel better enough to get through each day. Maybe even the tough ones coming up. She shuddered at the thought of enduring another anniversary of The Day, as she had come to call it. Now, Ms. Carson was prodding her to reveal this, too. But she just couldn't say the words out loud. Instead, she buried her face in her hands.

Ms. Carson hesitated, and Heather had come to learn that this meant she was deciding whether to give some advice or dig deeper. "Does this issue concern your mother?"

So, she'd decided to dig. Heather dropped her hands and shook her head, refusing for the fourth time to talk about it.

Standing up, Ms. Carson went to stare out the window. Another adult tactic—wait it out. Her father did it all the time. After a moment, the counselor turned to face her and slipped her hands into the pockets of her long, pretty, purple skirt. "Have any of our sessions helped you feel better?"

"Yes," she answered truthfully. "A lot."

"And why do you think that is?"

Absently, Heather pulled her hair off her shoulders and held it up behind her head in a mock ponytail. This was some sort of trap, she could sense it. "Because you help me to look at things differently. They don't seem so...big...anymore."

Ms. Carson smiled and casually leaned back against the window frame. The light from outside made her hair shine like a golden halo. "Then, how about letting me help put this in perspective, too."

She'd been right, she'd gotten cornered on this one. Heather smiled weakly at having fallen for the counselor's ploy. Then she felt those terrible tears pushing from the insides of her lids like a landslide and she hung her head in shame. She fingered the seams on the sides of her jeans. God, she'd promised herself she wouldn't cry today.

Ms. Carson grabbed some tissues and came to kneel before her. "Here, honey." Handing her the Kleenex, she looked right into Heather's eyes and spoke in such a convincing voice that Heather almost believed what she said. "It's okay to cry. You don't have to be brave with me. It's *better* if you let it all out. Keeping it inside is the worst thing you can do."

"But... but... I'm big now... I should be able to handle all this." She had to stop between words because the sobs were coming so fast they kept her from talking. She gripped the edges of the chair for support.

"Big people cry, too," Ms. Carson said, and Heather glanced up sharply at the counselor's choked words. It sounded as though the woman had felt this way before, maybe even cried over it. A sudden image of her father flashed into Heather's mind. He had cried that day at Nana's when she'd confessed just how depressed she was. She'd been shocked by his emotion. That experience, and Ms. Carson's reaction, made Heather want to open up, to tell this woman everything.

"Come on, you can tell me. You've already discussed how bad you feel for your brother, how much sympathy you have for your dad. Let's talk about *you*. What's hurting you so much?"

There was a long pause and finally the pain won out over her shame. "You were right earlier."

"It's about your mother." Ms. Carson stood and eased back onto the edge of her desk.

Heather averted her eyes and stared at her battered sneakers. She nodded, those words making her unable to speak. *Your mother.* God, she really did have one.

"What are you feeling about her?"

Heather sifted through the thoughts and emotions she'd had about this, all the ones no one had *ever* asked her to say out loud. Finally, she zeroed in on the most pressing one. "I wonder about her. What she's like, what she thinks about." Then, she barely whispered,

"Is she married again? Does she have any more..."
Heather couldn't finish the unbearable thought.

"How could you get some of those questions answered?"

"I don't know."

"Well, who would know this about her?"

"Oh, no, I could never ask him. No, Ms. Carson. I couldn't do it. Please, don't tell me to. Oh, God, what have I done? I shouldn't have said anything." Heather scanned the room frantically, ready to bolt from her chair.

Just then, the phone rang. Ms. Carson looked as if she didn't want to answer it. She glanced at her watch. "Heather," she said. "It's almost the end of our session, and the call could be for you." She grabbed the receiver. "Hello."

"Amanda, this is Beth DiMarco. I'm supposed to pick up Heather in ten minutes and there's no way I can make it. I'm stuck in a meeting that I've already canceled twice. Could she possibly wait there an extra half hour? I know it's putting you out, but I'm desperate."

"Beth, it's fine, don't worry. Why don't I just run Heather home? It's on my way and you can meet her there. I'll stay until you get to the house."

"You're a doll, Amanda Carson. I'll take you out to dinner to pay you back. I'd like to get to know you better, anyway."

"I'd like that, too," Amanda said before she hung up, oddly touched by the other woman's gesture of friendship.

During the phone conversation, Heather had closed up tighter than a freshly sealed tomb. Amanda decided to let it go for now, gathered her belongings, put on her coat and waited for Heather to do the same. They chatted on the short drive to the DiMarcos' apartment.

Nick's mother was there, but was running late for an appointment. When she left, Amanda was once again alone with the children of the man who occupied too many of her thoughts. She looked around the small living room, seeing Nick's stamp in the orderliness of his house and smelling the faint aroma of his cologne that lingered in the air.

Jason lounged on the floor, propped up by the couch, his navy sweatshirt emblazoned with a colorful Batman. As soon as his grandmother left, he eyed Amanda with relish. "What do you get when you cross an insect with a rabbit?"

"A hairy aunt?"

"Nope! Bugs bunny."

Amanda ruffled his hair while Heather groaned and bent to pick up the baseball cards strewn around him.

"Heather, don't, I'm just checking out how many I have to trade."

Amanda was reminded again of Lisa. She had loved baseball, too, and Amanda had always watched the games with her, impressed by her interest and knowledge. Jason's obvious enchantment with it made her feel close to Nick's son.

Shaking off the sad reminder of her sister, Amanda turned to the children and told Jason an even cornier pun than his, and the three settled down to wait for Beth.

Forty-five minutes later, the kids' aunt flew through the door, her arms full of packages, her chestnut hair tumbling around her cheeks, her face flushed. Jason was reading stats to Amanda out loud from his cards, while she French-braided Heather's hair.

Amanda could smell the distinctive Chinese sweet-and-sour combination as Beth set down the cartons. "Sorry, I'm later than I thought," she said as she whipped off her coat. "I stopped to get dinner. And there's enough for you, too, Amanda. You've got to stay and eat with us."

Heather frowned at all the packaging.

"Don't worry, doll, we'll put the food in pans and plates and keep it warm in the oven," Beth said easily. "That way, he'll never have to see all the cardboard boxes and bags that make him crazy. Honestly, I'm not sure how my brother got to be such a neat nut."

But Amanda knew. He had to have some control, had to put some order in a world that had spun out of his grasp like an uncharted meteor. Though she sympathized with the man who felt this need, she was worried about its effect on his daughter.

After securing Amanda's promise to remain for dinner, Beth went to the kitchen to heat up the food. When she returned, she joined Jason on the floor.

"Turn on the game, buddy," she told him, picking up the cards and perusing them. Amanda watched as Jason maneuvered himself with his hands to the television, switched on the World Series and settled back with his aunt as if they'd done it a hundred times. They discussed each player and Amanda was amazed at Beth's involvement in the game.

"What would you like to do, Heather?" Amanda asked.

"Can we do a make-over?"

In a few minutes, the two were immersed in coloring Heather's eyelids and accenting her cheeks with makeup from a bag Heather had retrieved from her room. The effect on her widely spaced eyes and creamy skin was dramatic. The girl would be a beauty when she was a few years older.

At six-thirty, Amanda glanced at the clock and mentioned the late hour to Beth. Nick was not home and he hadn't called. As if by telepathy, the phone rang. Beth went to answer it. It was Nick, and Beth's frown gave them cause for concern.

"You *what?* How long ago?" After a pause, she said, "Oh, Nicky, why didn't you call us? You shouldn't have gone alone."

The atmosphere in the small room was charged, as if struck by a bolt of lightning. Heather left the couch and made her way to Jason, sitting down carefully next to him. The boy leaned into his sister, and they hugged each other as they listened to what was clearly something bad about their father.

After a moment, Beth hung up and went to the children. She knelt down, taking a young hand in each of hers. "Your dad is okay. But there's been an accident at the construction site. He hurt his head a little bit. They've bandaged it and he's on his way home from the hospital right now. He'll be here in ten minutes."

Jason began to cry first, then tears slipped down his sister's cheeks. Amanda joined Beth on the floor in front of them.

"Heather, are you all right?" The girl had gone as pale as November snow, and when Amanda touched her, Heather's hands were just as cold. There was terror in her glassy blue eyes.

"He...could...what if he...who would..." For the second time that afternoon, Amanda watched Heather deal with thoughts she couldn't utter.

"Listen to me, both of you." Amanda's firm tone made their heads snap up. "Your father is fine, do you

understand that?'' They nodded simultaneously. "But
let's talk about what arrangements he's made in case
one day he can't take care of you. Do you know what
his plan is?"

The children shook their heads simultaneously.
Amanda looked at Beth. "Do you know?" she asked.

Clearly surprised at Amanda's candor, Beth answered, "I get custody of them to raise as my own." She
smiled at Amanda as understanding dawned. Beth
turned to the kids and stroked a hand down each of
their cheeks. "Didn't you guys know that? I'd take care
of you until you left me to get married and have kids
and ask me to baby-sit for them."

Beth's lightness alleviated much of the tension in the
room. Both children visibly relaxed. Then Beth added,
"And I'd love every minute of it. You'll always have
me." She hugged them fiercely, her eyes moist. They
remained that way, a tableau of love, until their aunt
pulled back. "Uh-oh, Heather, your makeup is smear-
ing. And Jason, you're bending back the corners of a
Dave Stewart card."

Amanda was repairing eye shadow and Beth was
smoothing creases out of the ball player's face when
Nick walked in minutes later. He stood by the door and
looked around at the four of them, something close to
amusement flickering brightly in his gray eyes. Then he
held out his arms. "Well, you'd think I could get a little sympathy around here," he said, gingerly touching
the bump on his left temple, which had turned purple.

Heather flew across the room to him, encircling his
waist with her slender arms and burying her face in his
wide, safe chest. Jason eased into his wheelchair and
spun over to hug his dad. Amanda had to turn away
from the scene.

Beth got dinner on the table soon after that, and when they'd finished cleaning up, Amanda announced it was time for her to leave. Everyone followed her to the door and Heather gave her an impulsive hug after she'd donned her coat. Amanda returned it with fervor. She was surprised to see Nick grab his jacket and murmur he'd see her to her car.

When they reached the curb, he settled her into the driver's seat and went around to the other side and got in. She was acutely aware of him looming next to her in the small interior of her Honda Civic. It was dark out, but the faint streetlight allowed her to see him sink wearily into the seat and rub his neck. Then he turned to face her. "Thanks for everything you did tonight."

"You're welcome. Are you sure you're all right? You should be in bed."

The sexy stare he favored her with made her knees weak, and the words she'd said took on a whole new meaning. Her eyes riveted on the plain white T-shirt and how it outlined the muscles of his arms. She wished they were around her.

"I just wanted to spend a few minutes alone with you," he admitted, but the words were like a caress, and just as potent.

"You did?"

In answer, he smiled at her, raised his arm and settled it on the seat behind her. He slid a few silky strands of her hair between his fingers. "Yeah, I did."

"Why?" She was mesmerized by the huskiness of his voice and the feel of his hand in her hair.

There was a long, meaningful pause and Nick's gaze traveled from the activity of his fingers to her eyes. "Because I appreciate all you're doing for Heather, even though I was so wary of it. Because I like how you want to help all the troubled kids at Eastside." His gaze dropped to her lips and his voice turned whiskey-soft. "Because I want to kiss you."

Amanda swayed toward him and without censoring her words, she whispered, "I want that, too. I just don't believe it."

The intimacy shattered like broken glass. Nick withdrew his hand from her. "Oh? Want to tell me why, princess?"

Amanda detected the annoyance in his tone, and the self-protective shield that was beginning to mask his face.

"Well, for one thing, Heather is my student, and I'm worried about the blurring of roles here."

His face softened. "Conflict of interest?"

"Yes."

"Would you be willing to work on it? It isn't like either of us is married. And I think we could keep it separate. That is, if you want to try."

His vulnerability touched her. "I want to try, Nick."

"But that's not the only reason you're surprised, is it?"

She shook her head.

"Tell me, Amanda."

"I'm not sure I can. I've never talked about this with anyone."

"Tell me. Please."

Taking a deep breath, she finger-combed a shaky hand through her hair. "I . . . I told you I was divorced, remember?"

Nodding, Nick didn't speak.

"Well, with Porter, my ex-husband, I wasn't very good at this." She waved her hand limply in the air.

Nick's forehead creased and he shook his head. "I'm lost. You're not good at *what?*"

Embarrassed, Amanda buried her face in her hands. "At sex. I haven't had good experiences with sex. I'm not very... responsive, Nick."

She was stunned as he threw back his head and guffawed. The laugh was deep and from his belly. Pulling away from him, she said haughtily, "Well, I didn't expect you to mock me."

When he calmed to a near chuckle, he reached out to stroke her hair again. "I'm not mocking *you,* Amanda. I'm mocking *him.*"

"Why?"

Nick eased toward her and his closeness made her pulse accelerate. Shaking his head, he said huskily, "Lady, someone's been feeding you a big line."

"What do you mean?"

Instead of answering, he peered intently into her eyes. For a long time. Then he took her shoulders in his hands. "Come here. A little demonstration should clear this up."

Without waiting for her verbal acquiescence, he pulled her to him. First, his lips brushed hers, back and forth, then back and forth again. All her muscles turned to gel and Amanda found it difficult to breathe. Increasing the pressure, he settled his lips over hers and his tongue demanded she part them. When she did, he invaded her mouth, encircling her teeth, probing every corner and every recess. She inched closer to him, instinctively trying to press her body to his. Denim met silk. He pulled back and took her face between his callused hands. The after-shave he'd used that morning still clung to his cheek and its male scent filled her.

"Tell me what you're feeling right now," he said.

Though she blushed, she was helpless to refuse him. "Light-headed. Breathless."

His smile was masculine smugness personified. Moving one hand from her face, he slowly traced her jaw, then her throat with his fingers. When they skimmed her breasts, she started. "And here, Amanda. What do you feel here?"

"Achy. I want you to touch me there." She could barely breathe but she was under his spell and had no choice but to answer.

Nick's jaw clenched in reaction to her words, and she felt a spurt of feminine satisfaction. But all thought fled when he cupped her breast. He kneaded it gently, then more aggressively and she moaned. Caught in a current of desire so great it could carry her away like a tidal wave, she was further engulfed when his palm went lower, to briefly whisk her lap. "And here, Amanda, what do you feel here?"

This she could not answer, and she felt herself blush vigorously. She tilted her head and met his forehead with her own. "I can't say it, Nick." But she knew what she felt. Wet. Totally, gloriously wet. And she knew exactly what it meant.

He gave a low, male chuckle in her ear. "You don't have to say it, but I know what I'd feel if I touched you there," he whispered into the darkness.

Easing back from her, he lifted her chin. The desire she saw in his eyes nearly undid her.

"Listen to me, baby. You're responsive. I'd like to stay and convince you further, but we're on a city street in a parked car and my kids are waiting for me inside."

Skimming her cheek with his knuckles, his voice was hoarse with his own arousal. "But know this, Mandy.

Your ex-husband was a fool. However, I can't say I regret that. His loss is definitely my gain.''

He kissed her quickly, then opened the door fast, as if he no longer trusted himself. Amanda watched his retreating back, aching to run her hands from the top of those broad shoulders down his spine to what his denims so snugly encased. She started the car, and still surrounded by Nick's scent, pulled away from the curb in a fog of longing.

She was halfway down the block before it began to clear and she realized with a jolt that he'd called her Mandy. A name only one person on this earth had ever used for her. Her sister Lisa.

CHAPTER SIX

BETH DIMARCO KEPT her promise and took Amanda to dinner the following Saturday. As they pulled into Muscato's parking lot, Amanda gripped her purse and turned to the other woman. "Oh, Beth, maybe this isn't such a good idea. The last time I was here, my father was so rude to Nick."

Beth's eyes, so like her brother's, shone with pleasure. "I'm glad you're worried about his feelings," she said, her gaze direct. "But don't be. Actually, it was Nicky's idea that I bring you here. When I told him I was calling you to take you to dinner, *he* suggested it."

"Really? That's great." A warmth spread through Amanda.

Reaching out, Beth squeezed her arm. "Nick's had a tough life, Amanda. He's a lonely man and I don't think it's good for him. It's time he let a woman in his life again."

Unspoken, Amanda heard Beth's approval of her. And it scared her. The kiss and the caresses in the car had been wonderful but frightening. It wasn't exactly that Amanda had accepted her lack of sexuality—somewhere in her heart she'd suspected that the fault lay partially with Porter, or at least her lack of attraction to him. But to confirm that she could indeed respond, and wantonly, was charting new waters. Would she drown in her responses to Nick DiMarco?

You should be so lucky, she heard Lisa say. The thought made her smile as they walked into the restaurant and were seated at a coveted corner table.

Amanda saw the interior of Muscato's through different eyes tonight. She still appreciated its smart white tablecloths, red napkins and soft-focus lighting, which gave the place a subtly sophisticated ambience. But this evening, it seemed warmer, cozier than when she'd been here several weeks ago with Craig and her parents. Then it had seemed cold. She smiled at how things had changed for her since then.

"And what mischief are the two lovely ladies at table six plotting?" a deep voice from beside her teased.

"Hi, bro." Beth smiled at Nick.

"Hi, Bethy." Then he turned to face Amanda. "Hello, Mandy."

"Hello, Nick." Amanda's pulse quickened as she stared up at him. She recalled where she'd been three nights ago the first time he'd used the nickname. When she looked into his eyes, she saw them glimmer with a sensuality that told her he, too, remembered those few stolen moments in the car.

Poising his pencil over a pad, he never released her gaze. "What can I get you to drink?"

"Chianti for me," Beth said with a chuckle.

Amanda placed her elbows on the table, rested her chin on her folded hands and peered up at him. "I'll have a beer, whatever kind you recommend."

"Right." He winked at her and his smile made the act of breathing difficult.

Beth's eyes glistened after he left.

"What is it?" Amanda asked, concerned.

"That's the old Nick. I haven't seen it in years, but it's how he was before..." Beth stopped short of her declaration.

Taking the opening she'd unwittingly been given, Amanda addressed the issue. "Beth, I know about Nick's ex-wife. He told me the basic facts as background for helping Heather. What I don't understand is how all of you can just pretend she didn't exist. I'm not being critical, but as Heather's counselor, I don't think it's healthy."

Again, a gleam of admiration shone in the younger DiMarco's eyes, and she leaned forward on her forearms. "You don't pull any punches, do you?"

Though she felt a tremor of insecurity, Amanda faced Beth squarely. "If you think I'm out of line, you have to know that I'll risk anything to help Heather."

"No, no, you're right to ask. And yes, we all avoid talking about Suzanne. She left the three of them devastated and no one wants to remind the kids of her."

An insidious feeling coiled through Amanda. This was going to be a problem between her and Nick. She just knew it.

Then he appeared with their drinks and the biggest antipasto she'd ever seen, and she once again forgot her reservations. "Compliments of the chef, who, incidentally, has the hots for my baby sister," Nick joked. "But he thinks she needs fattening up."

Both women laughed, and Nick continued, "I, however, think the two of you are just perfect."

Amanda blushed and Nick gave a satisfied chuckle in response.

The meal was delightful. Linguine was interspersed with more teasing from Nick, visits from Tony Muscato and the clearly enamored chef.

After both women finished the last bite of spumoni, and pushed the dessert plates away with matching groans, Nick materialized one last time. "Are you ladies in a hurry?"

Amanda answered first and fast. Too fast. "No, no, I'm not."

Beth blessedly saved her from total embarrassment. "Me, neither. Want us to wait in the bar until you're done and give you a lift home?"

"I'd like that, since my car's in the shop again." Nick cocked his head. "Would you like that, Mandy?"

Amanda was surprised she could even find her voice. "Yes."

It all passed in a flurry of activity. One minute they were in the bar waiting, the next, Nick had joined them. He'd changed into scruffy jeans and a light gray plaid flannel shirt. They'd gotten into Beth's car with Nick driving. He dropped his sister off at her apartment and, with big-brotherly presumptuousness, declared he'd return her car tomorrow. Then, he zipped to Amanda's house, walked her to the steps and asked to come in. In the foyer, he looked around with surprise. "Doing a lot of remodeling, aren't you?"

His glance took in the newly installed unpainted drywall and the old flooring that was sanded and waiting to be refinished. It was the same in every room but the kitchen, her bedroom and a back porch. She led him there, to the cozy space that had been converted to a year-round sun-room. Windows surrounded them and there were two skylights in the sloped ceiling above a rough-hewn stone fireplace. Raw cedar paneled the walls. Large stuffed tapestry couches were accented with solid-colored chairs.

"Have a seat here." She indicated the sofa with a sweep of her hand and her tone was teasing. "Maybe this room won't offend your sensibilities so much."

He grinned self-effacingly and plopped down. "Picked up on my penchant for tidiness, did you?"

Amanda nodded and smiled. "Can I get you something?"

Nick closed his eyes and groaned. *Could she really be such an innocent that she'd ask that of a man who'd been devouring her with his eyes all evening?*

Forcing aside those thoughts, he agreed to coffee and scanned the room while she was gone. He could tell it was used frequently, and though it was cluttered, it was clean. Yet he couldn't help wondering if she'd tire of this unremarkable living and flee to the exclusive suburb where she'd lived before. Away from Heather. And him.

He stood up to distract himself from these forebodings and wandered over to a wall unit. No adolescent tomes graced these shelves. Stuck in every nook and cranny, crushed together like lovers, were hundreds of bestsellers. He plucked one from the shelf and leafed through it.

So, the princess liked romance. And love stories. At one time, so had he. That was when he'd believed in happy endings. Now he read law books, but when he had occasion for recreational reading, he chose Stephen King. Horror seemed to fit his life better.

Replacing the book, he picked up a picture on the desk. It was recent, as Amanda didn't look much different. She was with a woman about two or three years younger who had the same nose, high cheekbones and full mouth. Their hair was the exact color, though the shape of their faces was different. Amanda looked wary, but the other woman had a devilish gleam in her eyes. He'd seen that same spark in Jason, though he could be drawing the conclusion because of their most obvious comparison: the woman was in a wheelchair.

He heard Amanda enter and pivoted with the photo in his hand. "Your sister?"

"Yes." Amanda bit her bottom lip.

Nick fingered the silver frame gently. "How old is she?"

"In that picture, she was twenty-nine." Her voice was tinged with a pain that Nick's battered heart recognized. "She never made it to her thirtieth birthday."

"I'm sorry, Mandy."

Smiling sadly, Amanda asked in a seeming non sequitur, "Why do you call me that?"

"I guess because Amanda is too formal, too sophisticated. And I don't want to see you that way." Carefully, Nick placed the photo back on the table.

As she handed him a mug, she chuckled and sank onto the couch. Nick followed suit. "My sister, Lisa, had more unflattering terms for my name. She's the only other one who ever used that nickname."

Sensing this had deep significance, Nick said, "Then I'm flattered by the similarity." He looked back at the picture. "What was wrong with her?"

"She had spina bifida."

Nick's forehead furrowed. He stretched his free hand across the back of the couch. It hovered near her hair. "But you don't die from that."

"No," Amanda answered woodenly and leaned back, almost unconsciously, as if she was seeking his touch. "You don't. Not in the way you mean." She sat up straight and shook off the pall. "She was a lot like Jason in other ways than being confined to a wheelchair. She loved those corny jokes he tells."

"Ah, so that's why you're so evenly matched with him."

"You haven't been around to see that."

"No, but he told me all about it. In detail. You've got a kindred spirit there." Before she could respond, he snagged a strand of her flaxen hair and rolled it between his fingers. "You're great with him and Heather. You've got a real talent for listening, for helping young people."

Amanda's eyes glowed. But there was a flicker of insecurity there, too. "Do I?"

"Yes, you do." He scowled. None of this fit with his preconceived notions of her. "You're really dedicated to your career, aren't you?"

"Of course I am. I want to do something more than look good and spend money. No one thinks I can do anything worthwhile." She narrowed her eyes and looked over at the photo on the table. "But I will, for my sake and for Lisa's."

Uneasy, Nick drew back from her.

Amanda's eyes bored into him and he knew she was reading him like a familiar book. "You know what I mean, don't you?" she said.

"About succeeding, despite the odds or the opinions of others?" She nodded. "Yeah," he said. He was quiet a moment and she didn't interfere with his reflection. "I want to be the top lawyer in the city so badly I can taste it. I've wanted it so long, so much that it's become a way of life." He crunched a handful of her hair in his fist, his jaw hardening. "And I'll get it, too."

"Why is that so important to you, Nick?"

No one had ever asked him that. After a slight pause, he tried to articulate his feelings. "I didn't always feel this way. I was happy, even though we didn't have much growing up. But in the last ten years, Heather and Jason have had so few material possessions and life in general has been so grim that I've developed the need to provide more for my family. I don't want to have to worry about Jason's medical bills anymore. I want Heather to have nice things." He looked at her intently. "And, quite honestly, my male ego could use the professional success."

Nick sat up straight, picked up his mug and smiled. "Now that I've bared my soul, tell me more about your sister."

Amanda eyed him shrewdly, but let the change of subject drop. "She had a wonderful sense of humor and really helped to lighten up my serious side." Mischief glimmered in her eyes. "She loved lawyer jokes. Did you hear the one about the attorney who died and went to Saint Peter for judgment? The lawyer said it was too soon to die, he was only forty-six. Peter shuffled through a mound of papers, and answered dryly, 'According to the hours you billed your clients, you're ninety-three.'"

Laughing at the punch line, Nick took the cue to keep the discussion light. He set his coffee down on the table and stretched his feet out in front of him. They talked easily about the house, his kids, Tony and everything else. To distract themselves from the needs and hopes and aspirations that had just been confessed in this quiet, intimate room, Nick thought. They also needed distraction from each other.

Finally, he couldn't take it any longer. In the middle of yet another story about his family, he stopped talking, leaned over and removed the cup from her hands. He slid a palm to her face, caressed its silky texture, rubbing her bottom lip with his thumb. "Enough. I've been dying to do this all night and I can't wait another second."

Lowering his head to her lips, he touched them briefly, then trailed feathery kisses along her jaw to the exposed neckline of the jumpsuit he'd been fantasizing about for hours. His return journey was as slow and sensuous, and by the time he reached her mouth again, he could feel the restlessness in her body. She arched to get closer to him, and he obliged her by encircling her waist with his arm.

Once more, he was struck by how firm, how substantial she felt in his hands. Thought fled, however, when she ran her hands up his arms and threaded them through his hair. He took her lips again, demanding entrance to the wet recesses of her mouth. When he broke away, his lips found the pulse at her throat. Gently, he tongued it while his hand slid up her arm and hovered over her breast.

"I want to touch you, Mandy, in secret, soft places. Do you want that, too?"

He felt her swallow, then say, "Yes, Nick, I want that, too."

Smiling into the silk of her skin, he raised his head to look at her. Her eyes were closed and she was breathing hard. He cupped her breast and when he kneaded it softly, she groaned with pleasure. "Look at me, Mandy." She opened her eyes and he saw they had turned cobalt. "Do you like this?" He took her nipple between his thumb and forefinger and rolled it gently. She nodded. "What does it make you feel?"

She waited so long, he thought she might not answer. Finally, she whispered, "It makes me feel connected, part of you. I've never felt that before."

"Good." He continued his sensuous ministration on the other breast. As he did so, he felt her tense slightly.

"Amanda? What is it?"

She drew in a deep, exasperated breath and hid her face in the soft cotton of his shirt. "I'm scared, Nick."

Shock was too mild a word to describe his reaction. He raised a hand to her chin and tenderly forced her to look at him. "Are you afraid of *me?*"

Twin scarlet slashes burned her cheeks. "Not in the way you're thinking. It's just that, like I told you before, I haven't been very good at this. And Porter didn't mind so much. But you're so...so masculine, so virile. I'm afraid I won't be good enough. I'm afraid I won't *be* enough for you, Nick."

He experienced two conflicting emotions simultaneously. He was furious with her jackass of a husband who'd made her feel inferior, who'd made her think this nonsense was true. And he was thrilled that *he* was the only man she responded to. He stroked her flaming cheek then pulled her to him and wrapped her in the security of his arms. Holding her close, he whispered in her ear, "If you were any more *enough,* Amanda Carson, I'd be bursting out of my jeans right now."

She buried her face in his shoulder again, and he knew she was embarrassed. He eased back from her and met her eyes. "Don't be shy with me. You've got me so hot, I'm about to combust. How can anyone who does that not be woman enough, sexy enough for me? God, I'd like to pummel the jerk who made you think that about yourself."

Her sea-colored eyes darkened with the need to believe him. To convince her further, Nick released her head and took her hand in his, and brought it to his mouth for a gentle kiss. Then he trailed it down the front of his body and felt his muscles leap into the curve of its caress.

"Do you feel that? It's just from your light touch." He kept going, each muscle responding in kind. She smiled in surprise until he got below his belt. "Here too, baby. Feel what you do to me here. I've been hard for you all night and you haven't even had to lay a finger on me to do it. God, it feels like heaven when you touch me now."

He let go of her hand but she didn't draw it away. Instead, she pressed it against the swelling of his zipper. He was throbbing and he worried that, like a teenage boy in the back seat of his father's car, he'd embarrass himself.

"Oh, God, Mandy," he moaned, lost in sensation, reveling in her touch. After a moment of the exquisite torture, he yanked her hand away and found her mouth again.

This time the union was totally carnal. Amanda was more involved and less hesitant. She met his tongue with hers, dug her nails into his shoulders and pressed her breasts to his chest. He wished he had opened the buttons of her silky top so he could feel her against him, but he was so intent on her mouth and on exploring the lovely curve of her spine and then her bottom that he didn't want to backtrack.

The caresses went on as long as Nick could stand them. He stopped when he knew any more touching would lead them down a path he was certain Amanda was not ready for. She needed to explore her sexuality a little more slowly and he'd be damned if he'd blow it like the other man in her life.

Besides, buddy, there's still some doubt there. Some distrust. Isn't there?

Of all the mistakes he'd made in his life, and there were some beauties, Nick DiMarco had never lied to himself. And, as he pulled away from Amanda and began to wind down their passionate interlude, he admitted the truth, at least to himself. He was still wary of this beautiful and sensuous woman who trembled in his arms.

And not only for Heather's sake.

"WHY DIDN'T the husband report it when his MasterCard was stolen?" Matt Barone straddled his chair, propped his hands and chin on the back of it and grinned devilishly.

"Is this a sexist joke, Matthew?"

He rocked in his seat. "Aw, come on, Teach, you can take it."

"Okay," she said, smoothing the wrinkles out of her long coral sweater and knit pants. "Why didn't he report it?"

"Because the thief was charging less per week than his wife." Matt laughed boisterously.

"Oh, man, Ms. C., you gonna let him get away with that?" Sandi asked, rolling up the sleeves of her yellow jersey and crossing her denim-clad legs.

Amanda drew a bead on the offender. "I'll get him back, next time. I'll resurrect my worst adolescent-boy joke."

Again, everyone laughed at the implied threat, even Heather. It was mid-November and this was her sixth session with the group. Although she'd said very little about her own state of mind, she listened intently and had even made a few comments when the others had talked about their problems. They, in turn, had taken her under their wing, as Amanda had expected. There was something about Heather's lack of worldliness and her vulnerability that reached out to them like an open invitation to protect her.

Amanda relaxed in her seat and took advantage of the mellow mood. "How's everyone doing today?"

Both Sandi and Matt averted their eyes, as if they'd been caught with their hands in the cookie jar.

"Matt?"

"Aw, sh—" he began but stopped.

Amanda had made very few rules for the group but she'd insisted on no obscenities. Some *hell* and *damn* was tolerated, but she asked them to try hard to clean up the rest of their language, believing violent language was a precursor to the act itself. Matt made the most slips.

"Sorry." He ducked his head and fiddled with the zipper of his leather jacket. "Anyway, I know you know about English class this week. I got so ticked off at that lady. She keeps prying, wantin' me to write personal stuff." He jutted a stubborn jaw, his angular features softened by a lopsided grin. "So I did."

"Very personal, from what I hear," Amanda said dryly.

He shrugged his shoulders and arched his black eyebrows. "Well, she asked for it." His green eyes were wide and innocent. Just like Cain's before he did his brother in.

"Did she?" Amanda matched his raised eyebrows. "Tell me, Matt, aren't there certain codes of behavior that are simply understood?"

"Like? "

"Well, when you walked in here today, did you spit on the floor?"

The boy's eyes narrowed and his posture straightened. Amanda knew he loved a challenge. "'Course not."

"Did I tell you not to?"

Matt shook his head, light dawning in his eyes.

She went in for the kill. "But you didn't because you knew it was inappropriate behavior, right?"

Shaking his head, he grinned, caught as surely as if he were a rabbit in a trap. "Your point, Teach." Then, he scowled just like the English teacher in question was known to do, pulled in his chest, as she did her hefty bosom, and said with mock authority, "I'll try to 'control my impulses more.'"

Sandi and Heather laughed at his accurate, unflattering impression. Ron didn't crack a smile when Amanda glanced at him, and she saw he had headphones on. At her frown, he grudgingly removed them. Dressed in black jeans, a deep blue sweatshirt and a jacket the color of midnight, his appearance was somber. A sudden premonition made Amanda shiver. "Ron, what are you listening to?"

The boy's usually impassive face sparked somewhat. "Magenta. Man, they're totally rad."

"Which song?"

"'Blackout.' It's awesome. You listen to this, stuff, Ms. Carson?"

Amanda sat back in her chair and crossed her arms, buying time. "I know this particular song." It was about suicide and had been the cause of much controversy several years ago when it was released. Experts worried that it glorified the ultimate act of despair.

Amanda knew she was on shaky ground here. Leronne Marshall had already tried to kill himself. He
bore the slash marks on his wrists like a badge, a silent
testament to his depression. And she was grimly aware
that the people who'd attempted suicide once were at
the highest risk to do it again.

Interjecting just the right mixture of concern and
authority into her voice, Amanda asked, "Why do you
like that song, Ron?"

He simply shrugged his thin shoulders.

She leaned closer and folded her arms in front of her.
"What does it make you feel?"

Again, he shrugged, his black eyes staring at her
blankly.

"It makes *me* feel creepy," Sandi put in.

"Why, Sandi?"

"This guy says death is great. A peaceful way to escape. Gives me the willies."

Ron set his cassette recorder on the floor and
stretched his arms above his head in a deceptively casual gesture. "It shouldn't, babe. It's one way to stop
the pain."

"When nothing else will," a small voice from the
right side of the room confirmed, so softly it seemed to
have slipped out almost against the speaker's will. That
it came from Heather, who had said nothing about
herself in all their group sessions, made the statement
as powerful as if she'd shouted it through a mega-
phone.

Though she was glad Heather had finally contrib-
uted to the group, Amanda wished Heather hadn't
chosen this fact to respond to. Suicide's appeal to kids
was that it was just a way to stop the pain, not really a
wish to die.

Swallowing the lump in her throat, Amanda forced her voice to be low and even when she wanted to shout how wrong this reasoning was. "Certainly death does that. But there are other ways to stop the hurt, too."

Eight doubting eyes focused on her. They knew as well as she did that she had no magic to give them. But they all desperately wanted some hope.

Amanda pulled herself up straight in the chair and looked at each one of them. "You can talk about it. You can try to change your circumstances. You can know when something is going to trigger that suffering and take steps to prevent it."

"How do you do that, Ms. C.?" Sandi asked. "Like, we sorta got an anniversary coming up and my ma, she's already depressed over it. Makes me feel terrible, so I..." She trailed off.

"You what?" Amanda gently prodded.

"Ah, I smoke some pot to get rid of it." Sandi ran a shaky hand through her curly hair, her hazel eyes suddenly old. "I skip school and veg in front of the soap operas."

"Like you did this week?"

Before Sandi could mutter an excuse, someone asked, "What kind of anniversary?"

Again, Heather's involvement in the discussion and her shyly uttered question touched them like an invisible hand.

Sandi turned in her chair and stared at Heather for a long time before she spoke. "I'll tell you that if you tell us somethin' about your problems. You ain't said nothin' yet and it's cool, girl, if that's how you want it. But I'd like to know what monkey's on your back."

Tears formed in Heather's eyes and splashed down onto her very white cheeks. But she never broke eye

contact with Sandi. She tilted her chin, her long ponytail swaying behind her. "Ten years ago, when I was
three, and my brother was only two weeks old, my...
my...mother left us." The tears were still falling, but
the brave child dug her nails into her hand until her
knuckles were white and continued, "We never saw her
again." There was a long pause while Heather took a
couple of deep breaths and then spoke, "Jason's birthday is on Thanksgiving. The time between Thanksgiving and Christmas is always so...lonely."

She'd reached the end of her stamina like a runner
who had gone too far in a marathon. Her breath came
in gasps and she hung her head and dug her sneakers
into the floor. No one moved and the silence was deaf-
ening.

Finally, Sandi got up, went over to Heather, knelt
before her and took her hands. "Heather, my stepfather left us a year ago this week. He was a bastard, but
my ma went downhill after that. She says it helps to
spend time with me during those days. How about you,
who do you wanna be with when you hurt?"

Heather looked at Amanda. They both knew the answer to that question.

Time ran out for the session shortly after Heather's
confession. Sandi briefly hugged her for comfort and
Matt said a few encouraging words about Heather's
first sharing before he left. Ron only responded with his
eyes. The empathy he felt with the girl was obvious.

Amanda was shaken by it all. She made sure to set a
private counseling session for Heather two weeks after
Jason's birthday, and she was halfway satisfied that the
girl was calm and could cope when her aunt picked her
up. She said nothing to Beth about the breakthrough,

but telephoned Nick immediately. Although she
wouldn't share the specifics, she was going to tackle the
issue of his spending more time at home. At some point,
she would also have to address Heather's need for information about her mother. But it was too soon for
that. She just wished she didn't have such a sense of
foreboding about it all.

SEVERAL HOURS LATER, Nick pulled up the collar of his
bomber jacket and rang Amanda's doorbell. He'd been
unable to banish thoughts of her from his mind all
weekend and kept reliving how she'd felt in his arms.

She opened the door and stood before him dressed in
baggy jeans and a blue Syracuse U sweatshirt that made
her eyes glow. She looked sexy as hell and she made his
whole body tense. He dragged her into his arms as soon
as he stepped inside.

The kiss was drugging. His mind stopped function-
ing when his lips touched hers. Pure male reaction took
over as he tasted her. She opened to him willingly and
he relearned the recesses of her mouth with his tongue.
Her hands slid up his chest and every muscle leapt out
to those supple fingers through the heavy weave of his
charcoal shirt. He heard her groan, and was thrilled,
once again, with her response to him. He felt protective of her and seduced by her at the same time.

Her hands tangled in his hair and she held on tight as
his lips left hers to trail down to her exposed neck. His
arms banded around her and rested intimately on her
hips for a moment, then went lower to cup her bottom.
The denim was soft and pliable and he could feel her
flesh through it. She leaned into him and he melded his
body with hers.

"God, I thought I'd imagined how good you felt under my hands, but I didn't. You make me want, Amanda Carson," he muttered thickly into her hair. He was drunk on her flowery shampoo and womanly scent.

She peered up at him, her pupils dilated with arousal. "You make me want, too, Nick DiMarco. More than I should."

More than I should, too. Much, much more. He pulled away then, afraid of embarrassing himself with further declarations, and walked arm in arm with her to the sofa. He sprawled across the couch and patted the cushion next to him. When she shook her head, his eyebrows raised in question.

Pushing her hair off her face, she gave a very female chuckle and shook her head. "No, we need to talk, and being close to you turns my brain to mush."

"Sounds good to me."

She shook her head again, sending the golden mane over her shoulders, and took a seat on the chair opposite him. He shrugged off his jacket. "Okay, what's up?"

"Nick, things are happening between us that I really like." She blushed prettily. "And not just physically. I think you're a good father to Heather and I really admire your grit and determination."

His chest swelled with her praise. He could have said the same thing about her, but he didn't want to interrupt.

"Anyway, because I'm working as Heather's counselor, we have to keep our professional dealings separate from this personal thing. Otherwise, I won't be able to live with the lack of ethics." Then she added hastily, "I think we can do it, though, if we're very careful."

At her ominous words, he jammed his hands into the pockets of his black jeans, bracing himself for her message. "What exactly do you mean by that, Amanda?" He'd used her full name intentionally, and he saw the flicker of disappointment that crossed her face.

But the beauty before him forged ahead, anyway. She squared her shoulders and stared at him intently. "Nick, my first responsibility is to Heather, and I'll always honor that, no matter what conflict it causes between us. In other words, I won't let my feelings for you, no matter how wonderful they are, keep me from doing what I think is best for your daughter."

It was no more than he'd expected. Hell, it was what he really *wanted*. Yet, way down deep, it hurt that she'd asked to see him tonight because of Heather. Not because she'd missed him. He wanted badly for her to have called just to see him. To be with him. And not just physically. The last thought scared the hell out of him, so he steeled his voice when he continued, "Is there something you want to tell me about my daughter?"

"This is pretty touchy. You know I can't reveal what we discuss in the counseling sessions. As I've already told you, confidentiality is vital." Amanda got up and began to pace. "But she's only thirteen, so it's my duty to make sure you understand the seriousness of what's going on."

"Don't I *know* what's going on?"

"Partially." Amanda stopped her strides and circled to face him. "I can't tell you any more than I already have. The only thing I *can* say is that you need to spend more time with her."

He remained seated and looked up at her, his gut churning. He could tell by the lines of stress on her face that this wasn't easy for her, that confrontation was probably something else she hadn't done much of in her life. "Listen, Amanda, it's not that simple. I work at Muscato's and fill in at my old construction company to pay for necessities. I clerk for Joris, Beech and Stowe ten hours a week now, and their demands will likely increase after Christmas. I have classes most nights and I have to study for the finals coming up. Where can I find more time to spend at home?" His words were clipped and he hated how cynical he sounded, but there was no sugarcoating this truth.

She sat down and moved closer to him as a sign of support. Reaching over, she took his hand and laced her fingers with his. "Something has to give, Nick. She needs you with her, now more than ever."

In order to determine what was best for Heather, he quelled his irritation at the fact that Amanda wouldn't see his position. "Why now?"

"I can't go into detail. You'll have to trust me that this is a crucial time for her, in the upcoming months. I *can* tell you that suicide attempts during the holidays reach all-time highs. Hot lines and crisis centers are inundated with calls and visits. Depression peaks during this season. There's more to it for Heather, but just that should be enough for you to change something."

Nick shuddered anew at the thought of Heather's suicidal tendencies. He felt closed in by his dilemma. Just a little while longer and he'd have what he wanted, what he needed. How could he jeopardize that now? Yet, if his daughter truly needed him...

He stood up, trying to bear the weight of this better. He wanted it all—Heather's mental health, the law degree and a good job—maybe even this woman before him. So he tried again. "Amanda, I have to study for these exams. If I don't maintain my grade point average, Joris and the others who are wooing me won't be interested any longer."

"Then what about the job at Muscato's? Can't you let it go for a while?"

That one statement crystallized the differences between them, and reminded him, unhappily, that she was more from Suzanne's world than his. "It's about *money*, princess. I have to worry about it, even if you don't." He winced at the edge in his voice.

Amanda rose to meet him, squared her shoulders and stared him down. "Don't get defensive with me because you're frustrated with the situation. I can help."

He had to give her credit. For such a fragile-looking woman, she stood her ground solidly. That worried him even more—he liked her moxie, he liked so many things about her. Exasperated, his thoughts slipped out. "We're so different, Amanda. This whole conversation makes me realize how little chance we have of making a relationship work. Add that to the conflict of interest and professional concerns we face..."

"But you said the other night you thought we could do it. You just kissed me like—" Her blue eyes widened, then darkened with pain.

He couldn't bear to hear his foolishness recounted so emotionally. He cut the air with his hand to silence her. "I know how I kissed you. What I said. But maybe I was wrong. I can't let you rearrange my whole life. I did that once before and it's what got me into this mess in the first place."

He saw the hurt etch itself first on her mouth, then glimmer in her crystalline eyes. She took a deep breath, and clasped her hands behind her back in a gesture he'd come to realize gave her confidence when she felt shaky. "Fine, Mr. DiMarco. I get the picture now. All personal stuff aside, will you think about easing up on the work load to spend more time with your daughter? It's my *professional* opinion that she needs you now.''

Her voice broke and so did his heart. If he'd been a more optimistic man, if life had been a little kinder to him, he might have reached for her, as he wanted to. But he'd learned not to read things into a woman's pleas, and *never* to trust the vulnerability in a pair of guileless blue eyes.

''All right, I'll go over my finances tonight. If you think it's best, I'll find a way to be home more.''

Making his way around her, careful not to touch her, he headed for the door. He was afraid if he came too close to her, he'd drag her to him to erase that haunted look in her eyes with a kiss and give her promises that he knew he couldn't keep.

CHAPTER SEVEN

"HI, HONEY. Is everything okay?" Slouched in a corner phone booth, Nick looked around the huge foyer of the Syracuse Law Library.

"Yes, Daddy, we're fine." Heather's voice was soft and sweet, as usual. "Mrs. Castellana made supper and I cleaned up. She just put Jason to bed."

"Did you eat enough?" he asked, trying to mask his concern. She *had* been been eating more, and sleeping a little better in the last few days, though she still stayed up late in her room.

"Yes, Dad." Teenage exasperation seeped through.

"All right, I'll be home in half an hour."

"Great, I'll wait up." Her enthusiasm reached clear across the phone lines.

He hung up, closed his eyes and leaned against the wall. His presence at home nights had made a difference already. He'd never forget the joy on Heather's face when he'd told her he was giving up his job at Muscato's for a few months. Winning the lottery couldn't have come close to causing that look.

As he walked the few feet to where he'd dropped his things, he realized again how right Amanda had been last week. Just thinking about her hurt. Damn, he'd really blown it.

After he'd left her house that night, he'd thought long and hard about her warnings about his daughter. And in the subsequent days, he couldn't ignore the way Heather prowled around late at night and how she picked at her food. The crying had been the worst. He'd tried talking to her, but it didn't help. Frustrated and frightened, he'd taken steps to spend more time at home. She really did need him. Why hadn't he done more about it before?

Because you are a first-class jerk, DiMarco, he told himself as he sank into a chair in the corner and wearily rubbed his hand over his face. That had never been clearer to him than when he told Amanda he didn't think they could make things work between them. He knew how much her response to him had meant to her; he also knew she'd begun to care for him. Yet, he'd ended the relationship because of his fears.

But she hadn't backed down about Heather. No, not his princess. She had done precisely what she said she'd do: she'd asked him to put Heather's welfare before his personal conflict over her. God, that made him feel like a heel, that she had to *ask* him to do that. Closing his eyes, he could see her standing proudly before him, her jaw clenched, pleading her case for Heather.

"Hello, Nick." It was Amanda's soft voice.

Lord, DiMarco, now you're imagining she's here.

He opened his eyes and she stood before him, not a vision, but a very real woman whose flesh made the blood pump double time through his veins.

Sitting up quickly, he asked, "Mandy, what are you doing here?"

Her eyes flickered with pleasure before she doused it. He'd inadvertently used the nickname that meant so much to her. "I'm meeting someone. I saw you on the phone and wanted to talk a minute."

"Sure, sit down." He gestured to the empty chair beside him.

Amanda glanced around and shook her head. "No, I can't. I just wanted to tell you how pleased I am that you're spending more time with Heather this week. She really appreciates it." Her voice trembled and Nick's pulse rate accelerated with the hope that she was as affected by their meeting as he was. He stood up to be closer to her.

She looked so sad, he wanted to kiss away the anguish he'd caused. Instead, he jammed his hands into the pockets of his tan corduroy pants. "You were right," he said hoarsely.

Nodding, she asked, "How did you manage it?"

"Beth, of course. I borrowed some money from her. She doesn't see it as a loan, though. She says she owes me for helping to pay for her college and graduate school, years ago. She was only too glad to help out."

"But it still hurts your pride."

"Yeah, but my pride's gotten me nowhere in the last few weeks." He looked meaningfully at her and plunged in. "Listen, I've been thinking about what I said the other night. It wasn't—"

Refusing to let him finish, Amanda shook her head and clasped her hands behind her back. "No, Nick, it's okay. I took too much for granted. It was just more important to me because..." She trailed off, her face turning red.

He reached out and grasped her arm gently. "No, no, you've got it all wr—"

"Hello, darling," interrupted a smooth male voice. A tall, blond man wrapped his arm around Amanda's waist, drawing her away from Nick. "I've been looking all over for you."

What the hell? Nick thought. Then he recognized the guy from the restaurant the night he'd waited on their table.

"Craig," Amanda said woodenly.

Dressed in an Italian suit, silk shirt and tie, Coleman looked from Amanda to Nick with narrowed eyes. He took in Nick's cords and fisherman-knit sweater with disdain. The lawyer's gold watch winked in the light as he drew Amanda closer. "I'm Craig Coleman. Amanda's fiancé."

The words hit Nick like a bomb exploding mere inches away. To shield himself from the fallout, he backed up a step. He schooled his features to reveal none of his shock or pain. "I'm Nick DiMarco. Ms. Carson is my daughter's guidance counselor."

Dismissing Nick with a nod, Coleman let Amanda go. "I'll just grab the books I need and meet you here. Don't dawdle, Amanda," he said with one last glance at the two of them.

Nick clenched his hands into fists to control his anger. When Coleman was out of sight, he grabbed Amanda's arm and dragged her into an anteroom that served as a small sitting area. He closed the door for a modicum of privacy.

"How could you?" he said under his breath. "What were you doing, just amusing yourself with me?" He laughed bitterly, let her go and began to pace. "And I was just about to apologize for the other night. God, I'm a fool. I've been agonizing over what I said to you for seven days running, wishing I could take it back." He pivoted and stared at her. "Damn you!"

Amanda's emotions were careering out of control as she stared at Nick prowling furiously before her. First, she'd been startled by his explosive anger when he yanked her into the private room. But then she'd focused on the rest of his tirade. *He cared.* Somewhere deep inside herself, she had suspected he would regret his words of the other night. But then he hadn't called and she'd lost hope. Now, to hear him declare it aloud, even if it was in anger, thrilled her.

"Are you laughing at me?" he asked incredulously.

Amanda realized she must be smiling. She shook her head, the grin remaining in place. "No, Nick, I'm just pleased about what you said."

By now he was so angry he was practically sputtering, "You've got gall, lady," and headed for the door.

"Maybe I do, but I don't have a fiancé." She grasped the bulky material of his sleeve.

Stopping dead, he turned to look at her, his gray eyes wary. "That's not what Coleman says."

"Craig is a pompous, overbearing ass."

"Nice choice in men you have."

Amanda laughed, feeling freer than she'd felt in a long time. On impulse, she ran her hand up the sleeve of Nick's sweater to lightly stroke his neck. Involuntarily, he leaned into the caress. She reveled in the feminine power she had over him, even though he was still very angry.

"He's not *my* choice of men. He's my parents' pick. After I broke up with Porter, my father tried to replace him with a clone." Amanda giggled at her insulting remark. "I've refused the engagement all along, but no one listens. See, no ring."

She held up slender fingers and Nick stared unblinkingly at them. He looked at her hand for a moment, then took it in his, stroking the naked third finger. He raised his eyes to hers and they darkened to the color of stormy skies. "Coleman doesn't seem to understand that."

"That's why I asked to see him tonight. This charade has gone on long enough."

"Good." Nick gave her a satisfied grin and caressed her palm. "And I meant what I said, Mandy. I'm sorry for what I told you the other night. I reacted out of disappointment and stupid male pride."

Amanda retorted with a purely feminine smile. "I'm glad to hear you say it."

Slowly, Nick raised his hand and slid his fingers into her hair. She arched back into his possessive gesture. "Tell me he hasn't touched you. Not since I have, anyway."

The breath whooshed out of her at his seductive tone. Every muscle tingled and her lower body went liquid with that unique woman-to-man response. "He hasn't touched me, Nick."

She pulled away then, opened the door and took three steps out. But she returned, threw her arms around his neck and hugged him fiercely.

"Make sure he understands how things are, tonight."

"I will."

ON THE TENTH anniversary of Suzanne Sullivan's desertion, Amanda met with Heather for a private counseling session. They sat together in the small office on adjacent chairs. The wind was whipping around outside but the guidance suite was warm and cozy.

The teenager fidgeted with her books, looked around the room and chewed on the end of her pencil. "The group last Friday was heavy, Ms. Carson. I felt really bad for all the kids."

Recognizing the delay tactic, Amanda crossed her legs and folded her hands, temporarily allowing the evasion. "Was it upsetting to you?" When Heather nodded, Amanda asked her to elaborate.

"I felt so sorry for Sandi. Her mother doing drugs again so soon." There was genuine sympathy in the teenager's voice, no jealousy that at least Sandi had a mother.

Amanda marveled at Heather's selflessness, yet it was also part of her problem. "You like Sandi, don't you?"

Flipping through the pages of her spiral notebook, Heather didn't look at the counselor. "Yes."

"Why?"

"She likes me. And I know how she feels sometimes. Inside."

Amanda sat forward, listening as Heather continued to talk.

"I like Matt and Ron, too, but Ron's joke bothered me." Heather rose from her chair and walked over to the bookshelf. She fingered several tomes nervously. "Jason would think it was funny, why the cemetery was so crowded because people were dying to get in."

"But you didn't?"

"If anybody else told it I would. But not Ron. Every joke he tells is about death. It's almost as creepy as his coming to school on Halloween as the Grim Reaper."

Amanda shuddered at the image and hugged herself to ward off the chill. All the seniors dressed up for Halloween and some of the costumes were very imaginative. She could still recall a hooded Ron gliding down the hall carrying a scythe, the embodiment of death itself.

Resolutely, she turned the conversation to Heather. "How is today feeling for you?"

Heather blanched. She picked up a book and paged through it, refusing to meet Amanda's eyes. "Fine. Really, I didn't mean to make such a big deal out of today."

"But *I* think it's a big deal." When Heather didn't respond, Amanda continued, "Wouldn't it be better to tell me about these feelings you have all bottled up inside?"

Heather's eyes were anguished but she nodded in agreement. Yet she seemed unable to begin.

"Come and sit down, Heather." When the girl obeyed, Amanda asked, "How do you know this is the anniversary of the day your mother left?"

Heather stared at her for long tense seconds before she answered. "I told you before, I listen sometimes, late at night when Daddy talks with Aunt Beth." Her face flushed at the confession and she wrung her hands. "You won't tell him, will you?"

"Of course not," Amanda assured her. "When did you find all this out?"

"Two years ago."

Oh, Lord, and you've carried it around by yourself all that time. "How does it make you feel?"

Heather waited a moment. Then it was as if a dam burst and the words flooded out. Like a swimmer caught in the current, she was unable to stop the flow. "How could she just do that, just leave Jason when he was a tiny baby? And make Daddy take care of him. Doesn't she know that someday Jason is going to put this all together and think it's his fault? Which it isn't."

In the course of her outburst, Heather's words rose in pitch until she was shouting. Her hands trembled and her voice shook. It was the first time she'd shown any reaction but crying.

Scooting forward on her chair, Amanda clasped
Heather's frigid hands between hers and cut right to the
quick. "What about you? How were you hurt?"

The girl recoiled and then stared blankly at Amanda
with wounded eyes. But she didn't answer.

"Heather?" Amanda knew she had to hurt in order
to heal. "Aren't *you* mad at your mother?"

The teenager seemed to go into a trance. Amanda
rubbed Heather's hands for a moment, then let them go
and sat back. She'd seen this reaction in the past, when
she'd interned at the Teen Crisis Center. The staff had
a term for it, the CBS, the "calm before the storm." So
she waited it out. She said nothing, she didn't move, she
barely even breathed.

After a good two minutes, tears began to course
down Heather's cheeks, color returned to them and her
breathing picked up. "All right. Yes, I'm mad at her. I
hate her. Why would she do this to us? What kind of
woman is she? Why couldn't she just love us enough to
stay? What did I do to make her go?"

Moving off her seat, Amanda crouched before
Heather. "Look at me." When the teenager did,
Amanda brushed the pale hair from Heather's face.
"What you've said so far is true except that last thing.
You didn't make her go. Your brother may very well
blame himself at some point. But he'd be just as wrong
as you are to take responsibility for this. There's only
one person responsible here, honey. Your mother, Suzanne Sullivan."

Heather gripped her hands together, her face chalk
white. "Then why *did* she leave?"

"I don't know. But maybe you can find out."

The teenager stilled. "No! I can't. I can't ask him. I
can't talk to him about this. Not yet."

Amanda's heart caught in her throat at the last two words. *Not yet.* She breathed a silent prayer of thanks to whatever deity was watching over this family. Heather had gone from absolute refusal to postponement. It was a step in the right direction.

Thirty minutes later, when Heather was composed and even animated—a common aftermath of such an important catharsis—Nick knocked on the office door. When Amanda called for him to come in, he entered whistling. His eyes shone brightly and he looked less tired, less stressed than any time she'd seen him in the past.

"Hello, ladies," he said, smiling at his daughter and ruffling her hair. When he peered at her closely, he asked, "Are you all right, honey?"

"Sure," she answered.

His eyes lingered on Heather, then briefly sought Amanda's. When she shook her head slightly to indicate he shouldn't probe further, he said, "Ms. Carson. You're looking well."

"So are you. Good day?"

"Yep. I studied all morning for my last exam and then I made the DiMarcos' secret-recipe sauce. I was hoping Heather might want to invite you to sample it tonight."

Heather's eyes lit up like a Christmas tree. Amanda knew she couldn't decline the invitation, even if she'd wanted to. She glared knowingly at Nick.

You don't play fair, she said to him silently.

You bet I don't. Remember that, he answered with his eyes.

AN HOUR LATER, Amanda sat at the table across from Heather and Jason. The kids had set it with a red-and-white-checked tablecloth and stuck a candle in a wine bottle. They'd dimmed the lights and dished out the salad.

"This looks delicious," she said as Nick set spaghetti and meatballs in front of her and a cold beer next to that. His after-shave invaded her senses and his breath felt hot and prickly on the sensitive skin of her ear as he leaned close. She could feel his firm touch through the material of her blouse. His closeness made her pulse leap.

"What do you call a grumpy cat?" Jason asked, drawing her attention to him.

Nick pulled back from Amanda and said with mock exasperation, "Oh, no, please, Jase. Not again."

"Last one, Dad, I promise. Well?" The boy impatiently tapped his fork on the table.

Amanda smiled at him. "Sourpuss."

Jason's impish eyes widened, then crinkled with respect. "Wow, you figured that out all by yourself?"

"Wish I had, kiddo. But one of the guys at school told me."

As they ate, Heather was unusually talkative, mentioning the basketball game at school that night and a new friend she'd met. Jason was his typical chatterbox self. Amanda enjoyed it all, and tried not to think of the sullen meals she and Lisa had endured.

Nick sat next to her, and every time she glanced in his direction, he gave her a meaningful grin, an arched eyebrow and, once, an incredibly sexy wink. By the time the meal was over, Amanda was half-aroused by just his intimate looks.

A timid voice broke her absorption. Heather had begun to clear the table, but poised with her dish in the air, looking hopefully at Nick. "Daddy, could we go to the basketball game at school tonight?"

"What time does it start?"

She glanced at the clock and frowned. "In a half an hour. I guess it's too late."

Jason jumped in. "Geez, Dad, Heather never asks for anything. Couldn't we go?"

Scanning the kitchen that was strewn with pots and pans, he said automatically, "We've got to clean up."

Heather sank into her chair and the light went out in her eyes. Jason's gaze narrowed on his father. Seeing Nick's scowl, Amanda intervened. "We could clean up afterward. I'll come back and help."

Nick stared at her blankly. She'd forgotten his proclivity to neatness.

But Heather hadn't. "No, that's okay. Why don't you three go on in and play Monopoly and I'll clean up." She turned to face Amanda. "The sauce makes too much mess when it stands around. And Daddy doesn't..."

When Nick glanced briefly at Amanda, she saw pain flicker in his eyes. Then he looked at his daughter, who was trying to mollify everyone, and at his disappointed son. He seemed to make a quick decision. "Daddy doesn't want anyone to miss out on the game, sweetheart. The dishes can wait."

Both children's jaws dropped at their father's uncharacteristic behavior. But Jason rebounded fast and took off for the other room. "Way to go, Dad. Last one ready to leave has to scrub the pot when we get back."

THEY TOOK first-row seats at the basketball game so they could accommodate Jason's wheelchair on the floor next to them. As the players warmed up, Nick could still see the look in Amanda's eyes when he'd agreed to come to the game. She'd stared at him with such respect, such admiration, that he'd found himself wanting, no, *needing,* to keep that look there forever.

Not good, DiMarco. Not good.

Trying to shake off the gloomy thought, he turned his attention to the action on the floor. Next to him, he heard Amanda explain the starting jump to Heather and why one basket counted two points and another racked up three.

"How do you know so much about this?" Jason asked her.

Amanda grinned sheepishly and pointed to the floor. "See those girls in the short skirts there?"

"The cheerleaders?"

"Yeah. Don't tell anyone, but I used to do that."

Nick glanced down at her legs, which were exposed beneath a knee-length, slim denim skirt, and said dryly, "A sight to behold, I'm sure." His gaze traveled up her body and his mind flashed to what she might have on underneath the blue striped shirt and navy cardigan.

As if she knew the direction of his thoughts, Amanda blushed. Nick wanted to grab her hand, but he didn't. He had no rights to Ms. Carson, guidance counselor.

At halftime, Heather went to get some candy for herself and Jason. Then a group of teenagers paraded past them.

"Hey, Ms. C., nice to see you here," one good-looking but devilish boy called to her.

She smiled warmly at him. "Thanks, Jake. You, too."

"Ms. Carson, I love your hair like that," said a girl who whipped by them with three others who looked just like her.

"I'll remember that, Carly." The pleasure on Amanda's face was genuine.

Nick sat back and observed the scenarios. This vision of her as a respected, well-liked teacher was in direct opposition to the impression he'd had when they first met. Then, he'd seen her as a debutante. Now, he was ashamed by his blatant stereotyping.

The feeling intensified a few moments later when his daughter came speeding back, breathless. "Ms. Carson, you've got to come. It's Matt. He's in trouble. He's in a fight..."

In a flash, Amanda was off the bench and out of his sight before Nick even realized what had happened.

Heather's face was colorless. "Go with her, Dad, please. They've got knives."

"Stay with Jase," he ordered and bolted after Amanda.

A crowd of kids had gathered in the dim hallway. He elbowed his way through in time to see Amanda standing next to the vice principal, Tom Mannerly, each facing one of the combatants. The boys looked immense next to her. They were both about seventeen, muscular and very, very angry. Both were holding knives. One was higher than a kite, if Nick guessed correctly.

He watched as Amanda glanced at the two boys then at the gathering crowd. She spotted two security guards and pulled one aside, speaking quietly to him. In moments, they began to clear the area of spectators. *Smart woman,* Nick thought. These kids would never surrender in front of an audience.

Easing into a doorway, Nick shielded himself from the guards.

The principal was talking. "Back off, Chico."

"No way, man. He called me stud." The boy in question gripped the switchblade tighter.

Matt's eyes narrowed on Chico and he fingered the handle of his knife. "Yeah, you jerk. Sandi told you to get lost. Something wrong with your stupid hearing?"

"The weapons have to go, guys," Mannerly said calmly. "Particularly for you, Chico. You're on thin ice from the last fight. Any more trouble like this and you're out of school for good." The man's voice was even, but Nick could see the vein throbbing in his throat.

Amanda's face was flushed and she clasped her hands behind her back. But she turned to the first boy with assurance worthy of David facing Goliath. "Chico, I don't know you, but I do know Matt. If you two go after each other now, you'll both be expelled for having weapons on school property. What's more, you'll probably be seriously hurt. If I get Matt to stop this, will you?"

"What's it to you, lady?" Chico raked her with insolent eyes.

Fists clenched, Nick was ready to spring. But some intuition about Amanda's need to handle this herself held him back.

"I'm his guidance counselor and I care about him."

The boy-man looked her up and down, his eyes glassy and wild. Indicating the vice principal with a toss of his head, he asked, "What'll the dude do if we stop now?"

"Since no one attacked, you'll only be suspended for a few days."

"Ms. Carson's right," Mannerly said. "We can end this right now with minor repercussions."

Chico glared at the adults, then looked beyond them as if noticing for the first time that he'd lost his audience. That seemed to tip the balance. "Aw, hell, why not?" Then tilting his chin, he finished, "Get him to back down first."

Quickly Amanda turned to Matt, who had bristled at Chico's words, *back down*. She moved directly between the two boys, right in the path of Matt's knife. "Give it to me, Matt."

Cold green eyes stared over her shoulder at Chico for several tense seconds. Nick watched as they then focused on Amanda and warmed several degrees. But Matt said nothing.

"I want you to do this, Matt." Amanda's authoritative tone was implacable.

The boy held his aggressive stance for a moment longer, then his whole body slackened. "Sure. He pulled his first. I don't care about this crap. Just so he leaves Sandi alone."

"He will, Matt. We'll see to it."

It was over soon after that. Nick watched, open-mouthed, as Amanda accepted the knife from Matt and the vice principal took the weapon from the other boy. Mannerly led Chico to his office while Amanda pulled Matt to one side and began to speak softly to him. She looked at the teenager intently, and soothed his arm with her slender fingers. Matt shook his head and even smiled at something she said before he went off with one of the security guards.

Nick and Amanda were left alone. He felt fear, anger, respect and admiration simultaneously. As she walked across the hall, he realized she was trembling and her face had lost most of its color. "You okay?"

"Yes."

"That was quite a feat you pulled off."

"It was, wasn't it? I never would have believed I could do it, Nick." She smiled and dug her hands into her pockets.

He wanted to shake her for endangering herself, *and* hold her and tell her how much he admired her courage.

Instead, he raised his hand and stroked the side of her face with his knuckles. "Well, you did, Mandy. And all by yourself."

"Thanks for not pulling some macho rescue. I needed to do this alone."

"Yeah, I figured that. Don't think I didn't want to, though. God, Amanda, I wanted to throttle you for stepping in front of that one kid's blade." His tone softened, taking the sting out of his words. "And I could kiss you for your cool, calm reasoning."

Her eyes glowed at his praise.

To diffuse his reaction, he encircled her neck with his arm, pulled her to him and whispered gruffly in her ear, "But you took quite a chance and *that* I don't like one bit."

She smiled into his shoulder. "Well, that gives me food for thought."

Unfortunately, it gave him the same thing. And the conclusions he came to as he digested the events of the evening frightened him. Not only was Amanda sexy and desirable, but she was strong and savvy. It was easier to keep his feelings in check when he could view her as shallow and superficial. Easier to remember they came from different worlds and had a questionable future together. But, tonight, in a dismal hallway of Eastside High, she had seemed very much a part of his world.

True to her promise, she came back to the apartment after the game and cleaned up as he put his children to bed. The kids had been full of questions all the way home and had wanted her to tuck them in before she left. Nick knew they both wanted to assure themselves that she was all right.

Just as walking her to the car when she was ready to leave and easing in beside her filled a need he had.

"Shall I turn on the heat?" she asked innocently.

Nick didn't answer. Seized by something frantic, something desperate that began when he saw her standing in front of that damn knife, he pulled her to him and took her lips with his. He demanded entry into her mouth. He clasped her to him too tightly, wanting to meld her body with his. After a moment, he eased up a bit and trailed kisses down her jaw to her neck and sucked lightly. Her moan triggered a response deep in his gut.

When he pulled back and she peered up him, his eyes captured hers. "I need to be close to you tonight, Mandy. I'm not exactly sure why. Maybe it's because of the danger you were in earlier. Maybe it's because I didn't expect you to... never mind," he told her as he lifted his hand to her navy wool coat and parted it. It hovered above the buttons on her blouse. "May I?"

Her eyes told him yes even before her lips affirmed it. He eased each button apart, drinking in what his touch had bared. "Ah, Mandy, you're beautiful, exactly as I knew you would be." Slowly, he lowered his head and placed his wet tongue on her cleavage. He licked her gently. "Front closure, a woman after my own heart." He didn't ask permission this time. He just flicked open her undergarment and she spilled into his waiting palms. "Oh, Lord, I must be dreaming," he whispered as he felt her swell into his hand. "You're so full, you fit me so well."

"Oh, Nick, that feels so good. Touching me there. I didn't know. It's the first time I've really wanted . . ."

Leaning over and tracing the outline of her ear with his tongue, Nick's grin was all male. "You've wanted what, baby?" He felt her tremble. When he drew back, he looked in her eyes and saw her swallow convulsively. "Tell me."

Though she blushed an appealing shade of pink, her tone was confident when she answered him. "I want you to touch me."

He groaned. He couldn't help it. Sea blue eyes met silver ones and he admitted, "Do you know what hearing you say that does to me?"

"Yes, I think so." A smile as old as time itself touched her lips and she looked down his front.

He lowered his head and opened his mouth over one pouting peak. She started off the seat as if she'd never felt the sensation before. It made him more voracious. After a moment, he transferred his attention to her other breast. She raised her hand to his neck and fastened it there, as if afraid he would stop and the feeling would be gone, as if she couldn't count on him to continue.

"I want to touch you, too," she whispered into the darkness.

Reluctantly, he left her breast and lifted his eyes to hers. He took her hand and placed it over his heart, which lurched at even that innocent caress.

"I want that, too, baby. But this isn't the right place. We need to make some time for us, Mandy. To have some lengthy privacy."

Burying her face in his neck, she nodded.

"Not afraid anymore?" he asked.

She raised her head and met his gaze unflinchingly. "No, not anymore. Not with you."

"We'll take it slow, anyway." Stroking her hair, he said, "I'm going to enjoy every second of helping you to discover just how responsive this delectable body is." Pausing meaningfully, he added, "To me."

I'll just have to be sure to keep my emotions in check, he thought as he extricated himself from her, helped her right her clothes, kissed her soundly on the mouth and left the car. *I'll risk my body, not my heart.*

But after what he'd witnessed tonight, he knew he was in grave danger of doing both.

CHAPTER EIGHT

"WANT TO GO for a walk?" Amanda asked her mother after dinner on the Wednesday following Christmas. She needed to get out of the cabin, a cedar A-frame, perfect for skiing.

Holidays had been traumatic for the family since her sister's death. For her mother's sake, Amanda had agreed to celebrate this—the second one without Lisa—with her parents in Aspen. Lisa's loss still hurt. And she missed Nick. They'd been unable to juggle their busy schedules to connect before she left. That was part of the cause of her restlessness.

Spending so much time in such an enclosed space with her father exacerbated it. He kept bringing up her job, and she could feel her self-confidence drain with each of his cutting remarks.

As she and her mother walked a pedestrian trail at the famous ski resort, the muscles in Amanda's neck began to loosen. She watched her breath make puffs in front of her and felt the cold air prickle her skin.

"He doesn't mean it, you know," Joan commented without preliminaries.

Amanda didn't need to ask who or what. "Doesn't he, Mother? It seems his favorite pastime lately."

Joan frowned into the darkness. Amanda could see it in the dim walking lights spaced every few feet. "He's scared, dear."

Stopping midstride, Amanda stared at her mother for a moment and then said, "My father has never been afraid of anything in his whole life."

Joan rubbed her calfskin-gloved hands together. "That was true until Lisa died," she said. "After that, everything was different." When Amanda gave no response, Joan asked, "For you, too?"

Amanda felt the familiar inner chill that mention of Lisa's death brought on. Seeking warmth, she hugged herself tightly. "Yes. I saw just how empty my life was."

"That's why you made so many changes, isn't it?"

Feeling the sting of tears behind her eyes, Amanda wished she could attribute them to the wind which had picked up. But the moisture was caused by the realization that this was the very first time her mother had asked her anything about the reason behind her behavior in the past year and a half.

She and Joan had never been close. They'd never talked deeply about anything. It was always as if her mother was trying to adhere to her husband's ideas and codes and had none of her own. Only lately had Amanda had any inkling that Joan had opinions different from Robert's.

But she never blamed her mother. Joan was the typical wife in a typically wealthy family. Amanda herself had been just like her in many ways. *And maybe Suzanne Sullivan was, too.* This was the second time she'd compared Nick's ex-wife to her mother, to herself, and she filed the thought away for future examination. Tugging her coat closer around her, she glanced at Joan. "Yes, that's why I've made so many changes."

"I thought so. If it helps any, I think you've made some good decisions."

Again, Amanda was so taken aback, she stopped walking. "Surely you didn't agree with my decision to divorce Porter. You made your disapproval very clear at the time."

Joan halted a few steps from her daughter. "At the time, I did think it was a mistake. But in the last few months, you've seemed so much more alive and involved, like your life took on a meaning it didn't have before."

Warmth radiated through Amanda. "That's exactly how I feel."

"I'd like to hear about it, if you want to talk."

"Let me tell you about these kids in my group, then." Amanda reached out and linked her arm with her mother's.

They strolled and talked and Amanda was filled with an unfamiliar hope as they headed back to the cabin. The snow began to blow and the pathway narrowed, so they were forced to walk single file. When Amanda felt the icy mush hit her on the side of the head, she was stunned. She turned to find her mother hurling another ice-packed snowball at her.

"Mother, what are you doing? This isn't you," she blurted out and was rewarded with another direct hit to her shoulder.

Joan giggled, her cheeks glowing a rosy red in the path lights and her eyes sparkling. "I know, and it feels wonderful."

Another whack catapulted the daughter into action.

They were laughing like children, complete with runny noses and watery eyes from the too-long time they'd spent outdoors, when they arrived at the A-frame a half hour later.

Wet and bedraggled, Amanda preceded her mother through the door and stopped both her entry and her laughing as she came face-to-face with Craig Coleman. She blinked, hoping she was imagining him, when her father said, "Say hello to Craig, darling."

"What are you doing here?" she asked, instead.

"Is that any way to treat your fiancé?" Craig leaned against the doorway, looking deceptively innocent.

She had to shake her head to clear it. Had she heard him correctly? "Have you forgotten our conversation last month, Craig?"

He dropped the Southern-gentleman act. Straightening from the wall, he squared his shoulders. Amanda noticed how the navy-and-white patterned ski sweater accented his thinness. "No, I haven't. But I'd hoped you had. I've given you weeks to reconsider and I was sure you'd come to your senses by now. So when your father invited me up here, I came." The last bit was added smugly.

"Of all the..." But she stopped midsentence and turned to Robert. "You *invited* him? Father, I explained to both Mother and you that Craig wouldn't be joining us for the holidays. Why would you ask him here against my wishes?"

Her father rose from the leather chair where he'd been watching the byplay, his features pinched. "Oh, for God's sake, Amanda. You never did know your own mind. I've done what's best for you, as always."

Stalking over to him, Amanda went up on tiptoe so her face was close to his. "No, you've done what *you* think is best. I will not tolerate your interference in my life like this."

"Remember who you're talking to, young lady." Robert's tone was clearly warning, but there was a quiver of doubt in his voice and a trace of apprehension in his eyes as he looked down at his defiant daughter.

Without a word, Amanda turned on her heels and headed upstairs. Ten minutes later, she returned with a small Louis Vuitton overnight case. She spoke only to Joan as she donned her coat. "I'm sorry about this, Mother, but I'm forced to leave. Could you bring the rest of my things back with you when you come home?"

Joan nodded her assent. Amanda knew her mother wouldn't speak up against her father, but the approval in her eyes and the squeeze she gave her shoulder as Amanda bent to kiss her were silent support.

Pulling on her gloves, Amanda marched to the door. She was about to open it, when Craig spoke.

"I just hope this doesn't have anything to do with Nick DiMarco," he said silkily.

His comment brought her up short. She turned to Craig warily, hoping there was still color in her face. "What do you mean?"

"I mean, darling, that I hope that seedy little hug I witnessed in the foyer at the library a few weeks ago has nothing to do with your sudden decision not to marry me."

Amanda was still reeling from his comment when her father asked, "What are you talking about?"

"I think Amanda is involved somehow with the father of one of her students." Craig eased away from the chair he'd leaned against and slid his hands into the pockets of his navy wool sport coat. "I saw her with him and made a few inquiries, afterward. Robert, do you know Joshua Cohen?"

"Of course."

"Well, Cohen's wife, Suzanne, was married to Amanda's Mr. DiMarco years ago. It seems our struggling lawyer-to-be has a penchant for wealthy socialites."

Amanda felt the bile rise in her throat. She knew Suzanne Cohen by name. She'd seen the woman at various social functions, but she'd never made the connection that this was Heather's mother. Nick's ex-wife! And she was not flattered at the comparison Nick had made between her and Suzanne.

Craig smirked. "Really, darling, I'd have guessed it was his, how shall I say this, his virility that attracted you if I didn't know you better."

The attack might have hurt, but Amanda conjured Nick's words that night at her house. *If you were any more 'enough', Amanda Carson, I'd be bursting out of my jeans right now.*

She stared Craig down from the doorway. "You're a bastard, Craig. I always knew that, but I didn't know how much of one until just now. Goodbye, Mother. I'll call you when I get a flight."

Robert started toward her but stopped halfway. "You'll never get a flight on such short notice, Amanda, not on the holiday. Don't be childish. Take off your coat, now." Though his tone was peremptory, there was an underlying anxiety in it.

"I'd sooner sleep in the airport than under a roof with the two of you," she said, sweeping both her father and Craig with indignant eyes.

FIVE HOURS LATER, Amanda still felt the same, though she was exhausted and dispirited. There *were* no seats to New York, though she was on standby for several flights. She was tired and hungry but the satisfaction she felt at walking out on Craig's insults and her father's demands gave her stamina. It also gave her the courage to make a phone call. She drummed her fingers on the tinny surface of the booth as she listened to the ringing at the other end.

"Hello."

"Nick?"

"Amanda?"

"Yes."

"Where are you?"

"At Stapleton Airport."

She could hear his slight gasp of surprise. "Wonderful. I'm glad you're cutting short your holiday. When do you get to Syracuse?"

"Well, that's a good question." She started to giggle. Oh, God, she was getting punchy.

Nick hesitated, then asked, "Mandy, are you all right?" His voice lowered to that deep, familiar timbre it had when he was touching her. "I've missed you."

Amanda felt the warmth of his admission curl through her like hot cider on a cold night. "I've missed you, too."

"What's happened?"

Alternating between laughter and anger, she gave him an edited version, leaving out Craig's revelation.

When she was done, he swore colorfully. "Why do these men think they can do this to you?"

There was a long pause from her end. "Because they always have, Nick. I've always let them."

This time, the silence came from him. She never expected the chuckle that followed. "I find that very hard to believe, Mandy. It's certainly not a trait of the feisty woman I know."

She felt as if a hundred-pound weight had been removed from her shoulders. "It isn't, is it?" Amanda's response was slightly breathless.

Nick's voice got even huskier. "No. And I want the woman I know to come back here. Come home to me, Mandy, as soon as you can."

NICK SLID his hand around the back of the couch just to feel Amanda's skin again. He hadn't been able to stop touching her since he'd picked her up for dinner before the New Year's Eve celebration at Beth's.

He'd splurged on La Belle Gourmand, a fancy restaurant that Tony had recommended. As he'd sat across from her and watched her white teeth sink into a plump shrimp, he'd wondered *how* he would keep himself in check. The thought had plagued him the entire evening, as the gold of her one-piece outfit shimmered around her. Every time she moved, the slinky material glided over her body. When he caught a whiff of her perfume, it reminded him of dim bedrooms and satin sheets. And now, when she curled into his hand, her soft nape rubbing against his callused palm, he wondered if he had the strength to control himself. He wanted to be her guide and partner through a journey of discovery into her sensuality, but to do it he had to rein in his libido.

Beth snagged his attention when she sat down across from them. "I can't believe you came," she said to her brother. Then, facing Amanda, she smiled. "I have you to thank, for that and a lot of other things."

Amanda's face flushed becomingly at the praise and Nick settled his hand on her shoulder. *Would everything about her always please him so?*

Dangerous thought, DiMarco. Just enjoy the night.
No one's ever talked in terms of a future.

He leaned forward to catch the end of his sister's comment. "How long did you wait for a flight?" Beth asked.

Amanda laughed and threaded her hand through her hair. "Thirty-six hours. But it was worth it to get back here early."

Beth beamed and Nick realized his sister thought that Amanda was referring to being able to spend New Year's Eve with him. She was, however, indicating her relief at escaping from her father and Craig Coleman. Damn those bastards.

As he watched her talk to Beth, he toyed with her hair, loving its familiar texture, thinking about the day and a half it had taken her to get back to New York. He'd worried about her all night, and in the twilight hours just before the sun rose, he'd come to the conclusion that Amanda Carson needed gentle, careful handling or her fragile ego would be bruised. And he didn't intend to be another addition to the list of men who wanted her as a trophy, cared nothing about her needs and squelched the independence that she craved. Those were the very qualities that he admired in her, and he intended to nurture them.

Nick was distracted when she reached over and touched his knee in an unconscious caress. "I slept for fourteen hours straight when I arrived yesterday. I think it was the best night's rest I've had in years."

As the evening wore on and they mingled with the other guests, Nick felt Amanda gravitate toward him physically. She would sidle up to him in a group, inviting him to sneak his arm around her waist. He'd gently massage the slender indentation there and tug her a lit-

tle closer. Once, when one of Beth's bookstore friends
became overly eager and snaked his arm around
Amanda's shoulder, she politely eased from under his
grip and stood behind Nick so that his body half
shielded her from the other man. He could feel her
breasts against the back of his arm and his biceps tightened in response. Sensing it, she'd swayed into him and
rested her cheek briefly against his jacket. He swore he
could feel the satiny smoothness of her skin straight
through the wool. He was ready to turn and throw her
over his shoulder fireman-carry style, stalk from the
room, find any dark, private place and bury himself in
her warmth. Though the notion was appealing, he knew
he could never behave in such a Neanderthal way with
her because of her past. And because of his. Loss of
control was one thing he could *not* afford with her. Instead, he had pulled her around and hugged her tightly.

"Are you staying until midnight, Nicky?" Beth
asked.

He shook his head, ready for the protest from his
possessive sibling. But it never came. Arching an eyebrow, Beth quipped, "Got a private party planned?"

Nick looked to Amanda for confirmation. He hadn't
told her much beyond Beth's party. She stared at him
for a moment, then smiled slightly with her mouth but
her eyes were glowing with sexual intensity. He read all
sorts of age-old, male-female messages in them.

"Looks like we do, Bethy." His own eyes never left
Amanda's.

THEY REACHED her house at eleven-thirty. Nick
brought champagne that had cooled in the car. Pop-
ping it with ease, he filled the two fluted glasses
Amanda had placed on the table in the room that faced

the backyard. She could see snow falling softly beyond him, the delicate flakes a latticework against the trees. Her favorite soft music crooned in the background and a fire burned cozily in the hearth, but her senses were mostly attuned to the man before her. His navy jacket accented the sheer broadness of his back. She was dwarfed by it and it made her feel feminine. Other things about him did, too. The way he touched her with his large, work-roughened hands. The way his eyes smoldered when he looked down her body. The catch in his breath when she'd touched his chest.

He'd been staring out at the drifting snow, deep in thought, but he turned when she walked over to him, and handed her a glass of champagne. His slate gray eyes glittered with anticipation.

Clinking his glass with hers, he asked, "If you could have one New Year's wish, Mandy, one that wasn't for your kids or your family or for world peace, just for you, Amanda Carson the woman, what would it be?"

Startled by his question, she halted the drink half-way to her lips and was momentarily silenced. How honest could she be?

Reading her mind, he whispered, "You can tell me anything, Mandy." His voice was low and husky and he moved a step closer to her.

She held his gaze steadily. "I'd wish—" She broke off and sighed.

Raising his free hand, he stroked the underside of her jaw. "You can tell me."

Her face full of emotion, she turned her cheek into his palm. "I *have* told you, Nick. I want to be sure I can respond completely to a man like a normal woman does."

"Still think you can't?"

"Actually, with you, I think I can."

His eyes never leaving hers, he said, "Amanda, I think I want to know the whole story behind this. Tell me about your marriage."

"All right."

He took her by the hand and led her to the couch. With gentle pressure to her shoulders, he sat her down. "Have a few sips of the wine." After she did, he took the glass from her and disposed of it along with his, sank down beside her and pulled her into the security of his arms.

She laid her head on his chest as she began. "Porter is a nice man, but I think the relationship was as dull for him as it was for me. We grew up together, we'd been dating since high school and there was just no sparkle in anything...including sex."

Sighing, Amanda remembered those early days when she and Porter had had an unimaginative and uninspiring first few years as a couple. "Our sexual problem only got worse. I finally talked to a doctor who gave me reading to do on it. Porter was horrified. He felt it was an invasion of his privacy. When I tried to talk to him about it, to tell him I was..."

"Unsatisfied?"

"Yes," she admitted. "He told me he'd never had any complaints before." She looked up at Nick. "Frankly, I was shocked there *was* a before for him. We'd been engaged all through college and got married right afterward."

Nick's grip tightened around her. "So I take it he was your first lover?"

She nodded, then inched closer to him. "I really did try. Romantic dinners, lacy nightgowns, wine. Nothing worked. He just couldn't loosen up enough to take my suggestions. I guess Porter approached sex like he did everything else. Clinically. Neatly. At least with me. Finally, I gave up trying. We divorced amicably after seven years."

When she remained silent, Nick smoothed the heavy hair off her face. "Porter is a fool. He was also wrong to shuffle this off on you. It was his fault."

"It was *partially* his fault. And partially mine."

"Did you ever make love with Coleman?"

She burrowed deeper into his chest and shook her head. "No. I responded to him about as much as I did to Porter. It scared me, though, because I was beginning to believe it *was* all me."

"And now?" She could hear the satisfaction in his voice, but confirmed what he seemed to need to hear aloud.

"Now I believe it was just that I hadn't found the right man." As she said it, she drew back from him and looked into the face she was beginning to love.

He grinned at her, an elemental, male smile. "Well, a good lawyer always makes sure of his facts."

She smiled back. "Yes, he does."

"Shall we run a test case?"

"I think that's a good idea. Just to be sure."

Gently, he guided her onto his lap. "Better access," he said. She watched his hand open the first five buttons on her dress. Her heartbeat thrummed in her chest and her skin heated up quicker than sand on a summer beach. God, she wanted this the way she'd never wanted anything before. He gazed at her breasts, barely visible through the lace of a black camisole, and she felt her nipples pucker through it.

He brushed his fingertips over them. "Mmm, real solid proof. Real evidence. I love the lingerie. Is the rest of it like this?" he whispered. She could only nod her head. "Can I see?" Again, she gave silent permission.

The silky material of her dress slithered down her body like a waterfall, but his hands ignited every inch of skin he touched. He shifted her slightly and the outfit soon lay at his feet. "God, you're beautiful. So beautiful and so desirable. I want you, Mandy," he breathed in her ear.

Sensations bombarded Amanda. The definite hardening of him beneath her almost-bare bottom. His hand teasing away the silk of her bra and cupping her breasts firmly. As she'd done the last time, Amanda started and arched into him, surprised by the feeling. His other hand cradled her hip. Slowly, he slid his palm up and down, up and down. Amanda wanted more and she squirmed on his lap.

"Careful, baby. Do that again and I might embarrass myself."

She smiled at his confession. It all felt so good.

But she was soon distracted as he took his hand on yet another expedition. He brought it down the front of her and rested it on the panties that covered her triangle of curls. Carefully, he slid it inside the lace band and down between her legs. He looked her square in the eye as he sank his fingers into her moist warmth. Easing them in and out, he said, "Ah, more evidence. See how you respond for me. You're wet, and getting wetter. Just for me." He continued the motion for a moment, then removed his hand from its glorious discovery.

She moaned at the loss.

"Oh, Mandy, I love to hear that. Moan for me. Want me. It's all so much a part of you," Nick said.

Though his last words thickened the fog of desire, Amanda had enough awareness to say, "It is, Nick. You make me believe it." He sealed his mouth with hers. She moaned again, just for him. "I want..."

When she didn't continue, he encouraged her. "You want what, Mandy?"

"I want to touch you, too."

It was Nick's turn to moan. He seemed to struggle with the idea, and it took Amanda a moment to realize he was so aroused, he feared her touch. She smiled like a courtesan of ancient times.

Groaning, he warned, "Don't look at me like that and smile so seductively, princess, or you'll find yourself on your back in two seconds."

She couldn't help repeating the gesture. He relented when she whispered, "Please let me touch you."

He gritted his teeth. "Go ahead, I'll take it as long as I can."

Her hands floated to his body, as if they knew exactly what to do. Actually, they knew exactly what they'd always *wanted* to do to a man but had never had the chance. She slid off his lap and knelt next to him on the couch. Unbuttoning his shirt, she weaved her hands through the springy hair and familiarized herself with the coarse, male feel of it.

"I wanted to do this that first night at the restaurant. I wanted to know how your skin felt, to touch you here," she said softly as she bent to kiss his breastbone, and inhaled his woodsy scent. He jerked at her wet touch and grabbed her arms, but said nothing. She continued.

He leaned his head back against the couch and closed his eyes. "I can't bear the sight of you on your knees for me," he growled hoarsely.

She laughed with growing self-confidence, bent over and placed her mouth on him. She kissed her way up to his neck and sucked beneath his jaw. She made her way to his mouth and covered it fully with hers. She devoured him, biting his lip, giving it tiny kisses, biting it a second time. He groaned again.

"Oh, Nick, this feels so good, to touch you like this, to make you feel like this."

"*You* think it feels good?" When she returned to his chest and flicked a nipple with her tongue, he said brokenly, "I...oh, Mandy...I..."

"You what?" She mimicked the words he'd used when he had her under his control like this a few minutes earlier.

"I...think...I've...created a Frankenstein."

Amanda was awed that he could joke during this love play. In addition to the wonderful, responsive feelings it evoked, she realized that sex could also be fun.

LATER, when Nick jogged down the steps of her house, he felt like the wisest and most foolish man on earth. He had wound down the encounter with Amanda gently, allowing them both more kisses and caresses until he was sure he couldn't take any more without taking her. Some god somewhere had given him the strength to do that, despite the rampaging demands of his body.

He truly believed it was best for Amanda to take this gradually, to dip her feet into the pool of sensuality in small steps. And he'd been able to convince her that she could respond as enthusiastically as he. What he didn't know was why he'd done it this way. He *could* have taken her. He *should* have taken her. But he didn't because it was best for her.

Watch it, DiMarco, don't go noble or anything. She's still out of your league. Best to just enjoy her and not worry about afterward.

But he was slowly coming to fear that he might not be able to ever let her go.

CHAPTER NINE

"GLAD WE HAVE this chance to talk, Nick," Nathan Joris stated as he reached out to shake hands. Nick grasped the other man's hand firmly and greeted him. Though he'd been clerking here for a semester, this was the first time he'd been called to meet with this important partner. Nick knew what it meant. They'd decided they wanted him in the firm. And he wanted to be here. Today, January third, marked his entrance into the posh world of law and he intended to do everything in his power to stay there.

While Joris answered a call from his secretary, Nick sat down and looked around the offices of Joris, Beach and Stowe. They were a work of art. Located in a high rise in downtown Syracuse, only the best of everything graced the interior of the prestigious law firm. Buttery soft couches were scattered all over the suite and ranged in color from white to teal to conservative brown. Nick ran his hand across the supple leather that conformed to the body's shape. Picking up his coffee, he noted how the table was solid wood, finely crafted, cold to the touch and polished to a sheen.

A frown crossed his face as he thought about the last time he was in an office like this one. He'd come to Adam Sherwood to seek a divorce and an incontestable custody agreement. He'd gotten both and he'd also walked away with a promise to himself that someday he would return to one of these firms as a full-fledged lawyer. After his kids, reaching his goal had become the focus of his life, a driving force to succeed. This opportunity was the first step.

Joris hung up the phone. "I apologize for the interruption. It won't happen again." He sat behind a desk the likes of which Nick had never seen. It was teak with sleek curves and subtle crannies and alcoves. It shouted power, as did everything else here. All of which suited Nick just fine.

"I can't tell you how pleased we were when you decided to accept our offer in September."

Nick relaxed in the chair and kept Joris's eye contact. "I'm interested in this firm, Mr. Joris. I'm pleased you're interested in me."

Drumming his fingers on the desktop, the partner perused Nick shrewdly. "Third in your class at Syracuse is top-notch and very attractive. I'm certain you know that. Let's talk about some changes in your responsibilities here for the next few months, shall we? We want to see your grit, so we're going to give you meaty work."

Though his heartbeat sped up, Nick kept his casual pose. "By all means."

THE DAY FLEW BY after that. He began working with more important clients and some new lawyers. Each time he was introduced as the clerk the firm was courting, his self-esteem rose. Every comment about how pleased they were to get him gave him the sense of accomplishment he'd sought for ten long years, proved that he would be able to provide well for Heather and Jason and gave his ego that much-needed boost. He sank into a chair in his cubicle, which was probably

bigger and fancier than a full partner's office in another, less renowned firm, and thought, *I'm here to
stay.*

Over the week, following his interview with Joris, he
had to remind himself of his goal, for the escalation in
his responsibilities stretched him thin. The first night
after the meeting, he'd gotten home at a decent hour,
able to spend time with Heather and help Jason with his
homework. However, at five o'clock the next evening,
a partner entered his office and tossed a folder onto his
desk.

"This is the Connelly case we discussed at the meeting yesterday. I need you to research the statutes on an
obscure tax law passed in 1957." Then he paused and
smiled sympathetically. "By tomorrow morning at
eight."

Nick didn't even blink. He took the file and headed
for the library. On his way, he stopped to call his mother
to ask her to stay overnight. Though his family had all
pitched in and covered for him at home in the past, he'd
told them these next few months would be worse. They
agreed to help even more so he could finish in good
standing. That night, he rolled in at twelve thirty-five
and was gone before the kids got up in the morning.

The next evening, there was a seven o'clock meeting
with a client that he was *asked* to sit in on. Thursday, he
was supposed to see Amanda. Just the thought of
burying his hands in that thick honey-colored hair and
pulling her tight against his chest had him wanting all
day. But he'd had to delay it, canceling their dinner
plans to eat with his kids and promising her he'd pick
her up after her ballet class, which she'd decided to attend when he'd changed their plans.

In the doorway of the old, high-ceilinged room, Nick breathed in the musty odor of age and sweat. He was able to see why the latter permeated the air as he watched the group bend, stretch and leap through the air. Actually, he had eyes for only one dancer.

He hadn't realized she was so good. Her slender body contorted in every conceivable way and she moved with the grace and fluidity of a doe. He was mesmerized by her and aroused by the way her leotard outlined every single curve.

Thirty minutes later, when they settled into a booth at Ferrara's for dessert and coffee, Nick questioned her about her talent. "I didn't know you were so good. How long have you been taking classes?"

Amanda's eyes clouded for a moment, but she banished the memory of whatever had caused it and smiled self-effacingly. "Not long enough. I'm not nearly as good as the rest of them."

"Did you dance as a child?"

"Uh-huh." She picked up a menu and read it with absorption. When he yanked it out of her hand, she looked up at him with fake surprise.

"How long did you train?"

"Until I was sixteen." She sighed and slouched against the vinyl. The shadows were back in her eyes. "By then, I was studying with some of the best dancers in the city, each night. I went to New York every summer to train, too. I loved it."

"But you *quit?*" He leaned forward, propping his elbows on the table.

She nodded. Her eyes were hollow and hooded.

"Why?"

Tears welled in the beautiful cobalt depths and he watched her force them back. Reaching over, he took her hands in his. They felt as if she'd been in a snow-storm with no gloves. "Amanda? What is it?"

Shaking off the pall, she gripped his hands and smiled sadly. "One day, Lisa was watching me dress for a re-cital from the doorway. I had this beautiful costume, a white shimmery bodysuit with glittery stars all over it and a tutu so delicate it looked like it would dissolve if it was touched. Actually, the whole thing itched like hell." She chuckled at the memory but sobered again quickly. "I loved it, anyway. All of it, even the bleed-ing toes and strained muscles."

A waitress appeared and interrupted her story. But Nick wanted more information, so when the woman left, he continued his cross-examination. "Then why did you stop?"

"Lisa's face. If you could have seen the pain there. The longing. It hurt her, Nick, to see me dance. I never realized it before. So I quit. I told my parents I was tired of the pace and the pressure." Amanda stared over his shoulder and Nick could tell she was in another place and time. "My mother was disappointed, but she would have let it go without a fight. My father raged like a wounded bear. He yelled so loud, even Lisa was afraid—and she defied him constantly. But I wouldn't budge this time. I simply refused to go back."

He saw her forehead furrow. "What?" he asked.

Amanda laughed, but it wasn't a pleasant sound. "He'd win any way he could, Nick, even then. That's why he intimidates me so much now, he'll stop at noth-ing to get what he wants. He used Lisa to try to per-suade me. I think he told her that he'd guessed my real reason. She was furious in her own right and yelled at me almost as loud as he had. I lied to her, too. It was one of the few times I was ever dishonest with her. But it was better than knowing each time I danced, she suffered.''

Nick massaged her still-frigid fingers with his thumbs. "You're something else, Ms. Carson." Her eyes glowed at his praise. "When did you start again?"

Their dessert arrived and she began spooning vanilla ice cream covered with gooey hot fudge into her mouth. Her tongue darted out to catch a drip. Nick's groin hardened and it distracted him, so he almost missed the answer.

"Six months ago. Let's change the subject. Tell me about the clerking this semester," she said in between scoops.

He shifted in his seat, knowing she wasn't going to like this and he dreaded the confrontation. But he knew she expected an answer and he could only give her an honest one.

"It's getting more demanding now. I've worked my butt off to get this. It's exactly what I want, Amanda." Cautiously, he told her about his last encounter with Joris.

Her smile was forced and it twisted in his gut. "What have the hours been like lately? I won't see Heather until tomorrow so I don't know."

"Worse than last semester, which is typical." Nick knew he was scowling. "They want to see my 'grit.' But I'm trying to sneak away whenever I can. Like tonight. I had dinner with the kids and put Jason to bed before I left. Beth is at the house so I could see you."

Amanda stirred the remainder of her dessert into muddy puddles, having obviously lost her appetite for the ice cream. *Would she lose her appetite for him, too, if he let her down on this? No, damn it, he wouldn't let that happen.*

He reached over and grabbed her hand again. Deliberately, he traced each line in the soft skin. The callus on his thumb rubbed it roughly, sensuously, and she started in reaction. "Listen, baby, I'm doing the best I can. I won't let this get out of control. If I can't arrange everything, I'll make it up to them."

Amanda took a deep breath and removed her hand from his seductive caress. She pierced him with knowing eyes. "You won't be able to control it, Nick. No one realizes better than I how much this job will demand."

"Speaking from experience?" He bristled and sat back, breathing deeply to alleviate some of the constriction around his heart.

"Yes, of course I am. My father was never home when I was young, and when he was there, he was so preoccupied and grumpy we wished he'd go back to work. And Porter went through the same thing. The clerking and the initial years trying to make partner were the worst."

"I can handle it," Nick stated implacably.

She shook her head and leaned toward him, arms braced on the tabletop. "No, you can't. On paper the firm may put down that you only work the twenty hours a week allowed by the law school commission, but they expect more if you want a future with them. In addition to the rest of your course work, where in that schedule is there room for Heather and Jason?"

Exasperated, Nick raked his hand through his hair, in what was becoming a familiar gesture. "Okay, then, I'll have to work hard to get through these few months. I'll have more say once I'm on board. Heather and Jason will adjust temporarily."

"Heather needs you now, Nick. I told you that."

"*I* need *this,*" he said, raising his voice and attracting the attention of the other customers. "I've worked myself to the bone for it! I can't jeopardize everything now."

"Why?" Amanda asked simply.

"I told you before, I want to be able to give my children all the things I can't give them now. I want them to have every single opportunity you had, Amanda." When she didn't respond, he finished, "And I want to be successful for me. I admit, part of this is selfish, though not the whole thing. If my ambition makes you think less of me, then so be it."

She stared at him without flinching. "Nick, Suzanne's abandonment must have left you with all sorts of feelings of inadequacy. Are you sure this isn't just some vendetta against her that's turned into an obsession?"

"Absolutely not!" he snapped. "I want a good life for my kids. What's wrong with that?"

Chagrined at his loss of control, and the fact that he'd allowed himself to get to the place where he wanted Amanda's acceptance so badly, he tried to distance himself from her, physically and emotionally. He leaned back against the booth and crossed his arms over his chest in body language that would alert even a novice, let alone a trained therapist. "Funny, Amanda, you were there for Porter. You saw him through all this. But you won't do it for me. Apparently, I've misread what's between us."

Amanda's eyes flamed with angry sparks and she slapped the table with her hand. "That's unfair and you know it."

He arched an eyebrow. "Is it? Maybe the truth hurts. Look, I'm ready to go. Suddenly, I'm very tired."

Tossing a few bills on the table, he rose, grabbed his wool overcoat and stalked out of the restaurant, refusing to glance behind him to see if she was following. She was. He waited at the door, not wanting her to walk to the car alone.

On the drive to her house, she tried to make conversation. "I like the suit. Is it new?"

The topic was not a wise choice, but Amanda couldn't know that. He looked down at his charcoal gray suit and pin-striped shirt. It had bothered him to let Beth pay for the additional clothes he needed now that he was going to be working more at the firm. She'd gone with him to help him pick everything out and he'd kept an exact tab so he could pay her back, but the circumstances still grated.

He gripped the steering wheel. "Yeah, it's new." The terse comment cut off all further discussion and Amanda remained silent the rest of the way.

The tension was still between them like a stone wall as he walked her to her door. Trying to stifle his need for her, he stood rigidly before her, fists clenched in his pockets. He wanted to hold her. He wanted her to hold him and tell him everything was going to be all right, instead of crossing him on each and every issue.

She peered up at him with wary blue eyes. "Would you like to come in?"

He shook his head. "No, I don't think that's a good idea now."

Shrugging her shoulders, she angled her head. "All right, then. Thanks for the dessert." But she didn't turn to go in. She just stood there facing him, chin tilted, body straight, saying without words, "I won't apologize because I did nothing wrong."

God, how had her father and her husband bullied her all these years?

The thought of another man having her catapulted him into action. He drew her to him and melded her body to his. She dropped her gym bag and held on tight to his arms. Sliding her hands from his biceps, she encircled his waist. Then she laid her head on his chest and snuggled into him. "It won't work, Nick, distancing yourself from me. I won't let it."

She pulled away slightly and slid her hands inside his coat, up his shirt, to his neck. His body reacted with a start. She stood on her toes to bring her mouth close to his.

"Kiss me, Nick," she whispered against his lips.

He did. He devoured her. He bit her lip, soothed it, forced entry into the recesses of her mouth and dueled with her tongue. He released her mouth and made his way to her neck. He knew his rough beard abraded her tender skin, but he couldn't stop. The smell of her perfume inflamed him and he realized, too late, that he'd sucked too hard and had left his mark on her. "You make me lose control, baby. I'm sorry," he murmured into her throat.

Amanda shivered with his words and the fire of his embrace. She leaned into him with the lower part of her body as if she was trying to fuse it with his.

"I'm not sorry," she whispered. "I'm not sorry at all."

HEATHER DIMARCO shyly raised her hand and was rewarded with a bright smile from her counselor. She looked cheerful and perky in a denim skirt and fuzzy pink V-neck sweater.

"Heather's got a joke?" Matt teased, rocking his chair back on its back legs. When he saw her tremulous smile, he added quickly, "Hey, doll, I think it's cool. We been carrying you in the humor department for weeks."

Giving him a haughty look that, once perfected, would bring guys like Matt Barone to their knees, she said, "Why do they bury lawyers twenty feet underground?"

When no one could answer, Heather brushed back her blond bangs and giggled. "Because way down deep they're really nice guys."

Amanda wondered briefly if she'd told Nick the lawyer joke. And if he'd laughed. Had there been happiness in his life this week?

Ron Marshall played a drumbeat on his radio, which rested on his lap. "Oh, bad, girl, really bad. And mine is even worse."

There were groans from all around, but Amanda kept her eyes glued on the boy. She sensed that something wasn't right today. Ron was effervescent. He'd greeted her congenially when he arrived and had chattered until the others came. Dressed in a black sweatshirt, black sneakers and a black-and-white checked bandanna, he seemed like a typical, happy teenager, meeting with friends.

But Amanda knew Ron was a very troubled young man. These past weeks had been especially hard on him. He was the only one not making college or work plans. Even Matt had sent in a few applications. No, Ron's behavior was clearly suspect. She listened in time to hear his joke.

"Mommy, Mommy, why is Daddy so stiff?" He paused, then said, "Shut up and keep digging."

Ron's laugh was too hearty. Matt snorted and Heather smiled patronizingly.

The "Mommy, Mommy" death jokes had been popular two or three years ago. They were all sick, but tickled the funny bone of kids his age. Amanda thought they were stupid, but knew their appeal and had never minded them before. But she thought Ron's preoccupation with them was unhealthy. "Let's get on to how we all are, shall we?"

When no one volunteered, she turned to Sandi. The girl was dressed sloppily today, not her usual style. She had on army green stirrup pants that were worn at the knees and a drab T-shirt, torn at the shoulder. She sat in her chair, staring into space, saying nothing during the jokes. Something was wrong with her, too.

"Sandi, you're awfully quiet. Is something going on in your life that you'd like to share?"

Shaking her head, Sandi averted her gaze and tugged at the hem of her shirt.

"Why not?" Amanda prodded.

Surprisingly, tears welled up in the teenager's eyes and she swiped at them. Amanda had never seen Sandi cry before.

Matt stared at her. "The dude's back?"

Sandi's eyes widened and the tears abated. "How'd ya know that?"

"You're a pretty tough babe, Sand. Takes a lot to get to you. Had to be something heavy." Matt slanted his chair even farther back.

"Your stepfather's returned?" Amanda clarified.

Sandi wouldn't look at her, but nodded.

"When?"

"Three nights ago. And she welcomed the bastard back with open arms. And legs."

No one responded to her crudity. Sandi peered over at Amanda, then Heather, then threw up her hands in dismay. "Sorry. I'm so pumped about this, I get rude."

Amanda watched Heather reach over and squeeze Sandi's hand. "It's okay, Sandi, I feel bad for you."

"Yeah, well, kid, I do, too. They snort and smoke all the time. And he—" Sandi stopped midsentence. Her body went stiff and she gripped her hands together so tightly, her knuckles turned white.

Matt's chair came down with a thud. "He what?"

But Sandi refused to continue. She just stopped talking and shook her head again.

After a long and very uncomfortable silence, Amanda intervened. "All right, Sandi, if you want to pass for now. How about you, Ron?"

"Hey, man, I'm cool. Everything's cool. Life is bee-u-ti-ful today."

Narrowing her eyes on him, Amanda waited a moment before she responded. "Why is that?" she asked finally.

Ron squirmed a bit in his chair and then favored her with one of his rare grins. "The absence of pain, I guess."

Matt elbowed him in the ribs. "Really, buddy? Then maybe you'll finally sell me that watch I been wantin' to buy off you."

Ron batted Matt's arm away and fooled with the buttons on his portable stereo system. A genius in electronics, he excelled at restoring appliances. He'd practically rebuilt the radio, tape and CD player from scratch and he was as proud of it as a new father. "Just feelin' good, man, that's all." When everyone stared at him for his uncharacteristic behavior, he asked, "Is it a crime?"

"Of course not, Lee-ronne."

"All right, Matt, that's enough. Sure there's not more to this, Ron?" Amanda tried to hide her concern.

The boy looked to the floor for a few seconds, then raised his eyes to hers. The bleakness in their chocolate brown depths made her catch her breath. The despair there was so pronounced, she was rocked by it. "Naw, Ms. C., I'm cool. Pass me a chocolate chip, will ya?"

Since he'd effectively ended his sharing, Amanda turned to Heather. The girl smiled uneasily at her. They had all sensed Ron's unusual mood.

"I'm doing okay," Heather said, breaking the tension. She took a deep breath and folded her hands in her lap. "Things at home were real good for a while. My dad quit his waiter's job so he could be with us more. He was there a lot. I liked it."

Ron snorted. His own father, Amanda knew, drank heavily. She suspected some alcohol abuse from the boy, too. "Man, I dig it when my old man isn't home. He gets mean when he drinks, which is all the time. He's better off without me."

"You mean you're better off without him," Heather innocently corrected him.

Ron's look was blank. "Yeah, what did I say?"

Amanda's anxiety escalated. But Heather was still talking.

She was honest about her displeasure at Nick's absence this week, but defended him at all costs. "It's not his fault. I know he's just trying to finish law school and get a good job. But..." She bit her lip and didn't continue.

Amanda encouraged her. "But what?"

"But I'd rather have him than more money or a better place to live."

"Don't sound like you're doin' okay to me," Matt said with a frown.

Heather's eyes brightened. "Oh, but I am."

It seemed she'd met a girl at her bus stop and had been spending time with her. Nick had even let her invite her new friend, Tammy, to stay overnight tonight.

"I'm so happy. Aunt Beth brought over popcorn and soda and even bought me new pajamas." She scowled and the expression mirrored Nick's so much, it hurt Amanda to see it. "It's just too bad she forgot her stereo. She was going to set it up in my room. But that's okay, we'll have fun, anyway."

"Why didn't you say something, girl?" Ron picked up the box from his lap, rose and walked a few steps to her. "Here, you can have it," he said, handing her the portable stereo.

Heather blushed a deep red. Matt's jaw dropped. Sandi swore under her breath. And Amanda's heart plummeted.

Giving away prized possessions. A good mood for no reason. She stared at the slash marks on his wrists, the ugly two-inch scars that went horizontally across the arteries, and she knew for certain that Ron was in grave danger. Again.

When he just stood there, holding out the stereo to her, Heather finally shook her head. "Oh, no, I couldn't." But she stared longingly at the powerful machine.

"Why not? If you're worried about your daddy not liking the noise, there're two sets of ear phones for dual listening."

"No, it's not that. It's just..."

Amanda rescued her and tried not to offend Ron. "I think it's a lovely offer. Ron didn't mean for you to keep it, Heather. It's just a loan, isn't it, Ron?"

Ron's whole body went taut. Staring somberly at Amanda, he took a deep breath and sighed. "Sure, a loan. Enjoy it." Averting his gaze, he said, "Look, I gotta go. My old man said I had to come right home today."

He took a quick glance around the room, his gaze resting on his own seat for a moment, then it gently touched Matt, Sandi and finally came back to Heather. "Y'all take care of yourselves, ya hear?" and before anyone could react, he was gone.

Amanda bolted from her seat and ran after him. She followed him as far as the hallway but he was fast and he popped out of sight. *He is not all right. This time, I have to do something.*

Calmly, Amanda wound down the group as soon as she could without alarming the youngsters. She was dialing the crisis hot line, after having tried to contact the school nurse and the vice principal, when Matt returned to her office ten minutes later. His shoulders were tense and his ever-present cocky grin was gone.

"Forget something?" Amanda asked, surprised to see him.

"No. I found this in my pocket, Ms. Carson." In his almost-grown hand he held Ron's most precious possession.

"I don't understand. I offered him all that money a million times for this watch and he refused. Why would he just give it to me?"

AMANDA STAYED at school until late trying to call Ron Marshall's home. The hot line had encouraged her to get help in trying to locate the boy. She'd reviewed his file previously but she checked it again and found the same sketchy personal information on him. There was a blank next to who to call in case of emergency and no phone number for father's place of employment. No information was listed about his mother. The background check indicated she'd left when Ron was eleven.

She'd finally reached the school nurse, who said she would keep calling Ron's home, as well. Amanda also connected with Tom Mannerly, her supervisor, at 6:00 p.m. and he agreed to go to Ron's apartment immediately. An hour later, he called back to tell her no one was at home.

Later that evening, Amanda telephoned the Marshalls' house several times with no luck. She knew of no friends to contact and no other family members.

That night, sleeping fitfully, she dreamed morbid scenarios involving the teenager and was even more anxious when she awoke Saturday morning.

THE MARSHALLS' apartment was in one of the worst sections of the city. It was surrounded by abandoned buildings whose glassless windows stared back like accusing eyes. The stench of debris in the street assaulted Amanda. She shivered as she stood before the building and the wind played with the strands of her hair. She felt a twinge of guilt for the full-length leather coat and kidskin gloves that probably would have paid two months' rent here. It was amazing that Ron felt he could communicate with her at all.

The front door squeaked as she eased it open. Out of the biting wind, she was still cold. When the light reached the hallway, she felt, rather than saw, little brown things scurry into the woodwork. Her stomach lurched and she was thankful she'd been too worried to eat breakfast. Gingerly, she made her way to number four, grateful it was not up the rickety stairs. The walls were covered with grime and she was careful not to brush them.

When she reached the apartment, she knocked hard on the door, the sound echoing in the deserted hallway. No answer. Amanda banged again and she could feel her pulse quicken. Lord, she was afraid. For Ron. For herself right now. She needed to calm down. Let's see... *What do you get when you cross a lawyer with the Godfather?*

An offer you can't understand. She barely smiled at the joke as she knocked once again.

She'd purposely waited until ten o'clock, not too early to wake them and not too late for Ron to have taken off again. Finally, she heard a grumbling inside. She crossed her arms and gripped her elbows with each hand.

The door creaked as it opened and suddenly there was a man looming before her. She had to quell the urge to step back. "This better be good, lady. What the hell do you want?"

Taking a deep breath, Amanda prayed her voice wouldn't quake. Her chin tilted and she stared at him unblinkingly. "I'm Amanda Carson, Ron's guidance counselor. I was worried about him yesterday and I've come to see him."

The man was huge, bigger than Nick. Staring at her with bloodshot eyes, he reeked of alcohol. His face was rough with several days' growth of beard and his thick black hair was matted from sleep. "You that lady he been seein' at school?"

Amanda nodded.

"He in trouble?"

Yes, I'm afraid he's going to kill himself. But Amanda knew intuitively she couldn't tell this man that.

"Not like you mean, Mr. Marshall. He seemed unusually upset yesterday and I'm worried about him. I tried to call him all last night but there was no answer. Is he here? Can I speak with him?"

The father stared at her for a long time. "Guess it won't do no harm. Can't quite figure out why a white woman would care, but I'll wake him up."

Mr. Marshall closed the door in her face and Amanda breathed a sigh of relief. At least she'd get to talk to Ron.

But the older man returned alone. "He ain't there."

"You mean he's gone out already?"

Running a hand through his hair, Marshall's shoulders slumped and the lines in his face deepened. "No, lady, he never came home. Bed ain't been slept in."

Amanda forcefully quelled the urge to reprimand him for negligence. The hall suddenly seemed darker and the man before her larger. She pulled a piece of paper out of her pocket and handed it to him. "Could you give this to Ron when he returns? It's a note I wrote in case no one was home."

The man looked down at her for a moment and Amanda felt like a bug under a microscope. He snapped up the missive, opened it and read it, then nodded to her. The door closed again in her face.

HER PHONE RANG at six o'clock and Amanda lunged for it. "Hello."

"Hi."

It was the only other voice she wanted to hear besides Ron's. Still, her shoulders sagged. "Nick."

"Yeah." There was silence. The last time they'd been together was strained and the tension was thick even across phone lines. "You sound disappointed."

"No, no, of course I'm not."

Again there was a too-long pause. Finally, Nick took the initiative. "Look, Mandy, I know I behaved like a jerk the other night. Let me come over and talk about it."

Amanda hesitated. She'd like nothing better than to say yes, to let Nick come here and fling herself into his arms for comfort. But old fears sneaked up on her, demons from her past.

You can't do this by yourself, Amanda. Let Porter handle it.

Damn, she needed to do this alone. Could he understand that? Could any man?

Nervously twisting the phone cord around her fingers, she answered, "No, Nick, not tonight. I'm busy."

There was another long pause. "Tell me you don't have a date," he finally said. She couldn't identify the emotion in his voice.

Amanda sighed again and sank into a chair. She laid her head back against the caning and closed her eyes. Dissembling wasn't working. "I don't have a date, Nick. I have a student I'm extremely worried about. I've been trying to track him down all day with no luck. I'm going to keep trying till I reach him."

She heard his sigh of relief. Jealousy was a destructive thing, but she couldn't help being pleased by Nick's display. It meant he cared. All pleasure vanished, however, after she told him what she'd done the last two days.

"You went there all alone?" he said, his tone brittle.

"Yes, I did." The ice in her voice was unmistakable.

Amanda, darling, you're incapable of doing this by yourself.

Silence again. "Listen, I'm not trying to tell you what to do. I know you can handle this. I'm just worried about your safety."

Tears welled in her eyes. She willed them back. "Thanks for the vote of confidence, Nick. It means more to me than you know."

"Promise me something."

"Maybe."

"Just don't go prowling around that area by yourself again. Call another teacher to go with you. Or call me. I won't sleep tonight if I think you're going to be there." When she didn't respond, his voice lowered to a husky plea. "Look, baby, you know how tired I've been. Do you want to be responsible for my tossing and turning all night?"

Unfair, DiMarco. You know I worry about your fatigue with the schedule you keep.

Her own answer was low and sexy. "I think I'd like very much to keep you tossing and turning all night."

His chuckle warmed her.

"But not out of worry," she added.

"Out of what?" His tone could have melted butter.

Oh, God, I'm out of my league. And out of my mind, Amanda thought.

He laughed fully at her silence. "Someday, princess, I'm going to get you to say out loud all those sexy thoughts flying around in your head, all those sexy words to describe how you feel. But I'll let you go now, while I still can," he said, ending the banter. "Good luck with the kid. Keep me posted."

AMANDA CALLED Ron's house again Saturday night and got a drunken Mr. Marshall on the phone. Ron was right, he was nasty under the influence. Among other things, he told her he didn't know where the hell his no-good kid was.

By Sunday morning, she still hadn't reached him, and when she called Tom Mannerly again, he trekked to the Marshalls' a second time with no luck. The boy had been gone all weekend.

She was relieved to catch a glimpse of Ron in school on Monday. Snagging him right away, she questioned him as best she could. His responses were vague, but he did promise to come to the group that afternoon. She waited anxiously all day, but he skipped the session. On Tuesday, she hunted him down during his study hall and insisted he talk with her in the corridor. He looked exhausted and sad.

Amanda kept her voice calm, though she was truly worried. "You missed group yesterday."

Staring at the floor, he made circles with his black boot on the linoleum.

"I tried to reach you all weekend," she chided gently.

He looked up at her, but she couldn't see anything behind the mirrored sunglasses he wore. "Yeah, my daddy told me. I was with a friend."

"Ron, I'm worried about you." Amanda reached out and touched the sleeve of his battered jacket.

"I know you are, lady, but it's cool. I'm cool."

"No, Ron, you're not. I think you're dangerously depressed and I want to help. I *can* help."

When he refused to talk more, Amanda let him go back to study hall and went directly to the principal, whom she didn't like. But she had no recourse. Jack Thornton was hardened by his years at Eastside and it showed in his stubbornness and inflexibility.

He sat imperiously behind his desk, his hands folded in front of him. When she recounted her story, he frowned. "Amanda, I think you're overreacting. The kid's here. He didn't hurt himself in the last seventy-two hours. I don't think there's anything to worry about."

Superimposed on his face she saw her father discount all the ideas, hunches and feelings she'd had over the years. *Damn these men.*

"Well, *I* do. And I'm the one who's trained in this area. Maybe if we intervened right now, got a crisis mediator—"

"I said no!"

"You can't just brush this off, Jack."

His graying eyebrows arched in surprise and he leaned over his clasped hands. "I can do anything I think is right. Listen, Amanda, I wasn't so keen on hiring you in the first place, but the do-gooders won out. I'm telling you to let it go. I'd like nothing better than to bring you up on insubordination. You've lost your objectivity. You're too involved with these kids."

Amanda stood and looked down at him. "And you've lost your humanity, Mr. Thornton." With that, she exited as calmly and coolly as she could. She'd help no one if she lost her job trying to protect Ron.

And, since nothing happened on Tuesday or Wednesday, Amanda began to think there was some truth to Thornton's words. Had she lost her impartiality?

THEN, sometime between the hours of 3:00 p.m. and midnight on Thursday, Leronne Marshall slashed his wrists in the bathroom while his father sat drinking beer and watching television in the next room. This time, he did a better job than the last.

CHAPTER TEN

THE GUIDANCE SUITE was eerily quiet when Amanda entered Friday morning. She was running a little late, so there should have been the usual buzz of word processors and the din of counselors chatting over coffee. When she spotted Tom Mannerly at her door, the hair on the back of her neck prickled. Shivering, she tried to calm the churning in her stomach. The other guidance counselors were here and looked at her somberly. A secretary was wiping her eyes.

When Amanda reached the vice principal, she asked immediately, "What happened?" Mannerly put his arm out to touch her shoulder and she stiffened. "Tom, what is it? Tell me."

"Leronne Marshall's dead, Amanda. We just got word this morning."

Amanda's knees buckled and she grasped the edge of a desk. Tears welled in her eyes but she forced them back.

Though she knew the answer, by God she knew it only too well, she asked, "How did he do it?"

"Amanda, look, come inside and sit down. You don't—"

"*How*, Tom?"

The vice principal rubbed his jaw with his hand. "Same as last time. Razor blades."

An image of Ron's scarred wrists floated before her eyes. *God, we just didn't give him enough.*

Numbly she allowed Tom to lead her into her office. They turned when a secretary brought in some water. "Oh, Amanda, we're all so sorry. Is there anything any of us can do?" the woman said.

Shaking her head, Amanda leaned against the desk. "No, there's nothing anyone can do. It's too late." *Just like Lisa.*

"I won't let you blame yourself, Amanda." The vice principal's tone was firm but gentle. "You did everything in your power to reach him. For the last six months and this past week."

But it wasn't enough.

Amanda took a deep breath and forced herself to abandon the self-pity. It would drag her down like an undertow and she had to stay afloat for the long day ahead of her. The other kids needed her.

She straightened and removed her coat. "There's a lot to do." Addressing the secretary who had remained, she gave directions. "Have Heather DiMarco, Matt Barone and Sandi Berrios met at homeroom and brought directly here." She turned to the vice principal. "Tom, there needs to be an announcement, nothing that would glamorize the suicide, but some kind of acknowledgment of Ron's death." She heard her voice crack, but continued. "Let the other guidance counselors know we should all assemble in the conference room as soon as possible. We'll have support groups running all day for kids who need to talk."

"Are you sure you're up to this?" he asked.

The glimmer of admiration in Mannerly's eyes bolstered her courage. "I have to be. It's our procedure when a student dies, right?"

The vice principal gently squeezed her shoulder. "You're quite a woman."

The commotion in the outer office distracted them both. Amanda heard her name and went to investigate.

Inside the suite stood Ron Marshall's father. Shoulders hunched, he looked smaller than he had in the dim doorway of his apartment. His eyes were red-rimmed again but not from drinking. In his shaking hands, he held a white slip of paper. When he spotted Amanda across the room, he held it out to her. "It's . . . for you. I . . . didn't read it. I'm . . ." He couldn't finish. Silent, savage tears leaked from his eyes.

Amanda crossed to him. Taking his arm, she led him into her office. Handing Marshall some water, she spoke soft phrases to him. "No one's fault . . . he was a troubled boy . . . he's at peace now."

After a grueling fifteen minutes, Ron's father left, apologizing to Amanda for his former treatment of her.

She gripped the note, staring at it, wishing it away, wishing it would ease some of the insidious blame she felt eating away at her insides. Taking a deep breath, she opened it. The letters squirmed like snakes as she read:

This is for all the group. Don't blame yourselves. You kept me alive six months longer. I gotta stop the pain.

                                                    Leronne.

The words were cold comfort. She'd read a similar message nearly two years ago, written in Lisa's scrawl. *Mandy, it's not your fault. I would never have survived these last few years without you. Please, you're not to blame.*

Switching off her internal pain, Amanda's mind raced to the group. They would take this hard, especially Matt, when he saw the signature. But she had no time to consider a course of action because the three teenagers had been brought and were in her doorway.

Matt braved the first words. "Somebody die around here?" He was joking. And he wasn't.

Amanda didn't answer then, but ushered them in and had them seated before she spoke. "Yes, someone did die."

Sandi caught on right away. She pounded her fists on her knees. "It's got to be Ron. He offed himself, didn't he?"

Heather began to cry and Matt put his arm around her. "Did he, Ms. C.?" Matt's voice was ragged.

"Yes, he did."

"When?"

"Last night."

"How?" Sandi asked.

Amanda tried to hedge on the details. "Listen, maybe we should—"

"I said how?" the girl shouted.

"With razor blades."

"Just like the last time," Heather whispered.

Jerking away from Heather, Matt stood up and let out a string of obscenities. Then he buried his face in his hands.

Sandi hung her head and cried wrenchingly.

Amanda wanted to cry with them, but she knew in her heart that if she lost control, these kids wouldn't be able to cope. "It's not our fault," she said with more conviction than she really felt. "We helped him as much as we could."

Gulping back her tears, Sandi looked at Amanda. "He leave a note?"

Amanda unfolded the paper clutched in her hand and gave it to Sandi. They passed it around, each reading the death message. When Matt finished, he crumpled it, stood up and paced back and forth in the small space like a caged animal. Then he raised his hand and punched it right through the drywall. Heather choked back a scream and Sandi started to swear.

Amanda knew the signature had affected Matt. Crossing to the teenager, she grabbed his shoulders from behind. "Matt, listen, that name became a sign of affection after a while. He liked when you teased him with it."

"Sure."

"Why do you think he gave you his watch?"

Matt turned to her with too-bright eyes. "You think so?"

She willed every ounce of sincerity she felt into her voice. "You can bet on it." After a pause, she faced the girls, too. "Listen, all of you. Ron wasn't strong enough to survive his bad feelings. That doesn't mean it's our fault. Or that you can't survive yours. It just means Ron could not. Do you understand?"

When no one spoke, she went to Heather. She tipped the girl's chin up. "Heather, it's him, not you. Get it?"

The girl nodded.

"Sandi?" Amanda asked, taking her hand.

"Yo. I hear ya."

And now the toughest nut to crack. "Matt?" She walked over and grasped his upper arm again. "Matt? Tell me you believe me."

Big, masculine shoulders slumped. Then, he whispered, "I believe you, Teach."

After ten minutes, all three teenagers decided they would go to class and participate in their normal activities, promising to come to the library conference room if they needed to talk during the day. Amanda made a mental note to check on them in a couple of hours. They left, agreeing to return for the after-school counseling session.

Amanda started the phone calls as soon as the kids were gone. She got Sandi's mother to agree to pick her daughter up right after the group when she explained the circumstances. No one was home at Matt's and his brother couldn't be reached at his auto shop. *Damn,* she thought as she put a call through to Nick's office. She got him after only a moment.

"Amanda, what a pleasant surprise. I was thinking about you." His voice was soft and sexy and she wanted to curl up in it and block out everything else.

"Nick—" She started to explain, but she broke down, unable to continue.

"Mandy, what is it?"

"It's...it's...Ron Marshall committed suicide last night. He slashed his wrists."

"Oh my God, no."

Amanda heard real fear in his voice. She gripped the receiver tighter. "Nick, it doesn't mean that Heather is going to do anything like this. She's getting better, at least I think she is..."

"Yes, I know that. How did she react to the news?"

"She took it hard. All the kids in my group did."

"I'll bet. Should I come and get her?"

Running a shaky hand through her hair, Amanda said, "No, I don't think so. She says she wants to stay here. We'll be running support groups today for anyone who needs to talk."

"All right, if you're sure. Call me if anything changes."

"I will." She knew her voice was tremulous and tried to quell the quiver.

"What about you? I'm concerned about you, Mandy."

His solicitousness brought the shakiness back. "Oh, Nick, I'm not sure I can handle this."

"Yes, Mandy, you can. You're a strong woman." He was confident and it came as solid support through the phone lines.

"Am I?" She watched her hands tremble and wound them around the cord to stop them from shaking.

"You are. You divorced an insensitive man because he couldn't give you what you needed. You stood up to your father and waited thirty-six hours in the airport to follow through with your decision. And, much as I hate it, you *never* back down on one single thing with me." He ended with a snort that almost made her smile.

"Thanks." After a pause, she said, "I have to go, it's almost time for the first class. The reason I called was to tell you you'd need to arrange to be with Heather tonight, as soon after school as you can."

"Of course. I'll pick her up at three."

"Make it three-thirty. There's a general counseling session at the end of the day that she should attend."

"Fine. Do me a favor. When you see Heather, give her my love and tell her I'm thinking about her."

In spite of her sadness, Amanda felt an arrow of admiration shoot through her. "I'll make a point of it."

"You go now, princess." Nick's voice was low and sincere. "I have all the faith in the world that you can help the kids through this."

Those words sustained Amanda through the horror of the day. More students than they expected showed up each class period and several teachers came down to the library, too.

Amanda glanced up at the clock when there was finally a break in the flow. She hadn't even stopped for lunch. Two-thirty. Massaging her constricted neck muscles, she thought, *Just one more hour left, Mandy, you can do it.*

Her determination faltered when she saw Nick standing in the doorway. He looked so big and unbreakable and she wanted to fling herself into his arms. Instead, she remained composed and walked calmly toward him.

When she reached him, he touched her cheek and caressed it gently. "You all right?" When she nodded, he added, "That's my girl."

She smiled weakly. "You're early."

"No, I'm not."

Taking her elbow again, he steered her to a corner. "How did it go?"

Closing her eyes, she rubbed the lids. "It was tough."

"Have you seen Heather?"

"Yeah, she came down at lunch. She's sad, and confused, but she's hanging in there." Amanda looked up into Nick's eyes. "She's got a lot of you in her."

Nick smiled and squeezed her arm.

At the bell, several students filed in. Nick watched Amanda and wondered if her slender shoulders could tolerate any more today. She looked as if she was ready to collapse. He was worried about her, though he understood her need to see this through to the end.

When she pulled herself away from the wall and began to move toward them, then halted abruptly, his concern escalated. He followed her eyes to a tall man who had just appeared and started in her direction. Jack Thornton! Nick knew how the principal had sloughed off Amanda's comments about Ron earlier in the week. When Thornton reached Amanda, she stood erect and crossed her arms over her chest.

At close range, Nick could see the grim line of the principal's mouth and the skin pulled tightly across his cheekbones. He was clearly suffering. *Good.*

Thornton lifted his hands, palms up, in a gesture indicating helplessness. "Amanda, I don't know what to say."

Nick watched anger, regret and finally compassion cross Amanda's face. He knew from the way she smiled sadly that she was going to comfort the guy, but he was still stunned when she reached out and took Thornton's hands. "We all let him down, Jack."

Thornton's eyes widened in surprise. "No, that's not true. But thanks for saying it." His voice was ragged. "I'm so sorry."

"So am I."

Had he once called this woman superficial? Selfish? Nick thought. My God, he'd never seen a deeper, more humane response.

When the counseling session started, Nick stood in the back and watched Amanda field questions and offer suggestions to help the kids cope. All the while, her eyes looked so sad, it broke his heart. And he could do nothing for her.

He could, however, help the slight blond child who catapulted herself into his arms the minute the meeting ended. "Oh, Daddy, I'm so glad you came. Isn't it awful?"

Hugging his living, breathing child, he closed his eyes to keep back the moisture. "Yes, it's awful, sweetheart. But I'm here now. It's okay."

Amanda was a few feet away talking with an older woman and her daughter. The teenage boy from the knife fight was with them and the three left together. Then, she joined Nick and his daughter.

"Is that Sandi's mom?" Heather asked.

"Yes. They've invited Matt to come home with them for the evening. You all need to be with someone."

Heather's forehead furrowed in concern and she reached out to touch Amanda's sleeve. "What about you, Ms. Carson?"

Amanda clasped her hands behind her back and Nick was sure she was trembling. "I'm fine, honey. You go on with your dad."

"Come with us?" he offered. But he knew what she was going to say before she got it out.

"No, not tonight. You and Heather need to be alone." Staring into his gray eyes with glassy blue ones, she sighed. "She needs your undivided attention, Nick. I'd interfere with that."

He got the message. His daughter was in pain and her needs came first. He wanted to hold and protect Heather forever. But he also wanted to comfort this brave, hurting woman.

Before he could say any more, Heather turned and wrapped her slender arms around Amanda's waist. "Thank you, Ms. Carson. No one could have got through today without you."

Shutting her eyes, Amanda held on to the human warmth she obviously needed.

Damn, what can I do? Nick thought.

In the end, he had no choice but to leave her standing by herself in the emptying library. She'd helped the kids all day and now she would have to confront her own demons alone. It just wasn't fair.

Which was why, thirty minutes later, he found himself dialing an unfamiliar phone number.

A voice very similar to Amanda's answered, "Hello."

"Mrs. Carson?"

"Yes?"

"You don't know me, but I'm a friend of your daughter's. My name is Nick DiMarco."

"Why, yes, Mr. DiMarco, I've heard your name."

A little surprised, he said, "I'm calling to tell you that your daughter needs you right now."

"Has something happened to her?" There was a trace of panic in Joan's voice.

"No, no. I didn't mean to alarm you. Amanda's fine. Physically, anyway. But there's been a tragedy at the school and I can't be with her at the moment. I'm afraid she's alone now and she shouldn't be. She's spoken a lot of your recent...your closeness and I thought you could go to her since I can't."

"Of course," Joan answered automatically. "Tell me, though. What kind of tragedy?"

Nick blew out an exasperated breath. "A student of Amanda's committed suicide last night."

"Oh my God, no."

"She's taking it pretty hard."

"You have no idea how hard this will be for her, Nick. I'll hang up now and get right over there."

The hairs on the back of his neck tingled and he felt his stomach lurch the way it used to just as he got tackled on the football field. "Mrs. Carson, what don't I know?"

There was a slight pause on the other end. Then, Joan answered softly, "Amanda's sister, Lisa, committed suicide two years ago next month."

AMANDA LET her mother baby her as she hadn't done in years. When Joan arrived at her doorstep at five o'clock that afternoon, Amanda finally let loose the tears that had threatened all day. After they settled into the porch, a fire burning in the corner, hot cider in their hands, Amanda poured out the entire story. Joan cried for both her daughters, and so did Amanda.

The catharsis helped them and they had a light supper of omelets and croissants and a glass of chardonnay each. Still sad, though not as despairing now, Amanda tensed at ten o'clock when the doorbell rang.

"Oh, Mother, it must be someone from school checking on me. I don't want to talk to anyone now. Could you tell them I've gone to bed?"

Joan patted her hand as she rose. "Don't worry, dear, I'll take care of it."

She returned in a moment with Nick. Amanda was so surprised to see him that tears misted her eyes again. Quicker than a flash of heat lightning, she was off the couch and in his arms. He held her tightly against him and she felt safer and warmer than she had in a very long time.

"It's so good to see you," she whispered into his chest.

"You, too, Mandy. I've been worried all evening."

As if that reminded her of both her mother and Heather, Amanda pulled back. "Nick, you should be with your daughter. I'm okay, really."

He smiled and brushed a stray lock of hair from her eyes. "Heather's in bed fast asleep and Beth is staying overnight. I want to be with you now, Amanda."

She stared at him a moment, then turned to Joan. "Mother, this is—"

Stepping forward, Joan smiled. "Yes, I know who this is. We had an interesting conversation earlier today."

Amanda looked at them and took a hint of the conspiracy. She peered into her mother's face. "I wondered how you just happened by."

As she pulled on her ermine coat, Joan smiled. "I'll let you two sort this out. I'm leaving now." Facing her daughter, her expression became somber. "Remember all we talked about tonight, young lady." Her mother kissed her and was gone.

Amanda barely had time to say goodbye before she found herself in Nick's arms once more. Then, separating only long enough to shed his bomber jacket, he led her to the couch. He settled them on the nubby fabric, pulled her to him and held her next to his heart. Amanda cuddled into him.

"How's Heather?" she asked. "Tell me what you've been doing the last few hours."

Nick rubbed her back as he talked. "She was calm when she went to bed, but she cried a lot before that. She's sad, and mad, too, I think."

"That's a common reaction."

"We talked for the first hour or so, but then we managed to eat a little supper and play a bit with Jason. I stayed in her room until she fell asleep. I think that meant the most to her."

Amanda looked up at him. "It would. Trying to fall asleep after something like this is the scariest part."

Nick smoothed a hand down her jaw. "What about you? How are you holding up?"

With those few words of compassion, Amanda began to cry again. Nick pulled her tighter and stroked her hair, crooning phrases of comfort. When the fresh bout of tears passed, he handed her his handkerchief and she pulled away to blow her nose. All defenses down now, she muttered, "Oh, great, I spend all these months making sure I look good every time I see you and now you catch me with a puffy face and blotches."

His eyes glowed as he reached out and ran his fingertips over her mottled skin. "You're a beautiful woman, Amanda Carson, inside and out."

When she shook her head, he wouldn't allow her denial. "Yes. You helped a bunch of troubled teenagers get through the day. I heard about it, blow by blow, from Heather. You took care of the kids in your group and you didn't even berate Jack Thornton, though *I* wanted to punch his lights out. I'll bet you stayed and talked to other teachers, too, didn't you?"

She nodded.

He reached for her. "Come here, baby, it's my turn to take care of you."

Amanda settled back into him, feeling the softness of his velour forest green shirt against her face. "What made you call my mother, Nick?"

"I was so worried about you and so frustrated I had to leave you. It goes without saying that I wanted to be with Heather tonight. I'd give my life for her." His voice was soft as he told her of his quandary. "But it killed me to walk out of there and leave you alone to deal with this."

His hand moved rhythmically on her arm and his voice lulled her. "You'd talked about your mother's new interest in your job, her recent approval. So I called her."

Burying her face in his chest, Amanda inhaled the male scent of him. "Thank you."

"Did it help?"

Silent for several seconds, Amanda's voice was strained when she spoke again. "Yes, it did. For a lot of reasons. Nick, there's something you don't know about my family."

"Then tell me."

Suddenly, it all came flooding back. The shock. The horror. The unrelenting sadness. Amanda clutched a handful of Nick's shirt. "My sister, Lisa, she...she was very unhappy at the end of her life. I don't know how much you know about spina bifida."

"Some. I did a lot of research on birth defects when Jason was born."

"His condition isn't congenital, is it?"

"No, it's multifactorial. It had many contributing causes. But spina bifida *is* congenital, isn't it?"

"Yes. Lisa was born with an opening in the spinal column. They operated immediately, but even the best doctors couldn't stop the paralysis. Luckily, she had pretty good control over her bowel and bladder. Not all victims do."

He tugged her closer. "Something to be thankful for."

"Anyway, the symptoms stayed pretty much the same until she was about twenty-five. Then she developed ulcers."

"Is that common?"

"Initially it is. It's unusual for it to happen so late. She got progressively sicker, in more and more pain. Eventually, she just couldn't handle it anymore. She

took her own life, Nick, two years ago March fifteenth.''

Amanda began to cry softly. Nick held on to her, his
own eyes moist.

She mumbled the rest into his broad, comforting
chest. ''I should have been there for her. I should have
seen the signs, loss of appetite, bouts of crying, giving
away precious possessions. But I was so unhappy with
Porter and my own life that I wasn't there for her.''

Patiently he let her cry some more, then pulled her
onto his lap and turned her to face him. ''Amanda,
hindsight is always twenty-twenty. Of course there are
things you could have done. But ultimately, that doesn't
make you responsible for your sister's suicide. She took
her own life. She wasn't strong enough to survive her
pain, like you told the kids today. Hell, I don't know if
I'd have been strong enough to survive her pain. But
there was certainly nothing you could do to stop her
desperate actions. Not hers. Not Ron's. You can help
people, Amanda, but you can't live their lives for them.
And you don't end them, either.''

His words brought more tears, but this time they were
cleansing, healing ones. On a professional level, she
knew he was right. But on a personal one, it was so hard
to accept that there was only so much you could do for
someone else.

Finally, she relaxed back into Nick's embrace. She
dozed, then felt herself being lifted, cradled in strong
arms and carried to her room. She'd slipped into
lounging pajamas earlier, so he lay her on the bed as she
was, covering her with a huge, downy quilt. She heard
his shoes hit the floor and felt him sink into the mattress. He gathered her into his arms and held her ten-

derly. "Sleep, princess, it's the best medicine right now."

"Don't leave me," she murmured.

"Never."

AMANDA WOKE TWICE during the night, once in a sweat, crying for her sister. The second time, she called for Ron. Both times, Nick was there to hold her and soothe her fears.

At dawn, she was wide-awake as he eased from the bed. "I have to go, honey. I want to be there when Heather wakes up. Will you be okay?"

"Yes," she assured him, though she didn't want him to leave. What she wanted more than anything else in the world was to make love with him. In her professional mind, she knew it was a common reaction to the aftermath of death, to affirm life in so elemental a way. But she knew in her woman's mind that it was also a deep craving for the man himself, one that frightened her as much as it gave her joy.

NICK SPENT the next day with his daughter and it felt good to console her. But he worried about Amanda. He phoned her twice, once when Tammy called and asked Heather to stay overnight. Nick was surprised she wanted to go, and called Amanda for her opinion.

Amanda thought it was a good sign, and pretty normal, that Heather wanted to distract herself from Ron's death. After talking to Heather herself about how she was feeling, Amanda advised Nick to let his daughter find solace with her friend.

When his father called at four, Nick mentioned that Heather was gone for the night. Ever astute, Ange DiMarco asked if his only son might like a free evening and Nick jumped at the chance. He showered quickly and dressed. Then he packed up Jason, dropped him off at his parents' house and was at Amanda's by six. He hoped to surprise her with both his presence and his freedom for the night, but he was the one in for the unexpected.

She answered the door wearing a lightweight aquamarine sweat suit that made her eyes the color of the sea. Her hair was tied back into a ponytail and she wore no makeup.

"You look about eighteen," he said just before he grabbed her and kissed her soundly on the mouth. She hesitated, pulling out of his arms, something she'd never done before.

Nick held her loosely and frowned. "What's wrong?"

"I have company. Come on in." When he scowled, she whispered, "Don't be cross."

He found Tom Mannerly sprawled on her sofa drinking *his* beer. Nick wanted to grab the can and squash it with his bare hands. Instead, he jammed them into his pockets.

"Nick, you know Tom Mannerly from the high school. He just stopped over to see if I was all right."

Remembering the night before, Nick was ashamed of his jealousy. He turned to Amanda and touched her cheek in a proprietary way even a monkey wouldn't misinterpret. "Are you?"

The vice-principal didn't miss the innuendo. He coughed uncomfortably, stood up and reached for the ski jacket he'd thrown over the chair. "I'll be going now, Amanda. I see you're well taken care of."

Amanda stepped to the side of Nick. "Thanks for coming, Tom. It was sweet of you to be so concerned."

As Mannerly walked by her, he touched her arm. "I...we all care about you. You're a valued member of our staff."

Nick stared at the other man's hand and fisted his own, trying to keep his reaction in check. *God, DiMarco, she's had a hell of a time. The poor sap came to see if she was all right.* But despite his admonition to himself, he eased his arm around her shoulders and the gesture spoke volumes.

After Tom left, Amanda looked at him quizzically. "What was that all about?"

"Territorial rights," Nick said, only half joking, and pulled her back into his arms, his eyes glowing with sexual intensity. "And I just established mine loud and clear."

Staring at him for a moment, she giggled, buried her face in his chest and hugged him. "I shouldn't like it, but I do."

"Good." He held her close for a minute. "Guess what?"

"What?" she asked, looking up at him.

"Heather did stay overnight at her friend's house."

"I think sometimes kids can help each other more than we can help them."

Nick nodded. His gaze was darkly sensual as he added, "And my dad has Jason."

"For the whole night?" Amanda pressed herself to him intimately.

"Uh-huh."

Peering into his stormy eyes with promise in hers, she whispered, "Then take me to bed, Nick."

His arms tightened around her. "God, I thought you'd never ask."

Gently, he scooped her up into his embrace and found his way to her bedroom once more. He'd been so concerned about her last night, he hadn't noticed the interior.

Soft. Everything in the room was soft. Pale pink walls, mauve covers, shimmery silver blinds. It smelled the way she did, a mixture of her lotions, shampoo and perfume. It was a large room containing a teak bed with a rounded headboard of slatted spindles, two low dressers and chairs and a large vanity. The bathroom opened off it and was decorated with the same motif. One muted torchlight was switched on in the corner.

"Like it?" she asked as she watched him study the decor.

He set her down on her feet and growled into her hair. "Not as much as I like you."

He kissed her thoroughly then and she leaned into him. Feeling a slight tension in her reminded him of her past experiences with lovemaking. Slowly, he stroked her back, a sudden inspiration coming to him. He eased his hands under her sweatshirt and rubbed her warm bare skin. "Did you hear the joke about the madam who ran the house of ill repute?"

Eyes wide, Amanda's jaw dropped.

"I take it that's a no," he said with a chuckle. "The women who serviced the brothel were all professionals during the daytime and were grouped by floors at night. After a few months, the madam noticed that every time a man returned for another visit, he'd ask for the third floor."

Placing his hands on the hem of her top, Nick pulled it over her head. "The madam couldn't understand it," he continued, kissing the exposed tops of her breasts underneath the demi-bra. It was pale peach and she filled it to capacity. His voice sounded hoarse to his own ears as he went on. "Because on the third floor were the plain, ordinary schoolteachers."

He nuzzled her cleavage and then his mouth trailed the silk to her nipple. He bit it gently. "That night, she decided to eavesdrop on each floor to determine why these men preferred the plain, ordinary schoolteachers." Nick deftly unclasped her bra and began to knead her breasts. "On the first floor, where all the gorgeous models were, the madam heard, 'No, don't do that, you're going to mess my makeup.'"

Amanda giggled and groaned consecutively.

Sliding his hands beneath the waistband of her pants, he caressed her bottom. "On the second floor, where all the businesswomen were, she heard, 'Okay, let's get this over quickly so we can get on to the next thing.'"

Amanda chuckled but it soon turned into a whimper as he eased his hand around front and cupped her. "Then she listened into the third floor where the plain, ordinary schoolteachers were."

Pushing her sweats down, he knelt to pull them off. When he rose, she stood before him gloriously naked. "And what she heard one of the teachers say to the customer was, 'Okay, if we don't get it right this time, we'll do it over and over until we do get it right.'"

Amanda laughed as he caught her into his arms. He could feel her skin against his clothes and it made him painfully hard. Pulling back from her slightly, he brushed the mane from her face. Her eyes were dilated with arousal and her cheeks were flushed. "It's more than a joke, baby."

"I don't understand."

"That's right, you don't understand. If we don't get it right this time, we just keep trying, too. There's no pressure on you. Just enjoy it."

Amanda could have wept at his sensitivity. How had he known that humor was the perfect way to ease her reservations?

She watched him step back from her and pull his sweater over his head. It disheveled his hair appealingly and made her long to run her hands through the thick, coarse mass. When he went to unbutton his striped shirt, her eyes flew to his fingers. Noting her stare, he took her hands in his and brought them to his chest. "Do you want to do it?"

She nodded.

"Honey, do anything you want to me. Anything that feels good to you, on your body, will feel as good to me."

Encouraged, she released each button of his shirt. Tilting her head, she kissed the exposed skin and felt the hair tickle her nose. She breathed in his cologne. "You smell so good."

His chest jerked at her words. She smiled against his skin. Lord, she wanted this.

Continuing her delightful discovery of his body, she ran her hands down his back and felt him shiver. His response made her brave and she slid her palms to his buttocks. The muscles there went taut and she massaged them gently. He moaned, his hands flying to his belt. She liked knowing he was in a hurry. Batting them away, she took her time removing it.

"Tease," he mumbled.

She wanted to whoop. *Me, a tease? Oh, God, thank you.*

But she found herself on her back for her taunt. The full weight of him on her was exciting.

"Too heavy?"

"No, never."

"Feel good?"

"Unbelievable."

He thrust his hips forward and she felt him throbbing against her belly. "Believe it."

Then, he began his own slow, exquisite torture. He rained kisses all over her neck and chest, stopping to caress one beaded nipple with his tongue. "You like that, don't you, baby?"

"Yes."

He continued this for a moment, then went lower and licked her abdomen. He felt her start.

"What is it?"

She whimpered as he kissed the tiny indentation there. When his mouth went lower to nuzzle her curls, she all but arched off the bed. He stopped, as if trying to decide how far to go. She was entranced at the strange sensations caused by his mouth and was disappointed when he drew himself up. Peering into her eyes, he asked, "Too new? Too much?"

"New, but not too much. I just feel so innocent with you."

Bending over her, braced on his forearms, he took a long, hard stare at her. "Yeah, well, you don't look innocent."

She grinned. "How do I look?"

"Absolutely beautiful." He nuzzled her neck. "And sexy as hell."

"So are you. I've wanted to do this, too, for a long time." Her hands glided up his chest again.

He closed his eyes at the feel of her caress. "Do what?"

She drew designs in his chest hair. "Tell you how attractive you are. How I love looking at you. I've never told a man that before."

Opening his eyes, he smiled. "You can tell me anytime."

Slowly she eased up on her elbows. "In that case, you're gorgeous and sexy. Too sexy."

His laugh was low and he nudged her down with his nose. "There's no such thing as too sexy. Just like there's no such thing as too rich."

Before she could react to his reminder of their differences, he took her mouth. His tongue explored every crevice, then went back for more. Sinking onto the mattress, he pulled her over him. He caressed her bottom with long, smooth strokes.

On top of him now, she took advantage of the position, bent her head and kissed his chest again. He tensed when her tongue flicked his male peak. She traveled down and kissed his stomach, as he had kissed hers. He moaned and clutched the sheets. When her mouth neared the hair lower on his body, he reached up and grabbed the headboard. Her fingers closed around him and he arched his back. She ran her palm up and down twice and agonized sounds escaped from his clenched teeth.

"Hurt?"

"I'm in pain, baby."

"Too much?"

"Never."

"Want me to stop?"

"Don't you dare."

She didn't. Until his moans strung together into one long groan. Suddenly, she was flipped on her back and he hovered over her. "Don't you ever, ever tell me again that you can't arouse a man. I'm near to dying from your touch."

Her smile was as old as Eve's. He kissed it off her face and ground his body into hers. She knew he was near the end of his restraint and she gloried in it.

Reaching for his jeans, he fumbled with his wallet. He yanked out a foil packet, tore it open and had its contents on in seconds. He kneed her legs apart and spoke softly. "Look at me, Mandy." When she did, he entered her slowly. She was slippery and very, very wet. He inched his way in and she wanted to raise her hips to hurry him, but he held them firmly to the bed. "You're mine, baby," he whispered just as the length of him reached her womb. She felt full and feminine and she was moved to tears. But when he began to thrust, she lost all conscious thought. Soon—too soon—the exquisite oneness gave way to shattering pleasure that kept coming and coming. The world continued to explode around her as he pushed in longer and harder strokes. She cried out several times, his name, endearments, prayers, dimly aware of similar cries from him when his climax finally broke through. It lasted almost as long as hers before he settled down on her sated body and buried his face in her neck.

When he could finally move again, Nick eased off her. He'd never felt pleasure like this before, and it was more than satisfying to know he'd given her what no man had. But the oneness he felt with Amanda was his dominant emotion.

And it scared him to death. How had he risked his heart on this woman? No, how had he lost it to her?

"What is it?" She propped herself up on her elbows.

He forced himself to shake off his reservations and opted for teasing. "You wrung me out, lady. And I'm not sure I like my loss of control."

"I did?"

"Yeah. And I have the marks to prove it."

She blushed prettily.

"Don't you dare go coy on me. Not after what you just did to me. After what I just did to you. After what I'm going to do to you again." Turning her over to her stomach, he straddled her. "I've got lots more to teach you tonight," he whispered in her ear before he began tracing her spine with his tongue. "And no doubt, lots more to learn from my little Lolita-in-disguise."

The flattery was real, but the teasing was meant to distract her. And him. He'd deal with reality tomorrow.

CHAPTER ELEVEN

RON'S DEATH spurred Amanda to renew the resolutions she'd made when Lisa died. She vowed again to live each day to the fullest and make the most of the time she had with the people she loved.

It was Nick's thirty-fifth birthday two weeks after the teenager's funeral and she had persuaded him to allow her to treat the family, including Beth, to dinner as her present to him. It had taken all her negotiation skills on several fronts to pull this off.

First she'd had to convince her very stubborn man.

"Absolutely not!" he'd said firmly when she'd brought it up.

Instinctively, she'd known when to time her request. She'd picked a night after their lovemaking had been particularly satisfying.

"Why not?" She lay sprawled across him, her hair tumbling around her naked shoulders.

"I don't need charity." He tried to sound stern, but she knew it was difficult when she was drawing patterns in his chest hair and his whole body still hummed from their union.

"It can be your gift."

He cupped her bare bottom. "That's not what I want for my birthday." His voice was husky and he looked rakish with his hair falling onto his forehead and the sheet tangled around his legs.

She arched into his hands. "You can have that, too, if you let me take you all out. Please, Nick, I really want to do this."

"Why?" His gaze was shrewd as his steel gray eyes bored into her.

"For lots of reasons. Some I don't want to talk about now."

Sighing heavily, he tilted her chin up to see her face. "Okay, but I don't like it. Nor do I like being seduced into it."

She fit herself to him. "You don't like this, Nick?"

Growling into her throat, he turned her on her back and entered her quickly. "I like it very much, you witch. *Too* much."

His last statement had disturbed her, as it did each time he commented on their differences or expressed unhappiness about his feelings for her. But her world had spun out of control before she could worry about it.

Then, there was the delicate discussion she'd had with Heather. Right from the beginning, Amanda had been concerned about getting involved with a student's father. She had thought long and hard about the blurring of roles, about loyalty and confidentiality. Ultimately, she was satisfied that she would *always* put Heather's welfare first, and had made sure Nick was clear on the issue. In her heart, she also knew he would do the same.

They had agreed to tell Heather they were "dating," a mild word, Amanda thought, for their tumultuous encounters.

As they sat in the DiMarco living room, Amanda had brought up the subject. "Heather, I want you to know what's happening to the adults in your world."

Amanda saw Heather tense, a reaction to her past experiences with grown-ups over whom she had no control. The girl's father caught it, too. Rising from the chair across the room, he went to the couch, sat down next to her and took her hand. "It's nothing bad, sweetheart. In fact, it's good news."

Still, Heather looked wary. "What is it?"

Amanda took a deep breath. "Your father and I have started, and would like to continue, seeing each other socially. But we want you to have some say in it since it affects your life."

Averting her gaze, Heather didn't speak at first. Nick's eyes sought Amanda's for a cue, but she shook her head. Finally, the teenager lifted her chin and gave her father a look full of a woman's wisdom. "I'm not really surprised. It took you a long time to walk her to her car every time she was here, Dad."

Nick smiled sheepishly but faced his daughter squarely. "How do you feel about it?"

Heather didn't even hesitate. "Oh, it's great."

Suspicious of the rushed response, Amanda said, "Heather, you've got to express what you're feeling inside. You must have some reservations about this."

After a moment, Heather looked at her with pleading eyes. "Will you still talk to me at school?"

"Of course."

"Will . . . will it still be . . . you know, private?"

"Yes, it will—except to give your father progress reports, and unless I believe you're in danger of harming yourself. Just like you and I discussed before."

Heather glanced at her father then. "I'm sorry, Daddy, I don't want to leave you out but—"

Nick didn't give her a chance to finish. Instead, he grabbed her and hugged her fiercely. "Honey, you don't have to explain. We promise it will still be private. Amanda never *has,* nor ever *will* break your confidence." He drew back and grasped his daughter's chin. "But think about this. I want to share what you're going through. You can tell me anything when you're ready to, okay?"

Briefly, Amanda had closed her eyes to keep back the tears. It was at that exact moment that she realized how much she loved Nick DiMarco. . . .

Tonight, in the warm ambience of Muscato's, Amanda recalled the incident and glanced at Nick across the table. He looked devastatingly handsome in a lightweight navy wool blazer, gray shirt, striped tie and charcoal slacks. Despite his initial objection to this dinner, his eyes sparkled with expectation.

Tony himself brought out the wine and spoke to Jason as he poured it. "What do you get when you put one hundred deer in a pen with one hundred pigs?"

"Dirty deer?" The boy tugged at the collar of his blue-and-white-striped shirt as he guessed the answer.

"Naw. One hundred sows and bucks."

Jason laughed. "Yeah, I get it. Like the money, right?"

Conversation flowed easily. Beth talked about her plans to open her own bookstore and Nick teasingly offered his legal services cheap. More than once, Nick's gaze caught Amanda's, then narrowed meaningfully on her black sequined dress. Formfitting, it had a scoop neck, a low back and skimmed her knees. He hadn't been able to take his eyes off it all evening.

When Amanda saw her mother and father making their way from the back of the restaurant, it was as if a cloud had cast a shadow on a sunny day. What trouble would her father cause when he saw them? The Carsons were on top of them before she could warn anyone.

Amanda stood, and Joan kissed her on the cheek and spoke softly. "Hello, dear, how nice to see you."

Robert crossed his arms over his chest in an aggressive stance. "A sad day when the first time we see our daughter in a month is at a restaurant."

Covertly, Amanda's gaze flew to her mother's. Joan's expression remained unperturbed. Amanda had seen Joan two weeks ago, but Robert didn't know. Her mother was obviously keeping secret the visit she'd made to Amanda that fateful Friday.

Beth coughed and Amanda realized introductions were in order. Nick and Beth rose to shake hands. Joan kept eye contact with Nick. "Mr. DiMarco, how nice to see you again."

"Again? Have you met before?" Robert asked curtly.

"Yes, dear, at Amanda's house."

"You've been to Amanda's house?" He appeared to be dumbfounded, and in spite of his arrogance, Amanda felt sorry for him.

Joan's face remained bland. "Yes, of course. Didn't I tell you?" She turned to her daughter then. "How was your week at school, dear?"

Warmed by her mother's concern, she said, "We all got through it. Thanks for asking."

Robert directed his attention to Nick, who appeared calm and self-assured. "DiMarco, I've heard about you from . . . an associate of mine. Finishing up law school, aren't you?"

Nick's eyebrows arched but he kept his casual pose. His voice was even when he answered, "Yes, I am. I'm in the midst of last-semester clerking."

Oh, no, Nick, don't let him get a shot at you, please.

"With what firm?" When Nick told him, her father nodded. "Very impressive." Casually, he turned to Amanda. "You'll have to bring Mr. DiMarco to the lawyers' gala next month and introduce him around. It will be good PR for his career." '

Bingo. Show him my other life. Show him how he can't compete with old money no matter how sought-after he is in the world of law.

Squaring her shoulders, Amanda raised a defiant chin to Robert. She'd do what she had to do to protect Nick. "Actually, Father, I'm not attending this year. I've already spoken to Mother about my not being there to help her."

With a dismissive gesture, Robert said, "Nonsense, she needs you to assist her as hostess this year just as in the past." Amanda was about to refuse a second time, when he added, "In point of fact, she needs you more this year. The gala is scheduled for March fifteenth."

Amanda gasped. *The anniversary of Lisa's death.* It was like walking into a door in the dark. He'd blindsided her, backed her into that familiar corner and she was fourteen and vulnerable again.

Dimly aware of the comments around her, Amanda's head spun.

"No, Robert, really it's not necessary," her mother said, the edge in her voice unusual, but clear.

As if she sensed the friction, Beth tried to distract Robert. "Mr. Carson, I'd like to talk to you sometime about your firm..."

Nick encircled Amanda's shoulder and gave her a supportive squeeze, but she could feel the tautness in his corded muscles. "Amanda and I will discuss this..."

And the children, not knowing the circumstances, but being all too familiar with adult tension, also came to her defense. Heather quietly slipped her hand into Amanda's. And Jason, God bless his soul and sense of humor, said to her staid, unsmiling father, "Hey, Mr. Carson. With your being a lawyer and all, you'll like Heather's joke. You know why they bury. . ."

CHUCKLING, Nick flopped down on Amanda's living room couch two hours later. Beth had taken her niece and nephew overnight—her birthday gift to Nick—so he and Amanda could be alone.

"Did you see his face when Jason told him that joke?" Nick said with a smirk.

"Oh, Nick, you don't know the half of it. He hates lawyer jokes." Amanda laughed outright and dropped down beside him. "Lisa told them to him all the time. We took bets on how far she'd get before he'd storm out of the room. His face would get red like it did tonight but he didn't sputter like he did back then."

Nick sobered and brought his palm up to stroke her cheek. "I'm sorry about his dig, baby."

Amanda sighed and leaned into the caress, unwilling to let go of the mirth. *He will not ruin tonight for me.* "Don't be. The DiMarco Defense more than made up for it. The look on my father's face when he saw Jason's wheelchair did bother me, though."

Of course, Robert hadn't noticed the children. When Jason spoke up, then ribbed him with that lawyer joke, Amanda had caught the pain that flitted across her father's aristocratic features. The parallels with his daughter were too great to ignore. It made Amanda almost forgive him for his taunt. *Almost,* because she knew Robert's invitation to the gala was going to cause difficulty with Nick. But not yet. She wanted to savor the rest of his birthday first.

Slowly, she stood and removed her long leather coat and tossed it on the floor. She turned to Nick in the dim light of the living room. The remodeling in the whole house was finished now, and Amanda had furnished this area with wide comfortable couches and a thick rug that featured in many of her recent fantasies involving the man before her. Kicking off her shoes, she began to unzip the black dress. "I want you to see your present right away," she whispered as she eased the frock off her shoulders.

Nick rose unsteadily, and shrugged out of his overcoat. "I thought I told you I didn't want any presents. At least, the material kind."

She smiled and finger-combed her hair out of her eyes, holding up the dress precariously with one hand. "Oh, this is in keeping with, shall we say, the spirit of the law."

Then she dropped the DNKY creation to the floor, stepped out of it and stood before him in lingerie more daring than she'd ever imagined wearing. The charcoal bra was strapless and low-cut so her breasts strained for release. She'd forgone the matching panties and opted for the garter belt, which held up sheer, silky black stockings. With her heels left on, she stood proudly before him. "Happy Birthday, Nick."

He swallowed convulsively. He felt his heart slam into his rib cage and, as he watched her, he thought it might beat right out of his chest.

Shedding his jacket, he began to remove his tie as he inched in her direction. "You've had this on all night?" he asked. Thank God he hadn't known.

She nodded. "I wanted to tell you earlier so you could think about it, but there was no opportunity."

Her voice was like warm honey slowly running over his heated skin.

"Lucky for you, lady, or I might have dragged you off and embarrassed myself in front of my kids." Clumsily, he unbuttoned and discarded his shirt, still standing halfway across the room. "Come here, Amanda."

She crossed the space between them slowly, teasingly. "Anything you say, Nick. Didn't your mother ever tell you you can have anything you want on your birthday?"

He chuckled then groaned again as her warmth closed over him, thinking Rosa DiMarco had never had this in mind.

AMANDA LIKED the aftermath of loving almost as much as the event itself. She lay curled against Nick, spoon-fashion, his arms crisscrossing her breasts. His scent curled around her like fog and she closed her eyes to savor it.

He stirred. "What time is it?"

"It's not your birthday anymore."

Chuckling, he buried his face in her hair. "At least we made it to the bed the last time."

"I'm not complaining." She snuggled into him.

After a short silence, Nick said, "Amanda, we've got to talk about your father's invitation."

"Can't it wait until tomorrow? I don't want to ruin tonight."

She felt Nick tense behind her. Sighing, she turned to face him. The moonlight bathed his face. She reached up to smooth his roughened jaw. She shivered slightly, remembering how his beard had scraped the inside of her thigh.

"All right. Let's get it over with. My father's comments were a challenge, Nick, not an invitation."

"Oh. To whom? You or me?"

"To me. I know exactly what he's doing."

Nick eased back from her onto his own pillow, raised his arm and placed it across his forehead and closed his eyes. "Why don't you enlighten me, then."

Amanda propped up on one elbow and leaned over him, holding the sheet to cover her breasts. "He's trying to place us in a position where you see me as I used to be. Before I changed my life. He wants to point out our differences."

"You don't have to use euphemisms. He wants to show you that I don't fit in your world. That I'm not good enough for you."

"*This* is my world, Nick. And you do fit in it. My father simply won't believe I've chosen to earn my own way, live off my own income."

Nick opened his eyes and turned to stare at her. "And have you, Amanda?"

"Have I what?"

"Chosen to live this way?"

Amanda's stomach knotted and a deep foreboding crept through her. She hadn't expected this accusation. "I don't understand."

"Have you chosen to give up the luxuries, work hard, sacrifice yourself for others, or is this a stopgap, like...?"

He didn't finish the question. He didn't have to. His implication incensed her.

"I'm not Suzanne, Nick." Each word was clipped and angry.

He waited a moment before he went on. "I don't hear a denial."

"You shouldn't need one," she whispered. "Not after all this." Her hand swept the bed.

Nick laughed ruefully. "Oh, princess, I've been good
enough here before. I seem to make the grade in the
bedroom but not in the ballroom."

Amanda felt tears threaten. That he would still see
her so much like his ex-wife, after all they'd shared, cut
deep. She threw back the covers and climbed out of bed.
As she reached for a robe on the adjacent chair, Nick
grabbed her arm.

"Mandy, don't leave." Gently, he tugged and she
tumbled back to the bed. He gathered her to him and
stroked her hair until he felt her relax.

"Nick, there's something else. Suzanne could be at
the gala."

He didn't respond immediately. Then he said, "I
don't care. I can handle that. I just want you to be
proud enough of me, to trust me enough, to believe I
can make it in your world."

Amanda waited a very long time before she answered, "But I don't want that world anymore."

Holding her, he said quietly, "I do, Amanda."

NICK PRESSED the Save button on his word processor
and leaned back in the chair, closed his eyes and
pinched the bridge of his nose. The report was done and
not a minute too soon. He had to pick Heather up in
half an hour and take her and Jason to the movies with
Tammy. He'd promised them they could sit alone in the
theater; he and Jason would stay out of their way. He
smiled as he realized she was acting more and more like
a normal teenager every day.

Gathering his notes, he remembered receiving this assignment at the beginning of the week from Joris himself.

"Nick," the senior partner had said, "we need a clerk we can count on to research this statute. You'll have to dig through a ton of case law to find the appropriate precedents, but this could save our client thousands of dollars. I think the other clerks are too inexperienced to handle this. Your maturity tells me you can do it."

Hiding his satisfaction at the comment, Nick had thanked him for the compliment and was surprised when the old man added, "Sit in on the consultation this Saturday, why don't you."

Nick had been elated. It was rare to receive that kind of offer. He'd scrambled all week trying to balance his time and, though he'd been away from the kids more than he liked, he'd managed to mollify everyone with the promise of a movie tonight. *He'd have it all, by God, even Amanda.* He'd show Robert Carson exactly who'd succeed both personally and professionally.

Just then, the phone rang. "DiMarco."

"Nick. Benson here. I found some more data for the Smythe account. You'll have to research a second statute . . ."

As Nick jotted down the information, his heart sank. He was in for at least three more hours of work. After he hung up, he swore virulently into the empty office. He could try to come back after the movie, but if he ran into difficulty, it would be one in the morning and there would be no chance of getting help. It was too risky. He'd have to cancel with Heather. The thought of disappointing his daughter sickened him, but he promised himself he'd make it up to her.

Jason answered the phone. "Hi, Dad. Hey, why'd the golfer wear two pairs of pants?"

Nick reined in his impatience and forced himself not to answer the old joke. "I don't know, Jase, why?"

"Because he got a hole in one."

His son picked up Nick's perfunctory laugh right away. "Is something wrong, Dad?"

"No, buddy, just let me talk to Heather."

Too soon she was on the line. "Hi, Dad."

Gripping the receiver, he felt guilt curl through him. "Hi, sweetheart. I...I hate to do this to you, but I can't make it home tonight. Something vital's come up and I have to stay and finish it."

"But you promised."

"I know, but I can't get out of it."

There was a long, long pause. "Can Aunt Beth or Grandpa take us, then?"

"No. That's why you're there alone, now. Beth is at a conference and Grandma and Grandpa are in Buffalo visiting your great-uncle Sal."

"Oh, Daddy, please. You've just got to do it... Tammy and I already planned what we'd wear. I've been saving my baby-sitting money...oh, please."

He'd never before heard Heather whine like this. "Heather, if I could change this, I would. But I can't." His guilt caused him to snap at her and he pounded his free fist into the desk.

She said nothing.

Consciously, he forced his muscles to relax. "Listen, how about tomorrow night? Call Tammy and see if you can reschedule."

Again, another pause. "Heather, are you there?"

"Yes." Her tone was flat and void of emotion. It caused a chill to skitter through him. "Tammy has to go to her grandfather's tomorrow night."

"Well, some other time, okay?"

"Sure."

Nick closed his eyes, tilted his head up to a heaven that didn't seem to be listening to him these days and sighed under the awful burden of letting down his child. "Lock all the doors. I'm not sure what time I'll be home. I'll call Mrs. Castellana and have her check on you every hour until she goes to bed." When there was no affirmation from the teenager, Nick tried to appease her one more time. "Honey, I'm really sorry." Still no response. "I love you, Heather. Good night."

"Goodbye, Dad."

FOUR HOURS LATER, famished and exhausted, Nick walked into a still and quiet apartment. He'd finished the project, done a hell of a job and never felt worse in his life. Making his way to the kitchen, he picked up a note on the counter and read the missive, written in Jason's childish scrawl.

Hi, Dad. Sorry you had to work. We're okay. Mrs. Castellana brought meatball sandwiches and we left you some in the fridge. See you tomorrow.

Opting to forgo dinner, Nick popped a beer. He made his way to the bedrooms and opened the door to Heather's. She was sprawled facedown, her blond hair pulled back in a braid. At the bed, he brushed back her silky bangs and leaned over to kiss her cheek. "Sorry, sweetie," he whispered and left the room.

When he opened Jason's door, his son called to him, "Hi, Dad. Help me sit up, would ya?"

"Jase, you're supposed to be asleep," Nick admonished gently as he assisted his son. "You okay?"

Usually, Jason's eyes were bubbling with so much mischief that Nick wanted to check his hands, his pockets and behind his back to inspect for frogs. Tonight, they were clouded by apprehension. "Yeah, I'm okay, but Heather sure isn't."

Nick sighed heavily and sank onto the edge of his bed. "I know, son. I disappointed her. And you."

"Aw, Dad, it's not your fault. It's just that she was counting on it so much. She—" The boy broke off, as if he had second thoughts about telling his father.

Nick brushed the hair out of his son's eyes. "She what, Jase?"

"Geez, Dad, I've never seen her like that. She threw the phone onto the floor, and then she . . . she swore."

Nick had to hide the smile. Actually, he was glad Heather had had a temper tantrum. It was healthier than bottling it all up inside. "There's a time and a place for those words. Sometimes they make us feel better."

Jason's forehead creased. "Yeah, I know. You told me that before. But, Dad, she, well, she yelled at me, too. More than once." His big blue eyes misted with tears. "She never does that, Dad. Heather's never mean to me."

Grasping his son's slender shoulders, Nick pulled him close. He wanted to swear himself right now. But that wouldn't make him feel any better. Hugging Jason, he wondered if anything ever would.

CHAPTER TWELVE

NICK WON the argument with Amanda about attending the gala but he didn't feel like a victor as he entered the Hotel Conrad the following Saturday. She had given in the night of his birthday celebration and agreed to go, but he felt like a bully for insisting. Then he felt like a heel, as she'd further capitulated and agreed to help her mother with the hostessing. He was meeting her here now because she'd arrived early to assume her duties. God, he'd really blown this one, just like last Saturday with Heather and the movie. Things were definitely going downhill like a runaway snowball, and he didn't know how to stop it.

"Your invitation, sir?" a concierge asked at the door. Digging into his pocket for the card, he glanced at the nameplate on the door—The Ballroom—and winced inwardly as he remembered what he'd said to her. *Oh, princess, I've been good enough here before. I seem to make the grade in the bedroom but not in the ballroom.* Well, since he'd made her prove that accusation wrong, he'd damn well better enjoy himself.

As he stepped inside and looked around, he could sense the money in this room. It showed in the glittering dresses and the tailored lines of the tuxedos. It was revealed in the way the men strode with confidence and the woman carried themselves with poise and assurance. Nick thought of how he'd told Amanda this life was what he wanted—and how she'd said she didn't.

Heading for the bar, he heard behind him, "I don't believe my eyes."

He turned to find Adam Sherwood and his wife, Joanna, bearing down on him. "What the hell are you doing here, buddy?" Adam reached out to grasp Nick's hand.

With genuine pleasure, Nick grinned and shook hands enthusiastically. "A beautiful woman coerced me into this monkey suit and persuaded me to attend. Hello, Joanna." He leaned over to kiss her cheek.

"Well, I'll be damned," Sherwood continued, clapping him on the back. "I never thought I'd see the day. Where is this prize?"

"Helping with details. Her mother is hostess tonight and Amanda's pitching in." *Because of me.* Nick tossed his head, indicating the tables across the room, and felt another pang of guilt. "What about you? Since when did the public defender's office pay for you to come to these affairs?"

"Free tickets from the mayor. The charity aspect is good public relations. This job has *some* perks. You really should think about signing on with us."

Shaking his head at Adam, Nick sidestepped the broad hint and spied Amanda over his friend's shoulder. The floor seemed to drop from beneath him, the disequilibrium akin to going up in an elevator too fast.

She was breathtaking tonight. Her hair was loose— the way he liked it, all wild and puffy at her bare shoulders. Around her neck hung a row of sapphires. A fitted, velvet dress hugged every curve and ended in the middle of her shapely calf. The outfit was the exact shade her eyes took on when she was aroused, and the thought made him hard. He plucked a glass of champagne from a passing waiter and gulped it, trying to rein in his reaction to the woman who was making her way toward them. Though Adam was still talking, Nick's attention was riveted on Amanda.

When she reached him, she touched his arm with both hands and her subtle scent wafted over him. "Hello," she said, her smile forced, almost nervous.

Guiltily, he realized that dread for this evening was written all over her beautiful face.

Turning to the other couple, she held out her hand. "I'm Amanda Carson."

When the Sherwoods introduced themselves, Amanda turned to Nick. "How nice for you to have your friends here. Shall I see if they can sit at our table?"

He nodded, irritated at the reminder that Adam would be his only ally at this gathering. When Amanda left, he caught the other man's grimace. "Don't say it, Sherwood. She's different."

"She doesn't look different."

He was right. Tonight, Amanda Carson looked every inch the debutante that his ex-wife had been. Decked out in jewels. A dress that cost more than his monthly rent. And an obvious ease with these people one couldn't put a price tag on. He had trouble reconciling this image of her with the woman who'd faced down an adolescent boy with a knife and sobbed over another who'd slashed his wrists with razor blades. And her assertion that she didn't want any part of this life was even more suspect, Nick thought, watching her.

He had no time to dwell on this, as Robert Carson sauntered by with another man. Seeming to notice Nick accidentally, Amanda's father stopped and greeted him, but there was something about the encounter that put Nick on instant alert.

They shook hands warily—like boxers squaring off before a match. Robert turned to the man beside him. "This is Porter Erickson, my associate. Nick Di-Marco."

While Nick introduced the Sherwoods, he covertly studied Erickson. This was the man who had dented Amanda's self-confidence as a woman. Nick fought to control the urge to wipe the smug look off the man's face.

"Nice to meet you, DiMarco," Erickson said flatly. His eyes scanned the room, never really looking at Nick, who felt himself dismissed. But he held his head high and forced his hands to relax at his sides.

In moments, Amanda rescued him by insinuating her slender form between him and the two men. She perfunctorily kissed her father on the cheek and nodded to her ex-husband.

The younger man gave her a very male perusal as if seeing her for the first time...or in a different way. Nick wondered if he'd look so sophisticated without teeth.

"You look well, darling," her father commented. "Doesn't she, Porter?"

"Actually, I was just thinking that you look different, Amanda. Healthier, almost glowing." Erickson's eyes were fixed on her.

Amanda thanked him for the compliment and caught Nick's gaze. He winked at her. *You look well loved,* he silently told her. Amanda smiled, indicating she'd gotten the message. One look at Erickson's face told Nick her ex-husband had understood, too. The measure of satisfaction Nick felt at this surprised him. He'd never been into sexual prowess contests before.

But Nick's smugness changed to irritation when they sat down to dinner and Craig Coleman swaggered to the table and pulled out a chair across from them. Amanda's cheeks flamed and her eyes sought her mother. Joan's surprise was evident, too. It didn't take a Ph.D. to figure out who had manipulated the seating arrangements. Coleman was accompanied by a chic, trophy-date type. And he dominated the conversation.

"What law school did you attend, DiMarco?" was his first attack. After that, the siege came fast and furious. "Where do you live...not passed the bar yet...any prospects..." until Amanda put down her wine, leaned on her elbows and looked the man square in the eye. "Craig, save the interviewing for later. Your date is looking a little lost. Pay some attention to her."

Amused at her defense of him, Nick squeezed Amanda's knee under the table and was rewarded with an intimate smile. When he glanced at Sherwood, who held his napkin to his mouth to keep from laughing aloud, Nick had to quell his own chuckle. The fact that Coleman noted their mirth made the incident even more enjoyable.

It was when dinner was served that Nick saw Suzanne Sullivan DiMarco Cohen at the adjacent table. He stared at his ex-wife, intrigued by his first glimpse of her in ten years. He wasn't exactly surprised because Amanda had warned him that Coleman and Erickson would be here, and very possibly the Cohens. Amanda had also told him that, although she'd never met Suzanne, she'd seen his ex-wife on several occasions similar to this. But *he'd* apparently suppressed any anticipation of seeing Suzanne, or of his reaction.

Time had not diminished her beauty. Blond hair coiled at the back of her neck, but it was lighter than he remembered it. Cool blue eyes stared out from a classically sculpted face. She wore shimmery gold everywhere, at her throat, wrists, ears and even threaded through the metallic dress. She'd never looked more lovely. Or more remote. Or more bored. A man who had an easy fifteen years on her sat beside her.

Reaching over to cover his hand with hers, Amanda frowned. "Nick, what is it?" She must have seen the look on his face.

Before he could respond to Amanda, Suzanne spotted him. Color suffused her beautiful cheeks and neck and she dropped her wineglass, staining the pristine linen a bloodred. The activity distracted her, but Nick continued to stare. Amanda's gaze followed his and he felt her stiffen next to him. It was her concern that shook him from the shock of seeing his ex-wife again.

Amanda gripped his hand tightly and angled her body to face him. "Are you all right?"

"Yes, of course." Nick cringed at the hoarseness of his voice.

"I'm sorry she's here, Nick."

His whole body clenched as he looked at Amanda, silently thanking her for not saying he'd been warned. "It was another reason you didn't want to come," he said. "It seems I blew it for a lot of reasons."

Unexpectedly, Amanda's eyes filled with hurt. "Is it so hard for you to see her?"

Nick cocked his head and took another glance at Suzanne. "No, not hard." Studying her, he found his rage had dissipated and he felt only cold anger at her for having abandoned her children. He felt a sudden chill and glanced at Amanda. The two could be sorority sisters, he thought. Nobody could miss the similarity. It underscored every single doubt he'd ever had about Amanda Carson.

As soon as dinner was over, Amanda, who had called on old patterns of control for the entire meal, excused herself to go to the ladies' room. She was angry at the situation and jealous of the woman who had once had Nick's heart; she needed to find some inner strength to finish the evening. On the way there, she thought about Lisa. It was the second anniversary of her sister's death, and Amanda sought some comfort in her memory. Lisa's favorite lawyer joke. *Why does Chicago have one thousand lawyers and New Jersey one hundred hazardous waste sites...? Because New Jersey had first choice.*

The humor, combined with the deep-breathing exercises she'd learned in ballet class, and the cold water she splashed on her face, calmed her enough to repair her makeup at the mirror. The door swung open, emptying the room of its other two occupants. Unfortunately, another person entered. Suzanne.

Amanda's self-confidence threatened to desert her, but she yanked it back with a silent pep talk. *Okay, I've done harder things. I buried my sister. I buried Ron. I faced down a very angry Nick. I can handle whatever she dishes out.*

Suzanne lounged against the wall and watched Amanda smooth rouge over her cheeks. Amanda kept her hand from shaking by noting the lines of stress around Suzanne's eyes and the slight puffiness there. The woman was incredibly beautiful, but the years had not been kind to her.

"I'm Suzanne Cohen," she said without preamble.

Briefly, Amanda held her gaze in the mirror. She looked like all the girls Amanda had grown up with, not the shrew Nick had made her out to be. "Yes, I know. I'm Amanda Carson. We've seen each other at these kind of events. But that was before I knew Nick and your connection to him."

A flicker of surprise flared in Suzanne's eyes at her candor, and Amanda calmed a little more inside. Taking out her lipstick, she averted her gaze.

"And now you know Nick."

"Yes. I know Nick very well."

Removing a cigarette from her purse, Suzanne lit it with trembling hands. Inexplicably, Amanda felt sorry for her, felt a connection, recognizing again how familiar her *type* was. Suzanne reminded her of Joan in some ways and of herself, a few years ago.

The woman took a long drag. "I didn't know Porter's wife had claws."

"Porter's wife didn't."

When Nick's ex-wife laughed, Amanda's sympathy fled. The sound was sultry and sensuous and images of Suzanne pleasing Nick in ways now familiar to Amanda taunted her.

"Ah, I see," Suzanne practically purred, crossing her arms over her voluptuous breasts and tilting her chin regally. The gold lamé of her dress shimmered with the movement. "I remember how Nick's energy and expertise in bed gave me that same kind of assurance. Tell me, is he still that *good?*"

Amanda straightened her spine and turned to face the woman fully. Tossing back her hair, she looked Suzanne up and down. "That's an adolescent question worthy of my students, and it doesn't merit a response. If you'll excuse me, I find this conversation extremely distasteful."

At the words *adolescent* and *student,* Suzanne's face crumpled. Clearly, the haughtiness had been a facade. Amanda didn't leave as she'd planned, some instinct telling her to wait for what was to come.

Obviously gathering her composure, Suzanne glanced at the small lounge area off the main bathroom. "Will you talk to me for a moment?" When Amanda hesitated, she added, "Please."

Only for Heather's sake, Amanda thought as she nodded, then preceded the gorgeous woman into the small room.

They sat across from each other, the door closed. Amanda was struck by the notion that they could be two classmates, reunited and about to have an intimate chat. The image was reinforced by the glimpse she caught of them in the mirror. They were almost the same age, had the same coloring, dressed in the same chic clothes. No wonder Nick had been so wary of letting Amanda into Heather's life.

Suzanne took in a deep breath. "Have you been seeing Nick long?"

"Why do you want to know that?"

The color drained from Suzanne's face. She wasn't attractive with pasty skin. Sinking into the chair as if some invisible weight were crushing her, she took a deep breath. Finally, she seemed to summon her courage. "Do...do you know Heather...and my son?"

The possessive tag cut Amanda like a knife. She wanted to shout, *He's more my son than yours.* She was shocked at her vindictiveness, and at how acute her feelings had become for both of Nick's children. Instead, she assumed her best professional voice and answered, "I know Jason. And I work at Heather's school, so I...see her often."

"Yes, I'd heard you had . . . a job." Suzanne looked perplexed.

Amanda wanted to laugh at her puzzlement but knew the situation was deadly serious.

"How are they?" Suzanne asked. Amanda would bet her next paycheck that was one of the hardest questions the woman had ever posed.

But how to answer? And why did she want to know? "Heather's turned into a beautiful young woman. And Jason's got a wonderful, clever sense of humor."

Suzanne's eyes glistened. Instead of being moved, Amanda was instantly angry. "Why, Suzanne? Why, after ten years, do you show such concern?"

The harshness of Amanda's voice must have stunned Suzanne. She blinked to force back the tears, stood and began to pace the small area.

Amanda was very good at waiting. At last, Suzanne began to talk in a raw, halting voice. "Life didn't exactly . . . turn out as I expected." She laughed ruefully, and it was an ugly sound. "What an understatement! I . . . loved Nick a great deal when I was twenty. He was so different from all the men I knew . . . so earthy, so masculine."

Carefully schooling her features to reveal nothing, Amanda remained silent. She knew only too well that particular response to Nick.

"But it wasn't just sex, though that was stupendous. I loved his carefreeness. His ability to have a good time without money. How laughter and family and friends were enough for him. Ironically, it was the very things I loved about him that drove me away," she said, peering down at Amanda. There was a deep sadness in her eyes.

"I don't understand."

Fumbling for her purse, Suzanne took out another cigarette and lit it. Inhaling seemed to calm her. "*I* couldn't live without the luxuries. Nick didn't need things, but *I* did. When Heather came along, I was intrigued by her and I loved her in my own way. For a while, I thought I might be able to handle everything. But I couldn't. It was too hard giving her all my time, all my energy. I didn't know how to sacrifice for an infant or a toddler. Then, when Jason was born..."

"Disabled," Amanda supplied for her. "Jason is disabled."

Suzanne must have caught the disdain in Amanda's voice for a mother who couldn't admit to her child's flaws, because her face flooded with color. "Yes, disabled. I simply couldn't do it. I wasn't strong enough. So I...left." There was a long pause, then Suzanne continued, "It took me years to get over Nick. I know how shallow that sounds, that I could leave the children easier than him, but that's me." She laughed again with that horrid, self-disgusted humor, then took a deep breath. "I've come to terms with who and what I am, Amanda. I can't do anything about it, but I don't necessarily like it."

Moved by her pain, but not her self-pity, Amanda said, "I'm not sure I agree that you couldn't have changed, Suzanne. But why are you telling me this? What exactly do you want now?"

"I've had a rough few years. Though Joshua is older than I am, I married him thinking I'd probably have other children, and nannies to take care of them. But Joshua wasn't thrilled about babies at his age and then...I had a hysterectomy six months ago. I did a lot of reevaluating of my life then and came to realize what I'd given up. Seeing Nick tonight..." Suzanne began to cry in earnest this time, but she forged on. "Made me even more aware of what I've lost. I know it's too late with him...but I've been wondering for some time if it's too late..." She straightened her shoulders, dabbed at her eyes and finished, "Do they ever ask about me, Amanda? Do they know I'm only a weak, shallow woman, not a monster?"

When the two emerged from the ladies' room fifteen minutes after they'd entered, Nick was standing ten feet away. His eyes were inscrutable as he watched them approach. Reaching out, he pulled Amanda to him, securing her next to his taut, safe body.

Amanda watched Suzanne's face crumple a second time and had an intolerable thought. *Oh, no, please, what if she tries to get him back?*

"Hello, Nicky."

Every feature in Nick's face constricted. The pulse in his throat leapt and Amanda almost gasped at how tightly his fingers dug into her waist. Finally, obviously gaining some measure of control, he nodded sharply. "Suze."

Nicknames. They had nicknames for each other.

Though she knew how Nick had felt about Suzanne, she realized his subconscious remembered his ex-wife in pet names. Amanda had experienced excruciating pain in her life and more loss than anyone should have to endure. But this particular prick was of a totally different nature and it hurt every bit as much. She hadn't realized before how much fear was associated with jealousy. She looked at Nick, noting how the dark tux accented his golden skin, how its cut outlined his muscles and his long, lithe form. His newly trimmed hair set off his silver eyes and, though they glowered with dislike, they were sexy and stormy and alluring. Amanda turned to Suzanne and watched her stare at her ex-husband for interminable seconds, then finally walk away.

Unable to stop her trembling, Amanda buried her face in Nick's shoulder.

"Are you all right?" he asked gruffly into her hair.

She drew back slightly and looked into his stern, angular face. "Yes, but I'd like to leave."

Examining her taut features, Nick nodded, and said, "Then let's go."

All the way home, Amanda's mind whirled with the fact that Suzanne Cohen hadn't been able to tear her eyes away from Nick.

AMANDA WAS STRUNG as tight as a poised bow by the time they reached her house around midnight. She kicked off her shoes, threw her coat over the chair and tossed her gloves and purse on the table. Nick followed behind her, putting each item and accessory away. *Too much of his world has gotten out of his control. He needs the neatness.*

They made their way to the enclosed porch, and Nick said nothing while he lit a fire. Then he rose and stood near the mantel, slouching back in a deceptively casual stance. "What did she say?" His voice was tightly controlled.

Amanda knew it wouldn't do to lie, but it was her initial inclination. Instead, she faced him like an adversary. "She was taunting at first. She made some cracks about you sexually."

"Did that bother you?"

"No. I'm not the old Amanda."

His eyes glimmered with satisfaction for a moment, then darkened. "Tell me the rest."

Sinking into a chair, she curled her feet under her. Briefly, she remembered the discussion she and Nick had had last night about his canceling his movie trip with Heather. She'd challenged him on that, and he'd been upset about her lack of understanding. This discussion would be World War Three in comparison. Nonetheless, Amanda met his gaze. "She asked about Heather and Jason."

Nick clenched his fists and straightened up and away from the fireplace. "What did she do when you refused to discuss them?"

"Look, Nick, I..."

He moved like lightning and reached her in a flash. Pulling her up from the sofa, he held her tightly by the arms. She drew in a deep breath of surprise at his rough grasp and he gentled his touch immediately. But his eyes were steely. "Tell me that you told her to butt out, that it was no concern of hers."

For long seconds, Amanda stared at him unblinkingly, though she quivered inside. "It *is* her concern, Nick. What's more, it's Heather's."

He let her go so fast, she stumbled backward. He couldn't have looked more shocked if she'd told him she was entering a convent. "What are you saying?"

"I'm saying that in my professional opinion, Heather needs some information about her mother. Maybe even some contact with her." Amanda drew herself up and faced him squarely. "And judging from tonight, Suzanne needs the same thing."

Suddenly, Nick felt the familiar rise of rage inside him. It welled up as it used to when he'd walked the floor at night with a crying infant or when he'd held a sobbing three-year-old who begged for her mommy. Scowling, he turned from Amanda, trying desperately to quell the images. His back to her, he said, "You have no right to make that decision for my family."

"As Heather's counselor, I have that right."

"No matter what it does to us? To you and me?"

"Yes, Nick, no matter what. We've discussed this a thousand times. And if you're honest, you'll admit it's what you want, too."

Of course, she was right. He wanted what was best for Heather. The problem was, he could never agree to this suggestion about Suzanne because he could never believe that *this* was what Heather needed. Amanda hadn't been there ten years ago to see the devastation the woman had caused. He braced his arms against the mantel and hung his head. Intuitively, he knew that this conflict was going to cause an unbreachable rift between him and Amanda and he wasn't sure how he was going to handle it.

When he felt her come up behind him, encircle his waist and lay her head against his back, he stiffened in an effort to resist her, to protect himself from her.

"I won't let you do this to us, Nick," she whispered against him.

Because he could feel himself weakening, because he wanted to bury himself so deep inside her and force her to see his point of view, he threw back a familiar retort. "Do what, princess?" But the epithet had long since lost its sarcasm and came across filled with reluctant affection.

"Shut me out because you're afraid. Lump me with Suzanne. What is it, Nick? Am I getting too close?"

The truth hurt, so he rounded on her. "Don't analyze me, Counselor."

Plopping her hands on her hips, Amanda glowered at him. "Damn it, Nick. I'm not going to let you do this.

You're mad, I understand that. But you're not going to frighten me into silence with your anger."

Nick marveled at the woman who had emerged from beneath the cool exterior she'd presented all evening. As if to solidify that change, she threw her arms around his neck and wrapped herself around him. "This issue with Heather and her mother has to be addressed, just like your spending time with her has to be worked out. And I'm not going to back down on either of them. As I just said, I would never risk Heather's welfare for our relationship and you wouldn't want me to. But neither am I going to stand meekly by and let you alienate me whenever we disagree. Now shut up and kiss me. We'll deal with this later."

Nick didn't know what to do. She wouldn't back down from him and he'd never do anything to hurt her. He grasped her to him, not gently, but in passion, and she matched it. Before him, he saw Craig Coleman's clear condescension, Porter's mystified perusal and Suzanne's haughty presence. Need jerked inside him. All the facets of his life were converging—Heather's well-being, his past with Suzanne, his entrance into the world of law—on this one woman. He felt an elemental desire to possess her as he had never done before.

Raking his hands over the velvet that was almost as soft as her skin, he grappled with the zipper on her dress. It fell to the floor and he lifted her from her feet. She was climbing onto him as his hands deftly unhooked the wispy bra she wore. He turned, backed her against the wall and took a beaded nipple in his mouth.

"Yes, oh yes, Nick," she moaned. "I want this."

His hands went to her hips. The garter belt was a hindrance this time, and he struggled with it. "Unhook it, damn it. I'm as clumsy as a boy."

"Never." She got rid of the barrier.

He had no patience for the panties and tore them from her. The ripping sound was an aphrodisiac, as was the wetness he felt on them before he tossed them to the floor. He cupped her firmly and she arched into his palm.

"Like it?"

"Yes. Give me more."

He slipped his finger inside her and she whimpered, trying to get closer to him. He eased it in and out, joined it with another finger and felt her start at the fullness.

Her hands flew to his belt and she struggled to unbuckle it. "It's not enough, Nick. Help me."

He did. He flung the cummerbund across the room and unbuttoned his pants. She'd gotten to the zipper by then. "It'll never be enough, baby, never. God, I want you so much. So damn much." The hammer blow of desire pounded within him.

She released him from his slacks and took him solidly in her hands, then pulled back to watch his face.

It was set in a grimace. "Do you like what you're seeing? What you do to me?"

"Yes."

"Then, hang on, baby. You can have it all. Wrap your legs around me." Bracing her against the wall, he entered her in one sure, swift stroke. "Oh, Mandy, this is so good, so right. Oh, baby..."

In what must have been one of her last coherent moments, she grasped his head and forced him to look at her. "Yes, Nick, it is..." He kept pushing, harder and harder. "Remember that."

And then she lost it. He tried to catch her moans in his mouth but he couldn't. So he buried his face in her neck and listened to the wonderful sound of her pleasure as long as he could. Which wasn't long. His control snapped, too. Against his will, he joined her in the most intense, searing pleasure he'd ever experienced.

Much later, Amanda snuggled into him on the couch. After their tumultuous union, against the wall, for God's sake, he'd picked her up like precious china, cuddled her to his chest and made his way to the sofa. He'd covered her with the afghan, adjusted his clothes and cradled her on his lap. Once in a while, he would brush his lips across her hair.

The tenderness of all his ministrations brought tears to her eyes. She knew the problem between them could not be solved by lovemaking, but she'd needed that connection with him. As if to affirm her fears, Nick pulled away from her, lay her against the pillows and left the room. She heard his footsteps taking the stairs. He returned with a warm, white terry robe and handed it to her. "Put this on, baby."

She heard the unspoken *You're going to need it.* So it was to be settled tonight. She shivered, but not from the cold.

Easing her arms inside the robe, she stood and wrapped it around her like a shield. "All right, let's have it."

He touched her cheek gently and his smile was sad, as if he, too, found the confrontation unbearable. "It's out of the question to let Heather talk about, talk to or see Suzanne. I'm going to say this only once. The woman ripped our lives apart long ago and it's taken me ten years to piece them back together. I absolutely will not allow her the chance to harm us again."

"What if it's the best thing for *Heather* to see her mother?" Amanda bit her lip and swallowed hard.

There was fire in Nick's eyes when they focused on her. "Has she been talking to you about Suzanne?"

Wanting to back down under the blast of his gaze, she forced herself not to. "Nick, I can't answer that, you know I can't."

"You just did." He began to pace. "I don't like it, Amanda." No "baby," no "Mandy." But he'd called his ex-wife "Suze."

Ignoring her own fear, Amanda made her voice calm and even. "Nick, Heather isn't out of the woods yet. She was making some progress for a while, when you quit Muscato's and before the clerking escalated, but since things have gotten busy for you, and since Ron's...death, I'm more concerned than ever."

Sinking wearily into a chair across from her, Nick scrubbed his hands over his face. "All right, I'll compromise. I won't let her down anymore. I'll spend more time with her. But under no circumstances can she see or talk to Suzanne."

"It may not be enough now." It took all the courage Amanda had to cross him again. She clasped her hands behind her back for strength.

Nick's gaze was glacial. "What do you mean?"

"I think Heather needs some realism shed on her mother. She seems to have this larger-than-life view of her...she seems to see her as more than an ordinary woman. Suzanne's a weak and shallow person, but ordinary, just the same."

"She's anything *but* ordinary. She is a monster." He enunciated each word for effect. "And she ruined our lives years ago. I won't give her another shot at Heather. Neither will you." His last words held a tomblike finality.

Running a shaky hand through her hair, Amanda watched him carefully. She hadn't missed the use of the word *monster*. Suzanne's word. "Nick, I don't believe she's a monster. What's more important, I don't think it's healthy for Heather to believe that. She needs to see that Suzanne's priorities were wrong, that she was weak and selfish, but that she's just a human being with human foibles. Heather also needs to understand that she's not like her mother, she's much more like you..."

"That's your opinion, Amanda."

"My professional opinion." When he said nothing, she added, "Which you obviously don't trust."

"It doesn't matter, Amanda. I simply can't allow it. I have to protect my child the way I think best. And I want your promise that you won't do anything behind my back."

She could feel her face heating and her stomach churning. But she stood still and stared him down. "You shouldn't need to ask me for that. I would never do anything without your knowledge."

"Or my approval."

Silence stretched between them. Then Amanda said, "I honestly don't know, Nick. As I've stated before, Heather's welfare is my first priority. I will only see and talk to her with your permission. I'd never take her anywhere against your wishes. That's all I can promise."

Apparently, he knew that was all he'd get. He stared at her for one long minute, then turned wearily, picked up his coat and walked out of the room. She followed him to the door, feeling the private sting of his rejection. It intensified when he didn't touch her, didn't kiss her good-night. She thought he'd leave without saying anything at all, but when his hand reached the doorknob, he stopped and murmured a sad goodbye, not even facing her. He opened the door and was halfway down the steps, when she called to him, "Nick?"

He halted, hesitated, then backtracked and stood outside the archway. The moon cast shadows over his angular features, accented by a darkening of his beard.

Slowly, she lifted her hand and rubbed the roughness of his cheek. "It doesn't matter, any of it."

He scowled but turned his face into her hand. "What doesn't?"

"You can be as stubborn, as withdrawn and as angry as you want. It doesn't matter, because I love you."

Hot, thick emotion flared in his eyes. He didn't move, didn't speak, and something deep inside Amanda contracted. She removed her palm from his cheek and stepped back. Closing the door, she locked it and leaned against it. She brought her hand to her mouth and nose and breathed in the musky scent of him.

It was silent on the porch so she knew that he remained where he was for several seconds, as if in indecision. Then she heard him go down the front steps. He hadn't returned the declaration. Only his eyes had reacted, burning with volcanic reaction to the words she spoke for the first time to him. But she didn't regret saying them. There were too many things she wished she'd said to Lisa and to Ron. And she'd withheld this message long enough. She loved Nick DiMarco and he needed to know it. Realizing she might not have another opportunity to tell him, she began to weep.

CHAPTER THIRTEEN

HEATHER SAT in the guidance office waiting for the Monday-afternoon group. Nothing had gone right since Ron died. She'd just begun to feel better, had begun to believe that the pain would go away. Then, after his suicide, it had gotten worse. Though Ms. Carson had helped at first, the old hurt was back now and just as bad as ever.

Needing to move, she got up and prowled around the small room. The sun streamed in through the windows and she let it bathe her face for a moment. Warm, she removed the pale yellow cardigan Aunt Beth had bought her for spring and stuck her hands in the pockets of the matching pants. She moved to the desk and picked up a picture. She'd noticed it before but never up close. It was a woman in a wheelchair who looked like Ms. Carson.

"Hello, Heather," she heard from behind her.

The girl whirled, picture in hand. She felt funny about the photograph. "Who's this?"

Ms. Carson glanced at it. "That's my sister Lisa."

"How come you never talk about her?"

The counselor hesitated the way all adults do when they're not sure how much to tell you. It made Heather mad.

"You never told me you had a sister in a wheelchair. Like Jason." Heather scowled and gripped the picture tighter.

Frowning, Ms. Carson crossed to her chair and sat down. "No, honey, I didn't tell you about Lisa. Does that bother you?"

"Yeah."

"Why?"

Heather set the frame down, buying time. *Because maybe it makes me feel you're interested in me for some reason besides that you like me.* "I don't know."

Just then, Matt Barone sauntered in. He'd exchanged his leather jacket for a lightweight green windbreaker that made his eyes sparkle. He still wore denims and his boots. "Hello, Ms. C. How ya doin'?" Without waiting for an answer, he ruffled Heather's hair. "Hi, princess. I got a great joke today."

But Heather didn't turn to him. She was staring at Ms. Carson, whose face had gone all tight and her eyes all watery when Matt had used the term "princess."

Before she could figure that one out, Sandi arrived. She didn't look good. Usually, her hair was fluffy around her shoulders and it made her beautiful. But she'd pulled it back today. Her eyes were red and there was something wrong with the side of her face. "Yo, guys," she said as she plunked down into a seat.

Covertly, Heather watched Matt watch Sandi. His eyes narrowed, but when Sandi looked up at him, he winked at her.

Turning away, Heather took her own chair. Ever since Ron's suicide, the two had been closer and she was jealous. Tammy hadn't called her much, her dad's hours were crummy again, and Ms. Carson hadn't been to the house in over a week. Now she felt she was losing Sandi and Matt to each other. She felt stupid and childish about not liking it, but she couldn't help it.

Ms. Carson scanned all three of them. Her eyes were still sad. "Okay, Matt, let's hear your joke."

Balancing his chair on its back legs, Matt linked his hands behind his neck. "What do you call one hundred rabbits in a row?" When no one answered, he finished, "A hareline."

There was polite laughter. "What do you call one hundred rabbits in a row walking backward?" Again, no response. "A receding hareline."

When the humor fell flat, Ms. Carson rose, circled the desk and sat in a chair facing them. "How is everyone today?"

No one spoke. Everybody looked away. The counselor let the silence go on, the way she always did until somebody got uncomfortable enough to talk. Another adult tactic.

Matt finally broke the tension. "I got a B in English. Ms. Radson says my compositions are more 'focused and discreet.'" He giggled boyishly.

Suddenly, Sandi stood. "I'm gonna book. No offense, Ms. C., but this ain't helping me much anymore. Ever since Ron... Damn, we're not gettin' anywhere anymore. I don't feel better. I hurt. This ain't..."

Ms. Carson leaned over with her forearms on her knees. "Then we should talk about why this group has been on hold since Ron committed suicide." Her voice was shaky and it worried Heather.

Silence closed in around them like an early morning fog.

Matt righted his chair with a thud. "Because nobody's sharin' what's really bothering them."

Again, silence. Finally, Ms. Carson spoke. "Matt's right. It's got to happen here. Ron wouldn't share and he couldn't survive. You three have to open up."

Tears formed in Heather's eyes. The group was falling apart, too, and she wasn't sure she could make it without their help.

Ms. Carson eased off her chair to crouch in front of her and took hold of her hands. "Heather, why are you crying?"

First, Heather shook her head, sending blond locks flying. When Ms. Carson asked again, she blurted out, "Because it hurts so much, I can't stand it anymore."

Suddenly, Sandi moved and squatted next to her and Matt moved his chair closer. "Tell us about your pain, kid." When Heather didn't respond, Sandi added, "If you do, I'll tell mine."

Heather looked at her friend and smiled weakly. "Promise?"

"You got it, girl."

Then Heather glanced at Ms. Carson. "You won't like this."

She saw the look of surprise flicker in the counselor's bright blue eyes, but Ms. Carson moved back and perched on the edge of her chair. "I don't like spinach, either, but I eat it because it's good for me. Tell us, Heather."

Taking in a deep breath, Heather held her gaze. "I heard Dad and Aunt Beth arguing last week. You saw her, didn't you?"

She watched Ms. Carson grip the sides of her chair. *Now I'll know how honest she is. If she lies to me, it's all over.*

"Saw who?" Matt asked, a frown marring his handsome forehead.

Ms. Carson's eyes got all watery again but she answered firmly, "Heather's mother. Yes, honey, I saw her at the party I went to with your father."

"You been datin' Heather's old man?" Sandi asked.

Still watching Heather, Ms. Carson nodded. "Yes." After a moment, she looked at the two others. "Heather and I have discussed this. Does it bother anyone else?"

"Not me." Matt's voice was suddenly very male. "You're a great-looking broad."

"And he's hot," Sandi interjected.

Momentarily, Heather smiled at their remarks. But the tears came back when Ms. Carson's gaze swung back to her. "What did you overhear?" she asked.

Heather didn't want to tell the whole awful story, but it all came tumbling out. She fingered the watch Grandpa had given her for her thirteenth birthday as she talked and looked at the floor. "Daddy said that you'd run into her. That you'd talked to her. That you and him had a fight about it. Aunt Beth told him he was a stubborn mule and he told her to mind her own business. Then she used words I'd never heard her use before and she stormed out of the house."

Ms. Carson stepped forward to kneel in front of Heather. "Did you talk to your dad about this?"

"Of course not. It hurts him to talk about her." She was close to tears again. "What does she look like, Ms. Carson?"

"Honey, your dad's asked me not to talk to you about that night. I . . . haven't made any decision about that request, but if I do tell you anything, I'd have to let him know first. Not get his permission, but not do anything behind his back, either. Do you understand?" The counselor reached for Heather's hands.

Laying her head back on the seat, Heather closed her eyes. "I think so."

Ms. Carson gripped her hands. "Look at me, Heather." When she did, the counselor continued, "Why don't I promise to speak to him this week, and you and I will meet on Thursday and talk about it?"

Heather nodded.

"Are you okay with that?"

"Yeah."

Amanda stood and sat back in her own chair. Watching Heather, she knew the girl was not all right. She, herself, had put off another confrontation with Nick by not contacting him after the gala and he'd done the same by not calling her for ten days. But it was time for action. She glanced at Lisa's picture on her desk. She'd fight for Heather no matter what the cost. Unfortunately, Amanda knew in her heart exactly what price she would pay. Biting her lip, she heard Heather address Sandi.

"Okay, your turn. You said you'd come clean, too."

Sitting back and steepling her hands, Amanda watched Heather. There was a lot of her father in her.

"I...I don't know where to start," Sandi stammered.

Amanda turned to the girl. Sandi had been getting more and more morose over the last few weeks. Keeping her voice calm, Amanda suggested, "Why don't you tell us how you got that bruise on your face."

Absently, Sandi played with a loose tendril of hair and studied the floor.

From the corner of her eye, Amanda saw Matt's hands fist. She'd have to be blind not to see that Matt and Sandi were getting close, but she didn't know the depth of their relationship.

Finally, Sandi looked up with huge eyes that reminded her of a wounded fawn. "He did it."

Amanda swallowed and tried to keep from tensing. "Who, Sandi?"

"My stepfather." The words were almost inaudible.

Matt started to say something but Amanda raised her hand to stop him.

"He hit you?"

"Yes."

"Is it the first time?"

Sandi closed her eyes and sagged against the vinyl. "No, it's not."

Matt reacted then. Sliding to the edge of his seat, he smacked one open hand with his fist. "That son of a bitch, I'll kill him."

"No, please," Sandi begged, reaching over to him. "It's one of the reasons I didn't want you to know."

Staring at her for a moment, Matt sank back into his chair, his whole body taut.

Amanda waited for a moment, then said, "You know I can't allow this to go unreported, Sandi."

"Yeah. I want you to do it. I'm sick of this." She began to cry.

Heather got up and went to the girl and hugged her. "Ms. Carson will help you, Sandi. You don't have to do this alone."

Glancing at the counselor, Sandi said, "I know. She'll help us all, just like she always has."

WHEN SHE WAS ALONE in her own house at ten o'clock that night, Amanda felt the full weight of her responsibility. She was glad the kids had opened up again, and she hoped she could live up to the trust they'd placed in her.

She needed to start tonight. With Heather.

Staring at the phone, she sipped a glass of chardonnay. It hadn't taken her long to reach her decision, even though she knew the consequences. She simply had to broach the subject of Suzanne with Nick again. Heather was in crisis because of the unresolved issue of her mother.

Images of Lisa and Ron swam before her as she dialed Nick's phone number, wanting to get this over with as soon as possible. Heather had said he'd be home by nine.

"Hello." His husky baritone washed over her.

Amanda paused, then cleared her throat. "Nick, it's Amanda."

He paused, too, and his own voice was hoarse when he responded. "Hi, baby."

The endearment brought tears to her eyes. He obviously took this call as a sign that she was ready to make up. Instead, she was going to tear their relationship apart irrevocably.

After waiting for Amanda to begin, Nick asked, "Are you all right?"

"Yes."

"You sound upset."

"It's been a rough day."

"Yeah? Mom said Heather looked whipped when she came home. She had a little supper and went straight to bed."

So she didn't talk to you. Okay, Amanda, this is your opening.

But she couldn't do it. All her strength was gone. She should have waited until tomorrow to call him. Everything flooded her at once. Ron's suicide and her guilt over it. The loneliness she'd felt without Nick all week.

The constant worry over Heather. Amanda just couldn't let Nick go right now. *Not another loss.*

She began to cry. She knew it was unfair to do to him on the phone, but she'd lost control. Sobbing, she sank into the chair.

"Mandy, please, what is it? Stop crying and tell me."

"I . . . can't." *I can't stop crying and I can't tell you.*

After a few seconds, Nick said, "I'm coming over. The kids are both asleep and my mother's staying the night because I have an early meeting tomorrow."

A chill skittered through Amanda. "No, Nick, please, not tonight. I can't do it now, I just can't."

"You don't have to do anything, baby. Just let me take care of you." With that, he hung up.

Amanda berated herself for her weakness. She shouldn't have broken down on the phone. She should have demanded he stay away. Because she knew in her heart she couldn't resist his comfort tonight. She hurt too much, and she would take the comfort from him one last time before she told him of her decision. Hating herself for her weakness, she sipped her chardonnay and waited anxiously for him to arrive.

He pounded on the door fifteen minutes later. Amanda thought she had herself in control until she saw him standing there, hair ruffled by the wind, concern darkening his eyes. He came inside, closed the door and barely got his jacket off before she threw herself into his arms.

Clasping her to him, he soothed her hair with his hands and her soul with his words. "Shh, baby, it's okay, I'm here. I'm sorry I left you alone all week. I was pouting. I'm not mad anymore."

You will be, she thought miserably as she burrowed into his chest. She grasped his neck tightly and inhaled the familiar scent of him.

After a moment, Nick guided her to the couch and tried to seat her next to him. But she curled onto his lap, burying her face in his shoulder.

"Mandy. Is this about Ron? Come on, tell me."

Oh, God, no. If she told him, *when* she told him, he would never hold her again, never kiss the backs of her knees, never whisper into her ear erotic love talk of what he was going to do to her. Though she'd lived so long without that in her life, she wondered if she could do it again, knowing what it was like to be with Nick. So she decided to take one more time, just for herself. She'd tell him afterward. "No. Not now. Make love to me, instead."

He stilled. "I don't think that's such a good idea. You're overwrought. We should talk about this."

She began unbuttoning his shirt. "I don't want to talk. I don't want to listen. I want to forget about death and pain and making choices. I want to touch you." She ran her fingers up his chest. "I want you to touch me." Taking his hand, she covered her breast with it. She felt her nipple bead instantly against his palm. "I want to do everything to you I never dared before." Sliding her hands to his groin, she cupped him through his jeans. That got a reaction, literally and figuratively. He moaned into her mouth and grabbed her tighter. It cut her loose. She pulled at the rest of the buttons on his shirt and they went flying. Tearing it off his shoulders, she went for his belt.

"Easy, baby, easy."

Ignoring the concern in his voice, Amanda scrambled off his lap and onto her knees. She yanked at his jeans and dragged them down with his underwear. When his Nike running shoes got in the way, she tore at them and his socks. Finally, with free access, she buried her face in his lap. "Oh, God, Nick, I want all of you. Please," she begged, taking him into her mouth.

He groaned from above her and when she looked up, she saw him grip the pillow on the couch. "I couldn't stop you if I wanted to. Do you know what you do to me?"

"Tell me." She continued her gentle torture. "Tell me every erotic thought you've ever had about me."

He didn't, though. He only moaned again. Amanda kept caressing him until he dragged her up from the floor and pushed her back into the cushions. Hovering over her, he said, "Baby, you're so rare, so precious. You mean so much to me, I..."

But she grasped his long, hard length and guided him to her so he was unable to finish. He plunged deeply into her. Amanda felt his touch go straight to her soul.

"Yes, Nick, yes. Take me. Love me. Make me forget."

It only took a thrust or two, they were both so ready. "Baby...I..." But Nick could no longer articulate.

"I love you, Nick, I love you...love you...love you."

Minutes later, Nick gazed down at Amanda, sensing something was not quite right. It was more than the fight they'd had. He was ashamed of himself for not calling her, because obviously she had needed him. And not just physically, though she had wrung him out so fast and so completely that he wasn't sure he could get up from the couch. Easing onto his elbows, he studied her well-loved face. "Let me move, I've got to be heavy on you." Passion still clogged his throat. He smiled lovingly at her and was shocked to see her tears glisten in her eyes. Smoothing back her hair, he said, "Oh, Mandy, tell me. Nothing can be this bad."

Her eyes darkened and the depth of suffering, and the...what was it?...fear...he saw there alarmed him. "Amanda?"

"Please, Nick, just take me upstairs and love me again. Stay with me tonight. I'll tell you in the morning."

He wanted to object, to erase her pain now, he was so sure he could do it. But some primordial fear gnawed inside of him. *Do it her way, DiMarco,* it told him.

So he rose from the couch, picked her up and carried her to bed. There, he made love to her twice more through the night and completely forgot about his earlier foreboding. He left her sound asleep at 6:00 a.m., setting the clock for an hour later, and whistled his way home. It was a beautiful crisp morning, he'd had the woman he loved in his arms all night and everything was going to work out just fine.

HE WAS WHISTLING again at ten o'clock that night as he waited for Amanda at his house. The kids were settled down and he'd changed into clean white jeans and a navy polo shirt. He leafed through a law journal, passing the time. He didn't know why she'd called him from school today to ask to see him tonight, but he knew one thing that was going to happen.

He planned to tell her he loved her. He'd withheld the declaration for too long and last night he'd realized he had to verbalize it. He loved her and he wanted a future with her. The two of them and Jason and Heather. Wouldn't the kids love it?

Tossing the magazine down, his mind settled on Heather. She'd been skittish around him all night, but she would be fine when he told her he was going to marry Amanda. Everything would be all right. He wondered if Amanda would want to have a baby. The thought of her carrying their child made him ache inside.

Oh, God, DiMarco, you're lost. Completely and utterly lost.

And it had never felt so good.

When he opened the door to her, even the desperate look on her face and her shadowed eyes couldn't dull his pleasure. She was hauntingly beautiful in a grass green, long T-shirt and tight leggings. "Hello, Nick."

The sound of her voice gave him cause for concern. It was scratchy and hoarse. But she said nothing else until she was seated on a chair facing the couch. Her hands were clasped so tightly, her knuckles were white.

"Mandy, what is it?"

Taking a deep breath, she began, "Nick, I believe you're making a mistake with Heather. It's my professional opinion that she needs to work through some things about her mother. She knows I spoke with Suzanne."

Involuntarily, all of Nick's muscles tensed. "You told me you wouldn't do anything behind my back. Why did you tell her you'd seen Suzanne?"

"I didn't. She heard you and Beth arguing. She asked me to tell her what Suzanne said."

Amanda lost all the color in her face. Her pallor upset him but he steeled himself. God help him, he knew the worst was yet to come. "Why didn't she ask me?"

"She's afraid to ask you, Nick."

He scowled at the thought of his daughter being afraid of him. "I would have explained to her that

Suzanne is not worth discussing. I don't want to hurt her all over again by telling her what her mother did, why she left. I have to protect Heather and Jason from that."

Her posture brittle, Amanda warned, "I don't think you have a choice anymore. Heather is demanding answers. Someone has to give them to her."

And if I don't, you will, he thought.

To suppress his temper at her interference, Nick got up and walked to the window, jamming his hands in his pockets. He had to do something. Maybe Heather did have a right to know. Maybe if he agreed to let Amanda talk to her, it would be enough.

He pivoted, crossed to the chair and squatted in front of her. Grabbing her hand, he was startled by its iciness. Deep in his gut, he knew just talking about Suzanne wasn't what she was after. "What else, Amanda?"

"I'm going to tell Heather that Suzanne asked about her." She bit her lip so hard he was sure she'd draw blood. "I'm going to tell her Suzanne asked if there was a chance she and Jason might ever want to see her."

"No," he said hoarsely. "Absolutely not."

Amanda lifted her chin and took a deep breath. Swimming blue eyes looked at him from a chalk white face. "I'm not asking your permission, Nick. I'm just letting you know my intentions, as I said I would. I'm going to call Suzanne. I'm going to tell her how concerned I am about Heather's well-being. I'm going to tell her I think she's a large part of the cause of Heather's depression."

Nick rose slowly and stepped away from her, fear gripping him. The thought of Suzanne anywhere near his children made his stomach roil. "Don't do this, Amanda. You don't understand."

"No, Nick, *you* don't understand. You're too close to this to see it clearly. Heather needs to see Suzanne, to recognize her mother is simply a woman who made a mistake years ago. She needs to know that it wasn't *her* fault that Suzanne left. That the woman herself was responsible, not the child. And then she'll need help to recognize who she is and how she's not like this mother she's never known. How she's caring and loving and good." Amanda's voice broke. "Like you." She waited a moment before she went on. "I know I can help her to understand this if she gets to talk to her mother face-to-face. Nick, she needs this for her sanity. Actually, I think she needs it to survive at all."

Nick felt more helpless than he had the day Suzanne walked out. They stood facing each other. "Mandy, don't do this. I'll never be able to trust you again."

"You don't trust me now, Nick. Not enough to listen to me."

"How can you be so sure that you're right?"

"How can you?"

"She's my daughter. I was there ten years ago to see what happened to Heather when Suzanne left us."

"Heather isn't a baby anymore, Nick. And we'll be there to help her."

"No, *you* won't. *I* will."

He watched her suck in her breath, as if she'd been slapped. When she finally regained her composure, she stated, "All right, if that's the price I have to pay, so be it. I told you a long time ago, Heather is my first priority."

"You also told me you loved me."

Her shoulders shook, then tears coursed down her cheeks. "I do love you. I love Heather, too. And Jason." She brushed off the moisture on her face.

He clenched his fists and willed the tears from his own eyes. "And you'll still do this, in spite of what I think is best for Heather. And knowing it will mean the end of us."

She looked away. "Yes, if I have to."

He was silent for a long time. "You'll have to," he said finally.

"I knew I would."

"Is that what last night was all about?"

As if she couldn't speak, she nodded.

"Then there's nothing more to say."

"No, there isn't." She clenched trembling hands behind her. Turning, she crossed to the door and opened it. "Goodbye, Nick."

The click of the latch sounded like a bullet. But her words had been the real ammunition. She'd hit him straight in the heart with the message that she didn't love him quite enough.

He sank down into the chair and buried his face in his hands.

Oh, no, what have I done now? Heather thought as she crept back to bed from hiding in the doorway. She'd broken up her father and Amanda because she wanted to talk about her mother. His pain was all her fault and no matter how far she burrowed under the covers, she couldn't escape the sight of him sitting in the living room so unhappy. It was all her fault. Just like her mother's leaving had been. She'd rather die than hurt her father. She'd rather die than hurt Amanda. There was no way, she knew, as the salty tears of guilt soaked her baby-doll pajamas, that she could ever live with what she'd done tonight.

CHAPTER FOURTEEN

April Fools' Day, 12:00 noon

FOUR DAYS AFTER she'd overheard Ms. Carson and her father arguing, Heather clutched her books to her chest and walked down the senior wing of Eastside High School, listening to the banter, the cursing and the whispered words of love. She hadn't visited this area of the school much, but knew her destination. Kids jostled to get around her, others made snide comments about moving her butt out of the way, but she just stopped and stared at what she'd come to see. Locker number 453. Empty now for two months. Did anyone really miss Ron?

"Hey, babe, need some help?"

Pivoting slightly, Heather looked at the tall, gangling boy with spiked hair and a bad case of acne. "Yeah," she muttered. "I do."

As she turned and walked away, she heard him murmur to his buddy, "Cra-zy."

"That's me. Crazy."

No, Heather, you're just sad.

She spotted Sandi and Matt ten feet down the hall. But they didn't see her; they were glued to each other. Matt had his hand in the back pocket of Sandi's jeans and she held on to his rib cage. They talked in low, secret tones and Heather did a U-turn to avoid them. Their closeness made her ache.

"Everyone has someone else," she told herself, "but me."

You have your father. And Ms. Carson.

"But they don't have each other. Because of me. I drove her away, just like my own mother."

Nah, kid. Remember what the lady said. You aren't responsible for other people's decisions. Particularly the decisions of adults.

"Yeah, sure."

Heather traveled across the building with plodding steps. The guidance suite was a zoo, as usual, and she slipped into the office unnoticed. Scanning the room where she'd sat with people who cared about her, she pictured Ms. Carson teasing Matt into agreement, coaxing Sandi into talking and urging Ron to share. The vision was immediately transposed with the same woman, weeping in the DiMarco living room.

Barraged by memories she couldn't stand to think about, she removed from her backpack a small picture the school photographer had taken of her, scribbled something on the back of it and placed it in the corner of the metal frame that held Lisa's photo. Then she left, quietly and unobserved, like she did everything.

April Fools' Day, 1:00 p.m.

NICK HIT the punching bag as hard as he could, time and time again, but it didn't help.

"Nothing will, you fool."

I can think of one thing.

He landed a mean right jab. "Don't even mention it."

Listen, buddy, you can't kid me. I saw those scribbles on the legal pad. All the reasons you should call her.

"But I didn't call, did I?" he said as he pummeled the bag with five quick ones in a row.

No, instead, you tossed and turned for hours just like you have for five nights running. Ever since you gave her that stupid ultimatum.

He whacked even harder but finally had to stop and wipe the sweat from his eyes with his old football jersey. "Think of something else, DiMarco, like how happy Heather was this morning."

Almost bubbling, she'd come into the kitchen, kissed him and Jason a sunny hello and chattered through breakfast.

Pretty sudden change, isn't it?

She'd been morose for most of the past week, but he'd thought it was because his vile mood had rubbed off on her.

Viciously tearing off his gloves, he headed for the track. Joris, Beech and Stowe really understood the need to work off tension when they installed this gym on the ground floor, he thought as he hit the specially designed pavement. And someday it would all be commonplace in his life. This exercise facility. A chic office. And lots and lots of money.

"I don't need anything else," he told himself as he sped around the circle.

You need Amanda.

"No, I don't. I'll find another woman, sexier, more experienced, more understanding of my needs."

Fool!

April Fools' Day, 1:15 p.m.

"REALLY, Amanda, I can't believe you asked me to meet you in this hovel." Robert Carson sniffed at the fast-food restaurant with distaste, sipping coffee, the only thing he would risk ordering. He looked so out of place in his two-thousand-dollar suit that the sight was almost comical.

Amanda hid her smirk behind the greasy, dripping burger she'd purposely chosen, along with a biggie fries and milk shake. Robert Carson detested fatty food and eyed hers with derision. "I warned you this was a bad day for me to meet you," she said. "When you insisted, the only time I could spare was lunch. Since my break is so short, I thought it expeditious to meet near school."

All right, I admit I'm baiting him. But Nick said . . .

Her smile faded, feeling again the gnawing, aching hole inside her caused by Nick's absence from her life.

Robert was talking and she focused in to alleviate some of the pain. "I decided it was time for a heart-to-heart chat. Your mother and I are concerned about you and your involvement with this DiMarco family. I've done some investigating and there are things about him you should know."

Dropping the burger, Amanda stared openmouthed at her father. "You've investigated Nick?"

"Yes, I have. Craig mentioned his tumultuous marriage to Joshua Cohen's wife, but do you know the details?"

Amanda began to sweat. First her palms got clammy. Then her forehead. Robert recited information Amanda already knew . . . they'd married young, the two pregnancies . . . no money . . .

Leaning forward, her father uncharacteristically took her hand. "He isn't exactly the kind of man you're used to, Amanda. He's too earthy, too 'of the streets.'"

She stopped Robert's catalog of Nick's shortcomings with a vicious shake of her head. Her heart beat faster and her stomach churned. "When did you have Nick investigated?"

Scowling at the interruption, Robert pulled back and crossed his arms over his chest. "Right after you stormed out on us at Christmas." He peered at her for a moment, and his features softened. "I know we haven't always gotten along, dear, but I wish you'd listen to me on this. I care about you and only want what's best for you."

Somehow, Amanda believed him for a moment. There was something different about this whole conversation. "Father," she asked, "what did you hope to accomplish by inviting Nick to the gala?"

Robert kept his attorney's unflappable composure, but his eyes glimmered with conflicting emotions. "Don't make me spell it out, Amanda." When she remained silent, he sighed and said, "I believe you needed to see he doesn't fit in our world. You needed to see he tried it once before and failed miserably. You needed to see him beside Porter and Craig."

Amanda wanted to laugh. Porter and Craig looked liked milquetoast next to Nick. Neither had ever been able to set her pulse spinning with just a glance.

Very carefully, she folded her napkin and pushed her food away. She looked over her father's shoulder and tried to understand his point of view. Though she was angry at his machinations, she knew it wasn't his fault that she'd lost Nick.

"Father, Nick and I are no longer seeing each other for a lot of reasons, not because of what you've done. But I resent your interference in my life and you need to know that I won't tolerate it anymore. If you continue to do it, I won't be a part of your life at all." She held his gaze and was surprised by the hurt she saw there.

"Amanda," he said hoarsely, sitting forward to grasp her hand again. His was cold. "I've already lost one daughter. I can't lose you, too."

Her throat clogged. There had been too much loss, too much sadness in her life. But she had to be strong. "Then you need to think about what I've said." She stood before she could relent. "You have another chance with me, but I swear it's the last one." She turned on her heel and left Robert Carson alone in a foreign world, and with his foreign emotions.

April Fools' Day, 3:00 p.m.

THE DIMARCO APARTMENT was still and silent when Heather let herself in. It was never this quiet, because someone was usually here for them. Or occasionally it was just her and Jason. But she was never alone. Today, the eeriness of it suited her mood.

"I'm alone because I lied," she said into the emptiness.

She had called her grandmother from school and told her she wouldn't be getting off the bus at the older DiMarcos' house today, as planned. She'd said she was going to Tammy's for dinner instead and her father had okayed this.

"Doesn't matter anymore, though, does it?"

Of course it matters. Ms. Carson just told you yesterday how much you matter to her.

Carefully hanging her jacket on the coat tree, Heather straightened the throw rug and walked to her room. She put her books on the desk and stowed her backpack in the closet. Then she remade her bed and sat down on it. It would be good to be free from all this. Free from the constant worry over disappointing someone, from the fear of making anyone unhappy. She saw again her father burying his face in his hands.

"I sure blew that one, just like everything else. Well, no more. No more."

Unbidden, she heard Ms. Carson's voice. "Heather, I can help you through this. So can your dad."

But they just didn't understand.

Restless, she sprang from the bed, went to her dresser and removed a bag. Inside was a fragile porcelain unicorn. It was delicately detailed, and Aunt Beth had said it reminded her of Heather so she'd bought it at the World's Fair.

Jason loved this figurine. When he was sad or in pain, Heather would let him hold it, stroke it, and keep it on his bureau until he fell asleep. Quietly, she made her way to his room. She opened the door and strode over to straighten the bedspread and put his sneakers away. It was a chore for Jason to keep his room tidy, but he tried real hard.

Looking around at his superhero posters and his baseball photos, she scowled. "Why you, Jase? You're so sweet, so nice, so uncomplaining. Life just isn't fair."

But you know that, Heather. And Ms. Carson's right, you have to make it as fair as you can and tough out the rest.

Heather placed the bag on his bed where he wouldn't miss it, wiped at the tears that were flowing at the thought of never again seeing the brother she loved so much, and left his room.

Back in the living area, Heather took one more glance around. Her eyes lighted on a photograph. Her father was on one knee for the camera, holding her on his leg, grinning at the lens. For the first time, she realized her mother must have taken the shot. It was more than she could bear. She raised her hand and traced the outline of her father's face. "I love you, Daddy. I'm sorry."

Again, her counselor's words came through. "He loves you so much Heather, so do your grandparents, and Aunt Beth. Think about that when you're feeling down."

"No," she said aloud into the empty apartment. "They'll be better off without me."

But suddenly she wasn't so sure. To rid herself of doubt, she walked around the room, turning facedown every single picture of her that was there. Next to one on the bookshelf was a framed snapshot she hadn't seen before—it was of Ms. Carson, her and Jason. Heather was mesmerized by the happiness on the counselor's face as she peered out at the camera. And Jason looked happier than she'd ever seen him. But it was her own image that struck her the most. She, too, had that sense of joy. And it was thanks to the woman in the picture.

Holding the photo close, she walked to the bathroom, but slower this time, less sure.

April Fools' Day, 4:00 p.m.

NICK RUBBED his sore eyes and sank into the leather chair. The report he was working on was giving him a headache in more ways than one. It outlined several borderline procedures for yet another wealthy client to pay fewer taxes. Ah, the luxuries of the rich. Soon, they would be his, too.

Amanda doesn't want that kind of life anymore.

He slapped the papers down on the desk. "Well, I do."

But did he really? If it meant spending his days keeping the rich and their money together? Didn't he want to do something useful with his life? Like Adam Sherwood.

Like Amanda.

Swearing vilely under his breath, he leaned back and closed his eyes. It always kept coming back to her, to a pair of azure eyes that sparkled with laughter at some silly joke, that darkened with arousal when he brushed her lips with his thumb, that shone with admiration when he did something she approved of.

"So she'd rather see you in a job like Adam's," he said aloud again to no one in particular. "Who cares?"

You do. So does Heather. So does Jason, for that matter.

Nick forced his thoughts away from Amanda to Heather. Glancing at the clock, he wondered if she'd reached his mother's house yet. Something passed through him, some sense of foreboding like the one that he'd had the day he found her with the photo album of Suzanne. He picked up the receiver just as there was a knock on the door.

A young, well-groomed lawyer poked his head in the office. "Oh, good, Nick, you're here. Mr. Joris is ready to discuss the new file now." The junior partner was everything Nick wanted to be. Why did he seem so shallow and insipid today?

Shaking off the introspection, Nick replaced the receiver and made a mental note to try his mother as soon as he could. He followed the man out of the office, still feeling uneasy.

April Fools' Day, 5:00 p.m.

AMANDA BENT into the bar, mercilessly stretching her leg muscles. She tried to clear her mind, but images haunted her. Matt and Sandi groping for some direction in this crazy world. Her father's confusion as she left the restaurant. The look of horror on Nick's face when she told him she was going to call Suzanne.

But thoughts of Heather dominated. She did two *pliés* and knitted her forehead, remembering how she'd discovered the teenager had been in her office. It wasn't until she was about to leave that she saw Heather's picture tucked into the frame of Lisa's photo. By chance, she turned it over. There was something about the message that bothered her but she couldn't put her finger on it. She was touched by the declaration of Heather's love for her, but something was just not right.

The instructor led them through *ronds de jambe* and several *pas de bourrée*. Amanda lifted her foot, thinking about the counseling sessions. Nick had let Heather keep seeing her professionally, at least for now. She'd met with the girl once alone and once in the group. Heather didn't say much either time but Amanda noticed a strange calm about her that was frightening.

True to her word, Amanda had phoned Suzanne Cohen, but Heather's mother was out of town for a week, so Amanda hadn't been able to get that ball rolling, either. Heather had seemed to accept this delay with weary resignation.

The dance steps got complicated soon and she was forced to concentrate on them. But in the cool down, her mind turned to Nick.

God, she missed him, his long slow kisses, his hand trailing down her spine, how full she felt when he was inside her.

You could call him.

No, he'd made his position clear. She needed to concentrate on Heather. She was so vulnerable now, so like Lisa, she...

Lisa... Heather... the frame... I love you...

Amanda stopped in the middle of a long, low stretch. No. Heather's message had said, "I love you too." I love you *too.* Heather had obviously heard Amanda say she loved her. And there was only one time Amanda had done that. Five nights ago in the DiMarco living room.

No! No! Heather must have overheard their whole, horrible confrontation over Suzanne.

Lisa... Heather... Ron... Heather... Oh, my God, not again, please, not again.

Leaping off the floor, quicker and faster than she had done during any of the dance routines, Amanda rushed to the phone in the hall, found change in her purse and dialed the DiMarco home. It rang once, three times, six times...no answer. She spotted the directory and made a split-second decision. She'd call Nick, and if he thought this was a ploy, then so be it. She would not ignore her grim hunch about his daughter.

This phone rang only once before a brisk, efficient voice answered, "Joris, Beech and Stowe. May I help you?"

"I need to talk with Nick DiMarco. He's a clerk in your office."

There was a slight pause. Amanda wondered if perhaps clerks didn't get phone calls.

"Just a moment. I'll try to locate him."

Oh, Lord, Heather may not have a moment.

The woman came back after what seemed like hours. "I'm sorry. Mr. DiMarco is in with Mr. Joris."

"Then interrupt them, please," Amanda said, annoyed.

"We don't interrupt the partners for anonymous callers. Perhaps you'll leave your name and I'll have Mr. DiMarco return your call when he's available."

Amanda hung up. In the time it took for the receptionist to patronize her, she'd made the decision to go to his office. Her dance class was only five minutes from where she'd once dropped Nick off at the high rise in the city.

Fifteen minutes later, she strode through the marble and oak lobby to the receptionist's desk. She hadn't thought of how she looked until she saw the woman take in her appearance. Still dressed in mauve tights, leotard and baggy shirt, Amanda hadn't even changed her beribboned ballet shoes.

"I need to see Nick DiMarco," she said without preamble.

The receptionist scrutinized her with disdain.

Amanda stood tall and implacable before her. "I just telephoned. He's in with Joris. Call him immediately."

The woman sucked in her breath. "I told you, I can't do that."

Drawing herself up, Amanda assumed a combination of her socialite haughtiness and her best schoolteacher voice. "Yes, you can. This is a family emergency. If you don't summon him right away, I'll go in there myself."

When she saw the receptionist reach for the phone, she took a step forward so she came up flush with the intricately carved desk. "If you call security, a teenager's life will be on your conscience. Do you really want to live with that?"

It did the trick. While she waited for Nick, she tried to call his home again.

After three long minutes, Nick hustled through the door. "Amanda," he said hoarsely, scanning her exercise attire. "What is it?" His demeanor revealed no annoyance, no embarrassment, just genuine concern.

Pulling him aside and out of earshot of the clearly curious receptionist, she tried to remain calm. "Nick, where is Heather?"

"At my mother's. Why?"

Oh, God, had she just imagined all this because of Lisa and Ron?

"Why?" He gripped her arm.

She bit her lip. "I'm worried about her. A few things happened in school and I—"

But she broke off when he left her and strode to the phone. She followed him. As he dialed, he said, "I've had a bad feeling about her all day. She was unusually cheerful... Yes, Mom, hi, it's Nick. Is Heather there?"

Amanda watched him, holding her hands to her mouth, palms together, thumbs hooked under her chin. She knew the answer to his question before he confirmed it. "No, no, that's okay. Yes, she's probably at Tammy's and forgot to tell me. No, I know you can't go over there with no car. Stay with Jason and I'll call you back."

His face was ashen when he hung up and his whole body sagged. "Did you drive?"

"Yes. I'm illegally parked out front."

Nick grabbed her hand and ran for the door. They were inside the car and on their way before he spoke again. "You think she may do something to herself, don't you?"

It was the hardest question Amanda ever had to answer. "Yes, Nick, I do."

As they spun away, Amanda reached over and cradled his hand in hers. He held it tightly on the torturous trip to his house. Both were haunted by their own private demons and neither spoke.

April Fools' Day, 6:00 p.m.

HEATHER LINED the pills up next to each other and then sorted them into little piles by color. Frowning, she got up and took milk from the refrigerator. The painkillers her father used for his knee were in capsules and she had never learned to swallow those things. Deliberately, she broke open the few that were left and dissolved them into the glass of liquid. She knew she'd be able to chew the remainder of the codeine pills Aunt Beth had left here, but would have a harder time with Jason's prescription drug. Without touching any of them, she sank into the chair and closed her eyes.

"It'll be over. No more blame. No more guilt. And, the best—no more pain."

And no more Jason, no more of your dad, no more Ms. Carson.

She opened her eyes and glimpsed at the picture of the three of them again, which she'd set up on the table. "There's no other way to escape it."

But louder, and clearer than her own voice, she heard, "There are always other ways to stop the pain." Ms. Carson had said it a thousand times.

She's right, kid. There are other ways.

Slowly, Heather got up from the table, leaving the macabre banquet untouched. Picking up the frame, she trudged to the back of the apartment. She entered the bedroom, dimly lit from the fading spring sun, and inhaled all those wonderful, masculine smells that were her father. A tear trickled down her cheek as she thought of how she'd hurt him.

His ever-present legal pad was on his night table and she saw his hand-written notes. She read aloud. "Number one—You're just being stubborn. Number 2—She's probably right about Suzanne. Number 3—You aren't objective about this."

Heather read all nine reasons, then dropped onto the bed. Ms. Carson had said, "Adults have to make their own way, Heather. You can't change things for them. And you aren't responsible."

Was Daddy making his own way? Would he take care of this himself?

Suddenly, Heather was really tired, but she felt calmer and a little better, too. Carefully setting the paper down, but holding the picture close to her heart, she crawled up on the bed, hugging her father's pillow to her chest like a baby's security blanket. Its scent comforted her and she closed her eyes.

CHAPTER FIFTEEN

NICK UNLOCKED the door and rushed into the apartment. Amanda was seconds behind. He raced to Heather's bedroom and when he found it empty, he breathed a little easier. "She's not here," he yelled from the small space. Relief gushed through him and he turned to leave. But Amanda stood frozen in the doorway and her stricken look was like a sucker punch to the gut.

He saw the empty brown bottles clutched in her hand. "These are empty but there are pills strewn over the kitchen table. I don't know if she took any. We have to check the rest of the place." Turning, she headed for Jason's room.

Striding to his own room, he found his daughter lying still as death on his bed. "Oh, God, no. Please, no." He darted toward her, vaguely aware of Amanda behind him, touching his shoulder and picking up the phone.

Fear pumped through him as he lifted Heather's wrist. It was warm and her pulse was steady. The breath whooshed out of him as he sat on the bed and cradled her in his arms. "I think she's okay."

"The ambulance is on its way. We can't be too careful." Amanda moved to the bed and bent over Heather.

His daughter's beautiful, clear blue eyes opened. "Daddy?"

Nick held her in a hammerlock, and it was Amanda who kept calm. "Heather, honey, did you take any of these pills?" She held up the pernicious bottles.

Tears pooled in Heather's eyes, but she shook her head definitively.

"Thank God," Nick whispered.

Amanda's shoulders slackened and she knelt beside his daughter. "You thought about it, though, didn't you?"

Surreptitiously, she glanced at her father. "Yes."

"You even got them all ready."

Nick thought he might be sick. "Oh, sweetheart, why?"

"I wanted to stop the pain."

Nick tightened his grasp on his daughter. Amanda sat on the side of the bed and stroked Heather's hair. Several minutes passed, then the pounding on the door interrupted them. Rising, Amanda hurried out of the room, returning in seconds with the medics.

"They just want to check her," Amanda said. "It's common practice, Nick."

Stepping back, he glanced at Amanda and instead of the recrimination he expected, he saw remorse etched on her face. She said simply, "Nick, suicide thoughts are much different from an attempt. She still needs a lot of attention, but she didn't try to kill herself. At the last minute, she made the decision to live. It's such a good sign."

Wanting to believe Amanda more than anything in the world, he said, "Yes, I suppose it is. But I feel so guilty that it got this far."

Amanda's eyes glistened. "So do I. But she made the right choice, and we have another chance to help her."

He squeezed her arm gently. "Yes, we do."

"Daddy?"

Nick turned, spoke briefly with the medics and then let Amanda see them to the door. He returned to the bed, scooped Heather up and sat down on the mattress, resting his back against the headboard. "I'm here, sweetheart. I always will be. I promise."

When Amanda returned, she asked Heather a few more questions and seemed satisfied with her answers. Nick held his child until she fell asleep, Amanda watching from a chair beside the bed. The last thing he remembered before his own eyes closed, was the incredibly sad look in hers, as she got up to leave.

THREE HOURS LATER, Heather peered up at him from the bed. "I'm sorry, Daddy." Her face was as white as the pillowcase, and there were huge smudges under her eyes. She'd slept deeply and he'd left her side only once, to call his mother and father, fill them in on what had happened and ask them to keep Jason until Nick could spend some time explaining this to him.

He smoothed her hair back. "Shh, none of that, sweetheart. No one blames you, no one's mad at you."

Tears welled up in Heather's eyes and she grasped the covers tightly. "I've caused even more trouble."

"No," Nick said firmly. "None of this is your fault. You didn't drive Amanda away. *I* did."

Heather frowned. "How did you know I felt that way?"

"Amanda figured out you heard our conversation from the picture you left her." He tucked the sheet around her securely.

"But, Daddy, that's not all."

"All right, honey, obviously I don't understand everything." Feeling the fear flow through him like icy water, he took his daughter's hand and held it too tightly in his own. "But I promise you, Heather, I *will* understand. I'll listen to everything you say, do whatever should be done to help you through this...sadness. You'll never feel so desperate that you..." His voice broke, and he wasn't sure he could continue. But he remembered how he'd felt seeing her curled on his bed and he forced himself to say, "That you'll consider ending your life."

Just hearing the words seemed to calm her. The tears receded and Heather squeezed his hand. "Okay, Daddy, if you say so." Her eyes closed and she drifted off into a safe sleep.

Nick leaned back into the chair by the bed. He'd been here for hours, and he would stay the rest of the night, and every night after if he had to. Occasionally, Amanda drifted into his mind, but he banished thoughts of her, for now. *I will not think about her. I need to concentrate on Heather.*

An hour later, she awoke again. "Daddy, I'm thirsty." Nick was immediately roused from his doze. He helped her to sit up, poured water and urged her to take small sips. "Feeling better?"

Reaching to touch his scratchy beard, she said, "Yeah. You been here all night?"

The words twisted in his gut. "Of course I have."

"Aren't you going to work?"

Nick could only shake his head. The meaning behind the innocent questions made his stomach clench. "No, sweetheart, I'm not."

She knitted her eyebrows as if struck by a thought. "Jason?"

"He's at Grandma's. He said to tell you he loves you."

"He can't have the unicorn now." Heather smiled and lay back on the pillows.

Nick didn't understand the comment but he patted her hand. "Don't worry about anything. Just sleep."

She did. At two o'clock, she woke again and Nick stirred in his chair. She reached for his hand and gripped it again. "I was so scared, Daddy. After I got out all the pills, I realized I couldn't do it."

"I'm so glad." The words were wrenched from him.

"I kept thinking about everything Ms. Carson had told me, and how much I loved you and Jason.

He caressed the dry skin over her knuckles with his fingertips. "And we love you."

She studied his shadowed face. "Daddy, did you hear about the guy who dies and goes to heaven and Saint Peter tells him he can ask any saint a question?"

Nick's eyes flew to hers. The humor seemed so incongruous. But Heather was smiling. "No, sweetheart, I didn't hear it."

"He wanted to see Mary. When she appeared before him, the guy asked her why, in all the pictures he'd seen of her, she always looked so sad."

"What did Mary say?"

"Mary looked at the man, smiled sadly and said, 'I really wanted a girl.' "

Grimly, Nick chuckled, Heather grinned and then drifted off again. Closing his eyes, Nick willed the tears back. *Oh, baby, I always wanted a girl, too. And by God, I'm going to keep you!*

Heather woke again at dawn with the big question. "What's going to happen now?"

Too bad Nick had no answers. "What would you like to happen now?"

When he saw her lips thin, he added, "Heather, you can tell me. I know I haven't listened before, I've been overbearing and strict, but I promise I'll listen now. Give me another chance."

And so, in the early-morning hours, Nick and Heather had a father-daughter heart-to-heart talk. She spoke quietly of her guilt that Jason was disabled and she was not. She complained of the lack of a normal teenage life. She explained how she missed Nick when he was gone so much. She told of her deep feelings for Amanda and her guilt for causing the breach between her and Nick. But she never mentioned her mother.

Nick withstood all the information stoically, though each detail pierced his heart like a poison arrow. It was the withholding of the last issue that stung the most. She still didn't trust him. *Well, what do you expect, DiMarco? You've got to earn her trust.*

"I will, damn it," he muttered to himself after Heather fell asleep again. "I will earn it," he affirmed as he left the bedroom and went to the phone.

Slowly, deliberately, he dialed Suzanne Cohen's number.

"ARE YOU SURE you're all right, Amanda?" Beth asked over the phone the next evening. "You sound horrible, and your day couldn't have been easy."

Amanda coiled the cord tightly around her fingers. "Yes, I'm all right. And no, today wasn't easy."

"You saved Heather's life. She told Nick it was what you had talked with her about that changed her mind." Beth's voice was raspy with emotion.

"Yes, Nick called me briefly to tell me that."

"She seems to be doing well, too. I'm on my way over there now. Nick hasn't left her side in twenty-four hours."

Amanda sank into a kitchen chair. "That's a common reaction to such a close call."

"Did you get any sleep last night?" Beth asked.

"A little." Amanda hoped she lied convincingly.

She'd sat in her porch watching the sun come up, thinking of how she'd lost Lisa and Ron, and almost lost Heather. It was only Nick's call to tell her why Heather hadn't taken the pills that kept Amanda from losing all the confidence she'd worked so hard to build up.

"I'll let you go, you sound exhausted. Take a hot bath and go to bed." Beth hesitated. "And Amanda, give him some time. He'll come around."

Amanda shook her head as she replaced the receiver. He wouldn't come around. She'd lost his trust. It was over. Final. Dead.

After fifteen minutes of thinking about what would never be, Amanda straightened and trudged upstairs. She changed into her ballet attire and headed for her spare room. She'd had a bar, mirrors and wooden floor installed in one of the bedrooms, this one in the back of the house. She'd work off some of this despair and then do what Beth suggested.

Half an hour later, as she did *tours jetés* through the air, she heard the doorbell ring. She was sweaty and sore and didn't want to see anyone. But it might be her mother, or maybe even Tom Mannerly, who'd been in her office several times today checking to see if she was all right. Grabbing a towel, she wiped her face and went to answer it.

She never expected to see Nick standing before her. It was like being hit by a sledgehammer. His face was relaxed, free of the haunted look she remembered from the last time she'd seen him. He stared at her with his intense gray eyes, scanning her from head to foot. It was a surprisingly sexual appraisal.

"Starting a new fashion trend?"

She gave him a tremulous smile. "No, just working off some stress."

"Maybe this will help." He handed her an envelope. When she took it, he rubbed his arms, covered only with a light windbreaker. "Can I come in, honey? It's not quite spring yet."

"I'm sorry, I'm not thinking straight." She led him into the living room and sat on the couch near a light, while he dropped onto a chair across from her. The letter was addressed to her in Heather's precise teenage script. She looked at Nick questioningly.

"Open it. This was all Heather's idea. I had nothing to do with it, although she wanted me to read it to see if it was okay." He cleared his throat and his eyes darkened. "We've promised to try not to keep secrets from each other."

Amanda tore open the note and read:

Dear Amanda,
I hope it's okay that I call you that. Daddy says he told you that you saved my life. I'm glad you did. I don't want to die and I know now that with everyone's help, things will work out. You gave me a second chance and I love you for it and everything else.

Heather

Holding the piece of paper, she raised watery eyes to Nick. "Thanks for bringing this to me." She stood up. "I'm sure you want to get back to her now."

Nick remained seated and had folded his hands together, propped his chin on them and watched her. "Sit down, Amanda. I'm not leaving yet."

His soft, sexy tone unnerved her. Instead of sitting, she paced the rug. "Heather's going to need a lot of counseling. More than I can, or should, provide at this point."

Nick heaved a sigh filled with responsibility and love. "That's one of the reasons I came over here tonight. I need a recommendation for an adolescent psychologist and family counselor."

"A family counselor, too?"

"Yeah. I called Suzanne last night. I told her what happened and because of it that I wanted her to see Heather, but one condition was that we all go for therapy together. Including Jason, to prevent something like this from happening to him later on." His voice was hoarse but firm.

She stared at him, not caring that her feelings glimmered in her eyes. She'd never loved him more. "Oh, Nick, I'm so glad. I know it's the right decision. You'll all be much happier for this."

Nodding, he held her gaze. "Thanks to you. You never gave up, no matter what I did. You're a special woman, Amanda Carson."

She said nothing and simply stared at him, clasping her hands behind her back.

"Listen. Are we through with this?"

Telling herself not to be disappointed, she nodded. He'd only come about the therapists and the note. Not to see her. He probably wanted to get home. "Sure." She stepped back and kept her voice light. "You can leave now."

Purposefully, he stalked toward her. "Leave, hell! I'm not going anywhere." He grabbed her so quickly, she gasped for breath. She all but lost it when his mouth closed over hers. He devoured her, insinuating his tongue into her and increasing the pressure. She grasped his shirt for balance and tried to participate in the kiss, but the tears began to flow and she couldn't. He drew back.

"Hey, none of that. No more crying, Mandy. No more sadness. We're past all that." He brushed aside the tears with his fingertips.

When she continued to weep, his hand moved to her mouth and he stroked her bottom lip with his thumb. "If you stop crying, I'll tell you I love you. I'll tell you I want to marry you as soon as possible. I'll ask you to have our child. Between what I've learned the last few months and your training, we'll raise this one right."

She stopped crying.

He repeated all those wonderful things as he led her to bed. It was a night they weren't likely to forget.

THE DOORBELL RANG two hours later. Nick swore under his breath. *Who the hell is that?*

Amanda sighed in her sleep and moved instinctively toward him. He eased away from her, trying not to wake her. She was exhausted by more than just their vigorous lovemaking.

Pulling on his pants and shirt, he made his way down the steps and to the door in record time. He was shocked to see Robert Carson standing on the front porch. The feeling was obviously mutual as the father took in the lover's dishabille. Robert coughed nervously. Nick had never seen him anxious before.

"Hello, Nick," he said gruffly. "I...I've come to see Amanda. I take it she's here." He said the words with such paternal chagrin Nick almost laughed aloud.

When Robert entered the living room and both men were seated, Nick's amusement faded. Leaning over, he clasped his hands between his knees and faced the man squarely. "Look, Carson, Amanda's had a horrendous day. I won't let you upset her, even if I have to remove you from this house bodily."

The older man's shoulders slumped and his face crumpled. Nick was shocked.

"I won't do that to her. Amanda told Joan about your daughter. It brought back..." His voice cracked and Nick reluctantly felt sorry for Robert. He hadn't been as lucky as Nick had been. "All the horror of Lisa's death. I came to tell Amanda some things she needs to know."

"Tell me first," Nick said implacably.

"No," a sleepy feminine voice said from behind them. "Tell us together."

Each man turned to see Amanda standing at the bottom of the stairs wrapped in a fluffy white robe. "What about Lisa, Father?"

Robert Carson turned a sickly shade of gray. For a moment, Nick thought he might be ill. He lay his head back on the couch and closed his eyes. "This thing with DiMarco's daughter brought it all back, Amanda. Your mother and I talked all night and through the day about it. I... learned some things about my behavior that I want to share with you."

She crossed to her father. Sitting down next to him, she touched his arm for reassurance. "Tell me."

Always the healer, Nick thought.

Straightening, Robert faced Amanda bravely. In halting sentences, he confessed to his deep-seated guilt over Lisa's death. He told them how he'd always felt responsible for everything, the underside of controlling people's lives. Taking the ownership of their happiness, he also took responsibility for Lisa's despair. When she'd committed suicide, he'd known it was his fault.

He gripped his daughter's arm in a frantic show of emotion. "But, Amanda, what concerns me the most is my reaction to the changes you made in your life. I thwarted you. I tried to stop you for...selfish reasons."

She shook her head. "I don't understand."

"You went into counseling, then got involved in suicide therapy. I was afraid you'd see I was at fault, I was too controlling, I'd missed warning signs, I hadn't done what I should have." Burying his face in his hands, Robert Carson sobbed. "I should have...I should have..."

Amanda wrapped her arms around her weeping father in an intimate embrace. "No, Dad, it's not your fault. No one is responsible for another's happiness, another's life. That includes you, too."

In the intervening hour before Robert left, Nick made coffee and the three talked of guilt, despair and hope for the future. When Amanda's father rose to go, he hugged her and told her words Nick guessed she'd never heard from him before. "I love you, Mandy."

Then he turned to Nick and held out his hand. "I think you're good for her, DiMarco. You've got moxie and you'll make one hell of an attorney. Why don't we get together to discuss the possibility of your joining my law firm? We won't do much better than you, son."

Her eyes glistening, Amanda watched the interaction. "Take it, Nick. I'll stand by you no matter what. It's a chance to have everything you want."

Nick stared into her slate blue eyes, smiled at her and shook his head. "I've already got everything I want."

He'd never spoken truer words in his life.

EPILOGUE

NICK ENTERED the house at five o'clock. He tried to get home early these days because he worried about Amanda's pregnancy. She was seven months along and big as a house.

There was music from upstairs and muffled shouts from below, but she slept blissfully through it on the living room couch. He walked over to her and smoothed a wayward strand of honey-colored hair away from her face. Then he rested his hand on her very rounded belly and whispered a greeting to his son or daughter.

The blaring of the stereo from a bedroom of what used to be Amanda's house, and now was home to all four DiMarcos, told him his daughter was here. He bounded up the steps taking them two at a time. He remembered to knock, a nicety Amanda had taught him, and he heard giggles from inside before he was allowed entry.

Heather sat on the bed and two other girls sprawled on the floor. "Hi, Daddy, how ya doin'?"

Her hair was up in some fancy twist and she had on too much makeup. She even talked liked a typical teenager now. And he couldn't be more pleased. Every once in a while, he'd flashback to that horrible night almost eighteen months ago when he'd found her curled on his bed. The sights and sounds of teenagehood were blessings to him now.

"Hi, sweetheart," he said from the doorway.

"Hey, Dad, what do you call a man with five teenage daughters?"

"Insane." Glancing at the stereo, he said, "Turn that down, would you? Amanda's sleeping."

"Sure thing." Heather got up to adjust the volume and came over to him. "She okay?"

"Yeah. Just tired out from your sibling-to-be. Everything okay with you?" He knew he asked the question too frequently, but he couldn't help himself.

Heather groaned and he ruffled her hair. "Y-e-s, Dad." She strung out the response in complaint, but she reached up and placed a grateful kiss on his cheek.

Back on her bed, she plopped down and called to him as he started to leave. "Don't forget Jason and I are going out with Suzanne tonight. Mom won't have to cook and you both can relax."

Smiling, Nick closed the door. He loved it when the kids call Amanda "Mom." They'd asked if they could do so soon after he and Amanda had married. In the intervening months, Heather had gotten extensive counseling and he, Suzanne and Jason had also attended some sessions with her. Heather was slowly piecing together a view of her mother and herself that she could live with, and Jason seemed to be adjusting well to his biological mother's presence in his life.

Nick loped downstairs to see that Amanda had roused.

"Hi." Sleepily, she dragged herself to a half-reclining position. "Is it that late already?"

"Naw." Nick sat down on the couch and nuzzled her neck. "It's only after five."

She lay back and frowned at him. "Nick, you don't have to do this. I'm perfectly fine. You and the kids are like mother hens these days. I'm pregnant, not ill."

He eyed her Baby-with-an-arrow-pointing-down maternity shirt. "Really? I thought you'd just put on weight."

There was a crash from the basement. Nick leapt off the couch to investigate. He was laughing when he returned. "Jason's friend ran into a sideline marker. They play like they're in the NBA."

Nick had renovated the basement for Jason and put in an access ramp from outside so other physically challenged kids could get downstairs.

"Thanks to you." Amanda's eyes glowed. "You're quite a man, Nick DiMarco."

"Yeah, and you're quite a woman. How was work today?"

"Fine, although I'm getting anxious to quit for a while, just so I don't have to waddle around the corridors." She laughed at herself. "Sandi was in to see me. Her job at the temporary agency is going well. She's applied at local community colleges for the spring semester, too."

"She heard from Matt at Buffalo State?"

"Yes, so did we. Heather left his letter on the kitchen table. He says he misses us all, but if I know that one..."

Nick grinned and rubbed her stomach. "I saw your dad at the courthouse this morning. He asked how his grandchild's behaving."

Patting her belly, Amanda chuckled. "He was just over here yesterday. He and Beth are always checking on me. She came to school today to have lunch with me."

"You should feel honored. She's hardly left the bookstore in the six months since she opened it."

Taking Amanda's hand, Nick brought it to his mouth. He kissed it, made his way down her arm and up to her shoulder to nuzzle her throat. "Heather and

Jason are going to be gone in an hour." He gave her a sexy stare. "And the doctor saw no reason why we couldn't..."

"Sorry." Amanda buried her face in his chest. "I invited Adam and Joanna for dinner at six."

"Geez, Mandy, why did you do that? We share an office at the public defender's. I see the guy every day at work."

"But I don't see Joanna."

He took love bites out of her neck. "You drive me to distraction, woman."

"I hope I always will."

Nick sobered with thoughts of the future. Easing away, he studied her for a moment, then glanced upstairs as another crash reverberated through the house down to the basement. Finally, he rested his gaze on her stomach. It hit him how much he'd changed, and how much of that change he owed to Amanda. She'd helped him see what his priorities were and how to arrange his life accordingly. Strong emotion pulsed through him.

"Thank you," he said quietly.

"For what?"

"For saving Heather. For being a mother to Jason. For giving me a new baby to love."

Amanda smiled. "You're a wonderful dad, Nick. *You're* responsible for much of their happiness. I just help."

The firm conviction in her voice convinced him. He wondered how he ever thought money and prestige could make him happy. Coupled with her love, being the kind of father who really made a difference in his kids' lives was all he needed.

Lightly caressing his unborn child, he silently vowed it always would be.